EUROPE Late-1942

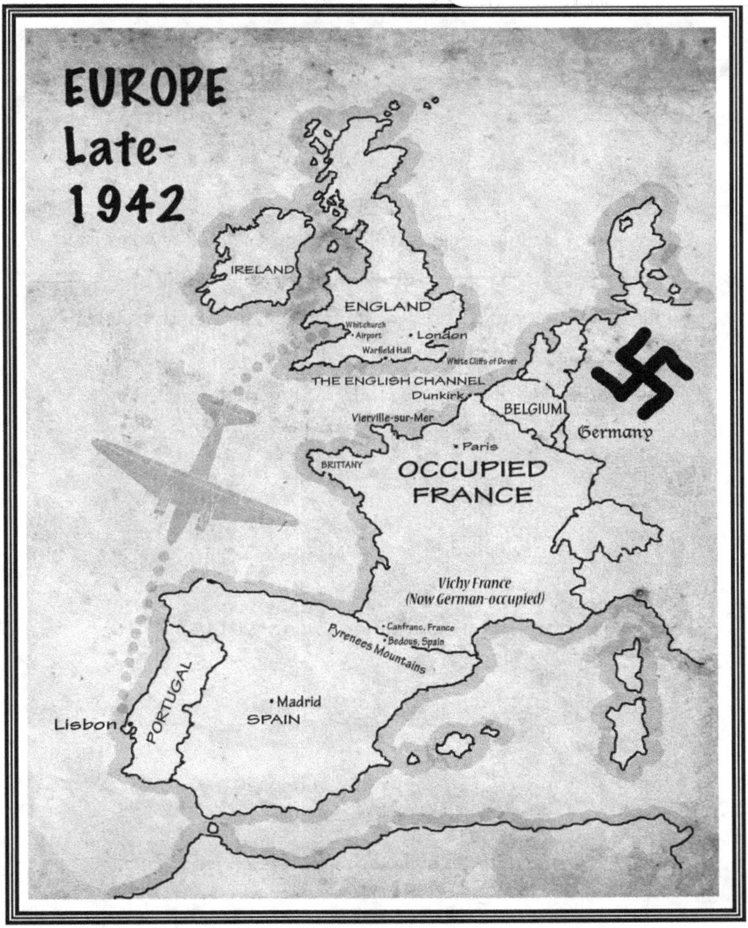

IRELAND

ENGLAND
Whitchurch Airport
Warfield Hall
London
White Cliffs of Dover

THE ENGLISH CHANNEL
Dunkirk
Vierville-sur-Mer
BELGIUM
Germany
Paris
BRITTANY
OCCUPIED FRANCE

Vichy France
(Now German-occupied)

Canfranc, France
Bedous, Spain
Pyrenees Mountains

PORTUGAL
Madrid
SPAIN

Lisbon

Foxford Press, Asheville, NC

First American Edition, August 2018

ISBN-13: 978-1-948907-04-0

Library of Congress Control Number: 2018956190

Printed in the United States of America

LETTER VIA PARIS

LETTER VIA PARIS

Cate M. Ruane

Foxford Press

To Jim Perretti and Mike Tesch,
my first writing teachers.

PROLOGUE

Somewhere in Berlin

THE FÜHRER, a man of middling height, leans over a marble-topped conference table, running his stubby hand over a blueprint that is spread out before him, pressing down on the curled edges. "Bring me a paperweight!" he shouts.

His secretary hurries toward a set of colossal oak doors; an Ardabil carpet silences her steps. With the brunt of her weight, she pushes the doors open. Her eyes fix on the golden eagle perched above the doorframe. Outside can be heard the shuffle of jackboots against a marble floor. Whispered voices, eager to obey, echo down a quarter-mile long reception gallery:

"The führer requires a paperweight!"

"Which paperweight?"

"Any paperweight!"

Within seconds, heels click together and the sought-after paperweight is produced, balanced upon an outstretched palm, biceps straining to hold up the cast bronze object.

The führer continues to examine the blueprint,

having forgotten his request.

At his shoulder, but a step behind, stands a tall and lanky architect, his hands grasped behind his back, his fingers opening and closing nervously. "Well, put the paperweight down, you fool," says the architect, slamming his hand on the table. *Contain yourself, Albert,* thinks the architect, immediately regretting the outburst, which still rings from the stone walls. *I ought to have specified mahogany paneling,* he thinks, surveying the 1312 square foot office. The echo fades, replaced with library-like silence.

Then finally the verdict: "You are a genius, Speer," says the führer, patting the architect's forearm.

"No, *mein Führer,*" says Speer. "The genius is yours. The Führermuseum will be your crowning achievement, the greatest collection since the destruction of the Alexandra Library."

"Greater than the Louvre," says the führer.

"Greater than the Hermitage or the Metropolitan Museum of Art," says Speer.

The führer pauses. A smile lifts below his square mustache. He motions to his secretary, "Bring me an inventory for both the Moscow and New York museums."

"Very wise, *mein Führer,*" says Speer. "Perhaps we ought to add two more wings to the Führermuseum?"

The führer leans over the blueprint again, taking up a pencil and drawing an X. "Here is where we will hang my centerpiece."

"Ah, the Vermeer, *mein Führer,*" says Speer. "And

where is it now? Here in Berlin, I hope?"

"Somewhere safer, Speer. Never you mind," says the führer.

CHAPTER ONE

England

CLINCHING MY TEETH and crossing my fingers did no good at all. The airplane was descending with too much velocity. Its fuselage tilted at the wrong angle and it wasn't banking tight enough. The wing grazed a pillar, and I flinched. The nose tilted downward and the plane went into a tailspin.

The phone rang right then. O'Reilly, the butler, stepped into the path of the spiraling aircraft. I crossed myself. There wasn't time to shout a warning. The airplane hit O'Reilly square in the head. He screamed at the top of his lungs:

"Tommy Mooney, you rascal!"

I crouched behind the banister, four floors up the spiral staircase. Peering between the railings, I saw O'Reilly crane his neck. "Homework, my foot," he said. At his feet were dozens of paper airplanes, all failed experiments.

The course was called *The Principles of Aviation Mechanics*, and I was the only student. Lord Thomas Octave Sopwith—my reluctant guardian—was my tutor.

He was an aviation pioneer and owner of Hawker Aviation, manufacturer of fighter planes and light bombers. "Safer to learn the principles with paper models, what?" he said after our first lesson, seated in a real airplane. I wouldn't pass until I designed a paper airplane able to descend like a vulture going for a wounded rabbit, circling the floors without hitting the railings and landing belly down. Lord Sopwith wanted the results of each launch recorded in a notebook: wingspan, fuselage length, and aileron configuration—also the paper's weight, as seen on the watermark. This way, once I hit on a successful design, it could be reproduced. *Mass production*, Lord Sopwith called it: the secret to getting an air fleet built fast enough to keep up with the German Luftwaffe.

I was crouched behind the banister and making notes when O'Reilly shouted, "Tommy! You are summoned to the telephone."

At first I thought it was a trick to get me out of hiding. But I looked down and saw that he was holding the receiver in his hand. As I slid down four flights of waxed banister, I wondered who could be calling me.

Maybe it was my ma calling from New York to tell me she'd found a way to get me over the *Kriegsmarine*-infested Atlantic Ocean. I ran away from home on Long Island two months earlier, first bicycling to the Brooklyn Harbor before stowing away on the Sopwiths' yacht. Later I made my way to Daphne, my brother's fiancée in London, and onward to German-occupied Europe, where together we rescued Jack, who was missing in action until we found him. Now I was back in England, with my ma missing me like a kid missing his front teeth.

If the Nazis didn't surrender soon, I wouldn't be home for Christmas. Ma said not to worry, she'd mail me a box of my favorite Christmas cookies: gingerbread men with maraschino cherry eyes. But it killed me to think my sister Mary would be the one licking the beater and bowl. She'd probably pick the cherry eyes out before my ma went to mail the box to England.

I couldn't remember my ma's voice, only that it sounded like an Irish jig. She sent me regular letters, written in cursive and sprinkled with apple blossom body powder. Pressing the paper to my nose was like getting a hug. Even if I *was* too old for that mushy stuff.

By the time my feet hit the marble landing, I was bracing for a disappointment. A transatlantic call would bankrupt the family, what with Da still taking odds-and-end jobs but finding nothing steady. It must be my brother Jack, I figured, which was just as good. He knew how to butter up a WAAF—the Women's Auxiliary Air Force—so'd she let him use the phone at the Royal Air Force base. My brother was a Spitfire pilot and the target of every dame in the British Empire, which stretched from British Columbia clear around the globe to Singapore. Jack had the pick of the litter, and was about to marry the cat's meow.

I grabbed the phone out of O'Reilly's white-gloved hand and yelled into the receiver. "Jack, is it you?"

"No, it's Daphne," said my brother's fiancée, the cat's meow herself.

O'Reilly wasn't budging. He stood one foot from

my toes, looking down at me with that Frankenstein face of his. "Give a fella privacy, won't you?" I said.

"Make it snappy and do not tie up the line," he said. "His lordship might receive a call at any moment—one of importance to the Nation."

"Thomas? Hello? Are you there?" said Daphne's crackling voice, coming from the earpiece.

I put the receiver against my flannel jacket and said to O'Reilly, "Don't you have anything more important to do? Counting bedsheets or wine tasting or something? Doesn't the silver need polishing?"

O'Reilly growled, but backed away. "No more than two minutes, you hear?" He pretended to inspect a flower arrangement, when the whole time he had one eye on a pocket watch.

"Daphne. Talk fast," I said.

"We've a letter from Paris," she said. "A very odd sort of letter."

"We?"

"Addressed to the both of us, and sent to my address in London. From the postmarks, it looks as if it was mailed from Vichy France."

That, I knew, was the part of France occupied by the Germans just a week or two before, but in cahoots with the Nazis from the get-go. Daphne went on: "Maybe the sender entrusted the letter to someone traveling to the South of France? Amazing that it got through the censors. Why, they've put their swastika stamps all over it."

"Did the censors black out parts? Maybe cut parts

out using a razor blade?"

"Actually, the odd thing is all that's in the envelope is a blank piece of paper with no marks of any sort."

"Smell it, would you? Does it smell like Coca-Cola?"

I knew without asking that the letter was from my friend Juliette. As I was leaving Paris for the escape over the Pyrenees Mountains with Jack and Daphne, I told her to write to me using invisible ink. Coke was the perfect fluid: it dried invisible. But once you heated up the letter the writing became visible again. Anything acidic will do the trick.

"It smells like salad dressing," said Daphne. "Vinegar, to be exact."

"One and a half minutes remaining," said O'Reilly, swinging his watch from the chain.

Rapid-fire I said, "Holdtheletteruptoalamp!" hoping Daphne could keep up.

"Hold the letter up to a what?" she said.

"A lamp! Then watch carefully. If I'm right, a message will appear like magic. Only, don't let the letter touch the lightbulb or it will catch on fire."

"One minute," said O'Reilly, tapping the toe of his spit shined shoe.

Daphne started hyperventilating. "Someone has written, *Help! Sophie is missing.* Oh, my, it's signed... *Juliette.* Why this is dreadful, Thomas. What could have happened to Sophie?"

Sophie was Juliette's big sister, and Daphne's best friend. We holed up at their place in Paris while we searched for my brother. I owed the Doumer family big-time. They fed me and everything; gave me a roof over my head; Madame Doumer even took me to see a guillotine. If they were in trouble, I was gonna help.

Heavy breathing come over the line. Daphne moaned.

I considered the situation from every angle and said, "My guess is Sophie ran away to work for the French Resistance and then got herself caught. The Nazis are probably torturing her. Those dirty rotten sons-of-female dogs, those lowlife—"

O'Reilly was making his way back to the phone. "Thirty-seconds," he said, tapping the face of his pocket watch. I gripped the receiver with both hands.

Just then, Lady Sopwith peeked her head out from the drawing room. "O'Reilly, oh, there you are," she said. "May I have a moment of your time? I need help with the radiator—it's leaking over the parquet floor again. The boards are warping. Come and see what can be done. The village plumber has been called up, you know, but you're just as handy in a pinch."

Thank Jesus, Mary, and Joseph for Lady Sop. She'd saved me out of more than one fix. It was her idea to invite me to stay at Warfield Hall while I was stranded in England. If it'd been up to O'Reilly, I would've been given a blow-up raft, a loaf of wheat bread, a jar of Marmite, and one oar.

Meanwhile, Daphne was sobbing on the other end of the line. "My dear Sophie. Oh dear, dear, darling Sophie. Oh Thomas, I hope it isn't as you said."

"Look, Daphne. Sorry I said what I said. You know how my imagination gets going. Maybe she *did* join the Resistance but had to go underground. You know, hide out in the woods, or in a basement, or up in an attic." I liked the idea of having another friend in the Resistance. They were my heroes, after all. Right up there with the Royal Air Force and General Dwight D. Eisenhower.

"Be off that telephone by the time I return," said O'Reilly, as he goose-stepped to the drawing room.

Daphne was hiccupping now. I said, "I betcha Sophie ran off with some fella. Probably one of them Frenchies who pose buff for her paintings." Sophie was an artist. Her paintings were what my ma would call indecent: fellas with everything hanging loose. I added, "She probably eloped to the Riviera wearing one of them berets and forgot to leave a note. Heck, Daphne. Would you stop crying already?"

"Perhaps you're right," said Daphne, all drawn out, like she was trying to buy my story. I helped her along:

"Something like that is how my ma ended up in New York. Her big sister was supposed to go and work as a maid, but ran off with an Irish farmhand the night before the boat was sailing. Didn't tell nobody, just sneaked off. My ma sailed in her place and had to work her fingers to the bone to send money home to Ireland. And all 'cause her sister disappeared with some country bumpkin."

Static electricity filled my ear while Daphne got herself together. Meanwhile, I let my wheels spin. I figured that my first guess was the right one: Sophie was in tight with her sister Juliette and with her ma, who she called *Maman*. She wouldn't've run off without telling them.

"Wouldn't she have left a note?" said Daphne, reading my mind. Even I'd left a note when I ran off—in my ma's top dresser drawer where she hid a secret stash of chocolate mints. But Sophie was practically a grown-up, eighteen years old. If she wanted to elope she'd invite her family along, her maman to bake a three-story cake, Juliette for flower girl and maid of honor.

It was obvious. The Nazis had her.

People in Paris were getting carted off left and right. Alvar Lidell talked about it on the BBC news, which the Sopwiths tuned into every night. Hitler's plan was to wipe out Jews, socialists, Gypsies, and jazz musicians. And Sophie was the artsy type, dressed like a Gypsy, listened to jazz, and hob-knobbed with socialists. You can't go around wearing berets and smocks without the Gestapo noticing. Not in German-occupied Paris, anyway. And her best friend, Daphne, was half-Jewish on her mother's side.

I was the first to pipe up. "We're got to act fast before the trail grows cold."

"But whatever can we do, stuck here in England?" said Daphne.

"There's an airline flying from Whitchurch to Lisbon, Portugal," I said. "I read about it in the paper. The Luftwaffe tried to shoot the plane down the other day."

"And you want us to book tickets?"

"From Lisbon it's an easy train ride to Paris. I'll

round up maps tonight and work out a route. Lord Sopwith has ones he keeps in the library."

"Thomas Robert Mooney, we are not going back to occupied Europe. My parents were frantic the whole time I was over there, not that they knew where I was at the time. They thought I'd run off and eloped." She laughed, but then her voice got serious. "If I'd had any idea how desperate the situation was over there, I never would have let you talk me into going. I'm not nearly as naïve now. So get the idea out of your head."

"Okay," I said, ignoring her. "Then we have a plan. Meet me at Whitchurch Airfield tomorrow morning at sunrise."

"Thomas Rob—"

As luck would have it, just then O'Reilly ripped the phone out of my hands and slammed the receiver down. As he grabbed my elbow, pulling me to a table full of tarnished tea sets and jars of polish, we heard the phone ring again.

"No need to answer," I said. "You know how girls can rattle on—all chatty when a fella wants a little peace and quiet."

O'Reilly sneered. "At your suggestion, I've decided it's time to polish the silver. Lady Sopwith is in full agreement." After a snicker he said, "It's high time you pay back for the food you consume. So get to work young man, and no dilly-dallying. Give it elbow grease."

CHAPTER TWO

Mrs. Balson, the cook, was applying her homemade salve to my elbow. We were down in the basement kitchen, sitting next to a cast-iron stove with the radio tuned into Josephine Bradley & Her Jive Rhythm Orchestra, playing "Torpedo Junction" live from London. Meanwhile, supper smells were coming from the oven, making my stomach rumble. Mrs. Balson was pouring on the sympathy:

"That O'Reilly works you too hard, if you want me two-cents. It's not right. A boy ought to be allowed to romp free. It's criminal, his making you do his work for him."

"Right-O," I said. "I'm like a boy trapped in a Dickens novel."

"*Oliver Twist*, that's the one. But when you ask for more soup, I'm going to give it to you with a big chuck of buttered bread, or maybe with bacon grease. Butter is becoming awfully scarce just now. The boys at the front line need it to keep up their strength, the dears."

"And they need butter to put on burns, Mrs. B. You know, the burns a pilot gets when his Spitfire gets blasted by German artillery and the cockpit catches in flames.

And then the canopy won't open, or the parachute. It's my ma's worst nightmare, what with my brother being a Spitfire pilot."

"What a picture. Gruesome, it is. But you're right about butter being soothing on burns. Some think it's an old wives' tale, but we know better." She winked. "No wonder there's a butter shortage. Those poor pilots." She dabbed the corners of her eyes with her apron.

The radio announcer said, "And now a word from our sponsor." Mrs. Balson got up to retune: "No use listening to the adverts when there's nothing on the shop shelves, not so much as a pat of butter."

"You could always try the black market," I said.

"Black market! If a cook is found with black market butter in her larder, it's off to Newgate Prison. No, no. These are times when we must, every one of us, make sacrifices for king and country. Even if it does mean dry toast."

"You figure the king eats his toast plain?"

"Oh, surely. You won't see butter on His Majesties' bread until Hitler surrenders. Neither on the princesses' crumpets either."

"I have to say, Mrs. B, that even with rationing you sure make good grub. You're a much better cook than my ma."

Mrs. B. pinched my cheek. "I'm glad someone notices, Tommy. Substitution, that's the trick. Most people don't realize that applesauce can work in a cake instead of the dairy. I'm not complaining. Why, we've got maple trees on the property, and syrup works as well as sugar.

Oh, but the extra work it makes tapping the trees. At the end of the day, I fall into me bed like a dead woman. But mind you, I'm not complaining. I'm happy to do me bit for the war effort."

"If you ask me, you deserve a vacation. Maybe a cruise," I said.

"A holiday *would* be lovely. But who would feed the Sopwiths when we're so short-handed? Half the staff, every young and able-bodied man, 'ah joined the services. Even Mavis is driving ambulances." She sighed, thinking about the shortage of able-bodied men, no doubt. "And no one's taking cruises these days, not with German U-boats patrolling the seas. The seashore would be nice though. Brighton's lovely." She rubbed her chin. "A bit cold this time of the year." She stood up and brushed flour from her apron, then patted me on the back. "It's nice to dream, Tommy."

She cut me a slice of her famous applesauce cake, knowing that nothing spoiled my supper. I said: "Go south, is what I'd do. Lisbon for example." I took a big bite.

"Portugal? Where ever do you get such ideas?" She started giggling. "Could you just see me in Portugal? I hear it's very exotic."

"I hear it's just the place to rest your weary bones."

"The perfect clime for me rheumatoid arthritis." She rubbed her knuckles.

"Did you know that Portugal ain't in the war? They're neutral like Ireland. You can go there and forget about the war, like it was a million miles away. Why, they're probably slobbering butter on their bread in Portugal."

"Wouldn't that be just the thing?" she said with a dreamy look in her eye.

Now was my chance to get the information I needed: "I heard there was an airline goes from Whitchurch Airport to Lisbon. Any idea where Whitchurch Airport is? 'Cause that's where you'll need to buy your ticket, Mrs. Balson."

She bit her lip she was thinking so hard, picturing herself in a bathing suit sunning on a Portuguese beach, her meals delivered on a polished tray.

"Whitchurch," she said, "I do believe that's near about Bristol. Lord and Lady Sopwith took a flight from that very airport once. I packed them a lovely hamper. Her ladyship said they'd be the envy of the other passengers, she did just. That was before the war. I made scones that called for half a pound of butter in the recipe. Not to mention the lard in the crust on me pork pie."

"And how'd the Sopwiths get themselves from here to Whitchurch?" I asked.

"In the Rolls-Royce, I'm sure."

The Rolls, I thought. I'd sat up front plenty of times, watching Nigel Duncan—the family chauffeur—shifting gears and applying the clutch and brakes. The only problem was getting the key off Duncan. Even if I managed to Jimmy-rig the ignition, Duncan slept above the garage and would hear the V12 engine starting up.

"I think the train is the best option for you, Mrs. Balson. You got a schedule?"

She slapped my knee and went to check on the supper. "You *are* a dreamer," she said. "Portugal. Could you just imagine me in Portugal?"

CHAPTER THREE

AFTER THREE HELPINGS of Mrs. Balson's Wartime Shepherd's Pie, I headed to the library where I found Lord and Lady Sopwith cozied up on a sofa, facing a roaring fire. The fireplace was so tall I could stand in it without bumping my head. One side of the mantel was carved to look like Hephaestus, the Greek fire god. On the other side was his wife Aphrodite. The ceiling was painted with a scene from Mount Olympus, Zeus throwing a lightening bolt. It gave me the willies to look up, thinking I'd get struck.

Since I might be shipped home at any minute, I wasn't enrolled in school. Instead, I spent my days in the library reading whatever caught my eye, usually adventure novels and Egyptology. Lord Sopwith said that airplane designers needed a knack for physics, so every once in a while I cracked open a textbook left over from his days at Seafield Park Engineering College.

There was so many books in the Sopwith library you needed a ladder to reach the top shelves. The ladder weighed a ton, carved out of solid oak. It had wheels and looked more like a lost staircase than a ladder. It had to be rolled to the right place along the railings—too much trouble, if you ask me. When Lord Sopwith wasn't watching, I climbed the shelves to get at a book.

Lord Sopwith had one in his hand and was reading out loud: " 'Why, such is love's transgression,'" he said.

Shakespeare.

I ducked under the library table. I'd been at Warfield Hall long enough to know *Romeo and Juliet* when I heard it.

" 'Griefs of mine own lie heavy in my breast,'" he bellowed.

My thoughts exactly. I crawled back out to the hallway. Unfortunately, the parquet floorboards creaked under me.

"Tommy? Is that you crouching behind the sofa?" said Lady Sop. "Come and join in the fun."

I popped up and said, "Heck, it'll be more romantic without me around to spoil the mood, ma'am."

"Oh, nonsense," she said. "We haven't gotten to that part yet."

Lady Sop was my English tutor and liked to nitpick every word that came out of my mouth. Her goal was to turn me into a proper English gent. Tough going for a kid raised by Irish immigrants, not twenty miles from Brooklyn, where everyone talked like they had marbles in their mouths and their noses plugged. But I knew not to cross Lady Sop. Her friends called her "The Dragon." So I said, "I shan't play Juliet."

"I'm to play Juliet, of course," she said. "Now come and sit down." She pointed to a spot on the rug where a mastiff was curled up. Dogs and me don't mix, so I inched my way over to the cabinet where they kept the maps.

"Just let me get my bearing, shall I?" I said—*shall* being one of them words you toss into a sentence whenever you want to sound hoity-toity. Other good options are *ought, shan't,* and *whilst.* I opened the cabinet door and pulled out a large, flat drawer. "*Romeo and Juliet's* set in Italy. That right?"

"Verona," said Lord Sopwith, scanning the play with a magnifying glass and picking up where he'd left off: " 'Which thou wilt propagate, to have it prest. With more of thine: this love that thou hast shown—' " He stopped mid-speech and swerved his head my way. "Boy, be careful with my rare maps. Put the gloves on before handling them."

"Dear, don't hinder the child when he's making an effort to educate himself," said Lady Sop.

Lord Sopwith lifted one eyebrow and kept reading: " 'Doth add more.' " He cleared his throat and began again a few notes down the scale. " 'Doth add more grief to too much of mine own. Love is a smoke raised with the fume of sighs—' "

"Dear, you read so skillfully." Lady Sop squeezed her husband's hand. This was exactly the reason I was allergic to the play. It wouldn't be long before they started making lovey-dovey eyes at each other. Lord Sopwith inched closer to Lady Sop. I saw their pinkie fingers hook together. But then Lady Sop patted the sofa and said, "Tommy, *do* come and join us. We'll let you play Capulet. You know how good Shakespeare is for improving one's grammar."

I knew no such thing, but I kept my mouth shut. Who said *doth* in 1942? Who even knew what it meant? I'd been in England for months and never met a single Englishman who spoke like Shakespeare. The only English play I liked was *Peter Pan*. I liked Gilbert and Sullivan too, but Lord Sopwith said those weren't plays but operettas. The Sopwiths took me to see *Peter Pan* in London's East End, where Lady Sop clutched her pocketbook, claiming that there were "unsavory characters about." We saw the new and improved version of *Peter Pan*, which "one simply had to see for one's self." Peter Pan was played by a girl, but that didn't ruin the fun. They'd strung the actress by a wire and she flew right over our heads. I told the Sopwiths right then and there: that was the part for me. Not Montague or Capulet. Besides, they had Bluebeard the pirate in *Peter Pan*. And you can't top that.

"Why can't we read *Peter Pan* again?" I said.

"Oh, balderdash," said Lord Sopwith to his wife. "Let the boy be. Give him a couple of years, what, and he'll be begging to play Romeo."

After that, they left me alone. Leafing through the maps, I found just what I was looking for: one of the British Isles. Didn't matter that the map was outdated— Rand McNally himself couldn't keep up, not with Hitler gobbling up Europe left and right. I scanned the coast of England and found Bristol just where Mrs. Balson said it was. All I had to do now was wait for an opportunity to roll the map and stick it up my pant leg.

"Take those grubby hands off my Elizabethan map," said Lord Sopwith, who had snuck up behind me. He lifted the vellum page from my bare hands, checked for fingerprints, and then put it back into the cabinet. After turning the key, he stuffed it in his vest pocket. "There's a perfectly good 20th century atlas sitting there on the library table," he said. "You will limit yourself to its use. Have I made myself clear?"

"Crystal," I said.

"You'll find Verona clearly marked. About 150 miles east of Venice."

I was perfectly aware of the atlas, but it was way too big to take along on my rescue mission. "The new-fangled atlas shan't be the same," I said in my best upper-crust voice. "I wanted a look at a map from Shakespeare's own day."

Lord Sopwith lifted an eyebrow, all impressed. "Would you listen to the boy, Phyllis? You've turned him into quite the scholar. Remarkable. He knows that Shakespeare and Queen Elizabeth were contemporaries."

It was a fluke I'd got that part right. Pure dumb luck. Hopefully it was enough to get Lord Sopwith to unlock the map cabinet. But he took me by the shoulders and walked me over to the world atlas.

"Can I take it to my room, sir? I mean, *may* I?"

"Yes you may," he said, dismissing me with a wave of his hand.

Now all I needed was a razor blade.

CHAPTER FOUR

I SHOULD'VE KNOWN Daphne would send up a smoke signal. Her and Lady Sop were in tight ever since a visit to Warfield Hall, when the two of them figured out they had things in common: archery, Jane Austen, fly-fishing, and "art appreciation," for starters. Sure enough, when I opened my bedroom door later that night, there was a chair blocking my exit.

"Would you be wanting to escape now?" said Fiona, the Irish maid. She grabbed the back pocket of my blue jeans, almost ripping it off. "I have strict orders to keep you from running off."

Fiona wasn't much older than me, but she was a tough cookie. Her father was in the Irish Republican Army and he taught her a trick or two. She had a rope handy, shaped into a lasso. Before I knew what was coming, she had me bound up like a runaway calf. If I didn't act quick I'd end up veal parmesan.

"Unhand me," I said.

"Unhand me?" she said mocking my accent. "You little turncoat."

"I got the line from *The Three Musketeers*," I said. "Frenchies." It was a flat out lie. The line came straight out of *Hamlet* and somehow she knew it.

Fiona yanked on the rope until my arms pinched against my ribs. "Rubbing noses with the Brits," she hissed, "reading Shakespeare. You're starting to sound like them. I have a mind to turn you over to the I.R.A. You know the penalty for joining up with the enemy?"

"Tar and feathers?"

"That's right. And worse: castration." Her lips peeled back, revealing a set of wolf-sharp teeth. My vivid imagination was working in ways I didn't like.

I switched to the Irish brogue I remembered from the cradle. "Can't you see I'm trying to escape the Brits, our *mutual* enemy? I'm escaping to Ireland, my motherland. The birthplace of my father, too." I threw in the Irish rebel chant, "Go Sinn Féin!"

Fiona let the rope slack. Her eyelashes started fluttering. "Ireland, you say?"

"That's right, Fiona. Ireland. Land of the free and the brave. Land of mashed potatoes and gravy. Land of leprechauns and four-leaf clovers." I reached into my front pocket, which wasn't easy. "Take a look at that," I said, handing over a crumpled card.

"What is it?" she asked. "A leaf?"

"It was a genuine four-leaf clover, but three fell off. My Irish grandma sent me the card straight from County Mayo. I've been carrying it ever since leaving New York. It's proof, can't you see?"

"Humm. Howda I know it once had four leaves? Only got one now," she said.

"What kind of grandma sends a kid a card with a

one-leaf clover?" I asked.

"You're telling the God's honest *tooth*? You're really escaping to Ireland?"

"Where do you think I'm escaping to—Portugal?"

She laughed. The tension went out of the rope. I could feel blood flowing back to my fingers.

"Would ya take me with ya?" she said. "I'm awfully homesick."

"Happy to. Just untie me first."

She hesitated and I started humming "Danny Boy."

"What's yer plan?" she said wide-eyed.

I told her that the plan began with her going off and packing her things. We'd meet up by the gatehouse in about an hour, after I raided the kitchen pantry.

Fiona ran off down the hallway, tearing off her maid's apron and cap as she went. We both had rooms up in the attic, hers on one side of the house, mine on the other.

I was traveling light, with only one small suitcase. It was patterned with little V's and L's, stamped with gold initials near the handle: T.O.M.S., which stood for Thomas Octave Murdoch Sopwith. Lucky thing it spelled out *Tom's*. If a customs officer questioned me, they'd be suckered into thinking the suitcase was mine. In the suitcase were the things you couldn't find in Paris: a spare pair of blue jeans, three Zane Grey Westerns (paperback editions my brother loaned me), two Cadbury chocolate bars, a bottle of ketchup—called tomato sauce in England—a baseball, maps of the British Isles and Europe, a compass… and, best of all, a diamond tiara.

The tiara was Lady Sops, but she wouldn't mind my taking it. O'Reilly let slip that the tiara was a fake. "Paste," he called it. It was the spitting image of the real tiara, too priceless to be let out of the safe at Lloyd's Bank in London. I figured I'd sell that tiara to some *fräulein*, maybe the wife of a storm trooper. If the paste version could fool Lady Sop's friends, it would work with the fräulein. It would serve her right too, kissing up to a Nazi. Daphne said that the *haute couture* was going to Berlin—haute couture meaning the good stuff—but now they'd be shipping home a fake. I'd use those Reichsmarks to hole up at the ritziest hotel in Paris: The Hôtel de Crillon. Last time I was there, Daphne and me watched Nazis sitting in the lobby eating éclairs, chocolate mousse, and crème brulee, us too broke to split a cup of tea. Next time it would be me eating the éclairs.

But first I had to shake Fiona. Balancing the suitcase on my head, I positioned myself on the banister. Just that day, I seen Fiona wax it. I picked up enough speed, four flights in under a minute, launching six feet across the foyer. I skirted around a statue of Venus and headed for the front door. There was a full moon that night, but the foyer was pitch-dark, what with the blackout laws, a tarp covered the ceiling dome. Lady Sop called it a *cupola*, but it looked like the nose of a B-25 bomber, if you ask me. Luckily, my sense of smell is highly developed, along the lines of a grizzly bear's, and I smelled the mastiff ten feet away. Figured Lady Sop would have a canine guarding the exit. She knew I was scared of dogs.

I opened my suitcase and took out a baseball.

Shame because it was a gift from my brother Jack, autographed by his buddy who played in the minor league. All I had to do was open the double-door leading into the drawing room, say, "Sic," and then pitch a four-seam fastball. The mastiff trotted into the room just as the ball smashed into one of Lady Sop's Ming vases. I slammed the drawing room door and heard whimpering from the other side.

Pumping my one free arm, the suitcase in the other, I ran full steam at the front door, unbolted the lock and jumped seven stairs, skidding onto the driveway gravel.

There was no sign of pursuit, not from Fiona or the dog. A light was on in one of the attic rooms: Fiona's. She was still trying to decide which getups to take and which to leave. She'd forgot to shut the blackout curtains, making the house a sitting target for the Luftwaffe. I felt guilty about giving her false hopes, but only for the split second it took me to turn my head. I wasn't going to Ireland, not in the near future anyway. Ireland was taking their neutrality too seriously. If a pilot bailed out of his plane and happened to get blown over to Ireland, they locked him up. Didn't matter if he was flying for the Royal Air Force or the German Luftwaffe. Didn't matter if he was an Irish-American flying a B-17 Flying Fortress.

The mastiff was in a frenzy by then, barking something fierce like he was face-to-face with a stray cat. A light came on in the drawing room. I seen it through a crack in the curtains.

It was time to move, and fast.

"'Ado, ado, much ado. Parting is such sweet sorrow,'" I said, facing the house and taking a bow with a flutter of my hand. The Sopwiths had been swell hosts. And I'd miss Mrs. Balson's cooking. But I was glad to see the back of O'Reilly. He could polish his own silver from now on.

CHAPTER FIVE

Turned out that Whitchurch airport was miles from the Bristol train station. Halfway there, my heels started blistering. I needed a hairpin to pop the blisters, but had to use my pocketknife instead. To make things worse, there weren't any road signs. The Home Guard figured it was a good idea to take them down, thinking to confuse the Germans but confusing a lost American instead. Striking on a plan, I stuck to roads with the blackest oil stains. Before long, the city was at my back and farmland in front of me. Not much grew this time of year. It was rutted dirt as far as the eye could see, with only a few barns and farmhouses to break up the view.

I took a break at a bus stop, hoping a bus might come by. Meanwhile, I ate one of my Cadbury bars. I kept a lookout for airliners, but saw not a one. Finally, a four-door sedan came into view and I put my thumb up. It had suitcases and steamer trunks piled on the roof and tied to the backboard. But when it got closer, I seen that the car was full of passengers. The driver gave me a shrug and whizzed past.

But before long, a tractor came rolling up. It looked like a tyrannosaurus rex: big, green, and ancient. I watched it make the turn from a field onto the road, and I tried out the thumb again when it got within range. A girl dressed in a green sweater with an armband yelled for me to hop on, not slowing down even a beat. I jumped up on the running board and plopped my suitcase next to the smokestack. There was only one seat and the girl was in it, so I kept standing. My blisters stopped screaming at least.

"You a soldier?" I asked, wondering about the two red diamonds on her armband.

"Land Girl," she said.

"What are the diamonds for?"

"Years of service to king, country, and cabbage."

I'd heard of the Land Girls from Mrs. Balson, who said that every last one of them should be awarded the Victoria Cross, being they were the ones who kept food on our table while the regular farmers were off fighting Hitler. I'd never met a Land Girl in the flesh. This one had dirt under her broken fingernails, and on the tip of her freckled nose. Hay stuck from her hairdo, the kind where the back is rolled up to look like a sausage glued to the neck.

"I'm only going a bit down the road before turning into that field," she said, and shifted gears so that the tractor jerked forward. We picked up speed, moving from five miles an hour to six.

"That's too bad," I said. "I like your wheels."

"Why, if you were any older I'd think you were being fresh."

It hit me just how pretty she was—something

along the lines of Dorothy in *The Wizard of Oz*, the Kansas version of a farm girl. I said, "If I were any older, I'd think about being a farmer right about now." It was the first time I ever tried out flirting. My stomach did an Irish jig.

"Say, you're cute," she said. "Now, unless you're serious about farming, you'd best make your escape here."

I waved goodbye and she threw me a kiss. She must've been desperate, I thought, trapped out there in the boonies with the bachelor farmers off fighting.

The last mile was torture. The only thing that kept me going was a vision of Sophie being tortured herself. I tried to imagine pain worse than any blister, worse than an amputated limb, worse than... Suddenly, my own troubles faded. I began trotting then, skipping even, making 10-yard dashes every once in a while. I walked the last bit barefoot, stringing my sneakers and bloody socks around my neck.

The Whitchurch airport—also called Bristol Airport—reminded me of Roosevelt Field, the Long Island airfield where Charles Lindbergh took off for his solo flight across the Atlantic. It had one tarred runway. I peeked through a chain-link fence to scope out the place.

A DC-3 sat on the tarmac. BOAC was painted on the fuselage. I'd never seen an airliner with my own two eyes, not at eye level, anyway. It wasn't much different from the bombers that flew overhead all the time. Only it didn't have bomb doors or a gunner's turret up on top. That made the airliner a sitting target for the Luftwaffe, and it was no wonder the Germans were trying to shoot one down.

A Spitfire was parked near the DC-3. I wondered if it was brought in to escort the airliner to Portugal, fighting off Messerschmitts the whole way. The pilot had his back to me. He was talking with an airline pilot who looked just like he'd stepped out of an advert for Pan Am Airways.

Both pilots turned to watch a stewardess sauntering toward them. She was dressed in a black suit with a little black cap propped on her head. My brother Jack would describe her as "stacked with a nice set of yams." The wind whipped up and she used one hand to keep the cap from flying off. With the other hand she balanced a tray with two teacups on it. The airline pilot took a cup from the tray and started sipping. The Spitfire pilot waved off the tea but leaned down and gave the stewardess a kiss on the lips. Spitfire pilots get away with murder. The stewardess didn't slap him or nothing. She just turned and headed back to the building. A sign ran the length of it and had letters big enough to read from the sky: Bristol Airport, it said.

I threw my suitcase over the fence and then followed behind it. Getting down on my hands and knees, I crawled to the back side of the building, so's I could look in the window. It was a one-stop shop: ticket counter, flight operation, and waiting room. There were racks displaying magazines, cigarettes, and donuts wrapped in cellophane. My mouth started salivating, but there was no way of getting at them without being seen.

Now the stewardess was talking to a man behind the counter. She laughed and I heard her voice clear as a bell. That's when I realized she wasn't a stewardess.

Not by a long shot.

That black getup was one I should've recognized.

I inched around the building and ducked behind a trolley cart loaded with luggage. I threw the suitcase on top of the stack and then crawled under the cart. Craning my neck, I saw a man in overalls walk to the trolley. He grunted and leaned into the load, pushing it in the direction of the airliner. My back scraped along the tarmac.

The cart stopped close to the airliner, close enough for me to eavesdrop on the two pilots. "You know how dames are," said my brother Jack. "They get in a tizzy at the drop of a hat. The kid's probably off climbing trees, while we're on a wild goose chase."

The airline pilot laughed, and said, "*Ja,* I don't doubt it."

A foreigner, I thought. I racked my brain trying to remember the news report, broadcast when a Messerschmitt shot at the airliner, almost bringing it down. If memory served me right, the planes once belonged to a Dutch airline, KLM, but the pilots flew the DC-3s out of Holland just as the Germans invaded. Now the Dutch crew were flying the planes for BOAC—British Overseas Airways Corporation.

Daphne walked over to my brother and held out her hand. I heard her say, "It's worth a try."

Jack reached into his pocket and forked over coins.

A minute later Daphne was back, waving a donut. "Thomas Robert Mooney!" she yelled. "If you are anywhere in the vicinity, come and get it." It took all my willpower not to rush at her, especially after she peeled off the cellophane and spun the donut on her index finger.

A few minutes went by like that, Daphne calling out, Jack laughing, the Dutch pilot saying, "*Ja, ja,* to be a boy again," while they watched a crewmen roll a staircase to the back end of the airliner. Meanwhile, a real stewardess—this one in a navy blue number—opened a door from the inside of the airliner and dangled one foot over the edge. A crewman whistled at her, but not Jack. He knew better, what with Daphne within striking distance. The staircase butted up against the airliner and the stewardess stepped out onto the landing, waving to the airline pilot and saying, "*Alles is klaar!*"

The wind blew up and my mouth filled with dirt. I swallowed, thinking it might be the only lunch I'd get. But I couldn't've asked for a better setup. The staircase was blocking me from view. If only the crewmen would scram.

Just then a man dressed like a New York City stockbroker stepped up to the luggage cart and said to the crewmen, "Be careful with that one. There's fragile items inside, you see."

"We'll handle her with kid gloves," said a crewman.

"Please see that you do," said the businessman, all pompous-like. I noticed that he didn't give a tip. His black wingtips did an about face and marched over to the staircase, where the other passengers were waiting to board. The crewmen chuckled:

"Give that suitcase an extra heave-ho, Ed."

"Be my pleasure, Fred."

The cart shook as they loaded the luggage into a small door, high up at the front of the plane. Any minute they'd roll the cart and the ladder away and I'd be done for, because I'd need a pole vault to get to the cargo hold after that.

My one-leaf clover was working its magic when a grandmother-type walked out of the building carrying a heavy suitcase in each hand. Ed and Fred rushed over to help her, giving me just enough time to leap up the ladder and throw myself into the cargo hold. No one'd seen me, but the cargo door was still open. I piled suitcases on top of me and laid out flat as a two-by-four. A few minutes later and Ed and Fred came back with another load. A hatbox landed on my head. The businessman's suitcase was thrown on my stomach, knocking the wind out of me, the kid gloves nowhere in sight.

"That's it," said Ed. "Did we get any tips?"

"About enough to split a half pint between us. A mingy bunch, this lot," said Fred. Peering down through a luggage handle, I seen them counting out change before walking out of view. A minute later and passengers were streaming out of the building, men carrying small suitcases and ladies with makeup and jewel cases—the kind Lady Sop travels with, the kind with built in mirrors that light up when you open the lid.

Daphne stepped out last, biting her nails. Her eyes

scanned the length of the airplane and she stood on her tippy-toes, thinking that would help. Jack came to her, grabbed her by the shoulders and spun her around. He tried to lay a kiss on her cheek, but she moved her head away, pushing him off. The donut fell to the ground, rolling on edge until it hit Jack's flight boot.

This might've been their first fight.

Next thing I knew, Daphne was making her way to the airplane. Jack stood in his place, shaking his head with his hands on his hips. I could see he was belly-laughing. He walked into the building after waving his hand in a way that said, "Women. I give up."

Daphne was out of my line of vision, somewheres off toward the passenger door. I hoped Ed and Fred would roll away the ladder before she came snooping.

My hand stretched and shut the cargo door, making the cargo hold black as a bomb shelter. I rubbed my hands together and said, "Well, that's that." By then my eyes were adjusting to the darkness. A little sliver of light came from around the cargo door frame and from tiny star-like dots where the rivets held the metal panels together.

Home free, I thought.

Until the door swung open and Daphne stood at the top of the ladder glaring at me. "I never," she said. Her head spun backwards and her mouth made a big O, like she was getting ready to holler for Jack.

I was done for. And so was Sophie.

I might be twelve and a half and Daphne eighteen, but I

knew a thing or two about wrestling. My hands flew out and got a grip under her armpits. Before she knew what hit her, she was laying flat on top of me and the cargo door was shut again. One flip and I was on top, pinning her to a steamer trunk. She was fighting like a girl, kicking in the wrong places. Lucky for me she had no fingernails to speak of, and she was using an open palm instead of a fist. My hand came down on her mouth and she bit me, but not hard enough to break skin.

It wasn't long before the props started spinning and we felt the airliner moving under us, the noise so loud I could barely hear Daphne screaming. The airliner felt like it would rattle apart. My stomach did a lurch when we lifted off the ground and hit turbulence. Wind blew in through the crack around the doorframe.

"We're flying, Daphne," I yelled over the noise. "Whoooooo-e!"

"You little devil, you rotten—"

"Aren't you glad you came along?"

That's when she hauled off and punched me in the jaw. It felt like Joe Louis, world heavyweight champion, slugged me. I moved my tongue around the inside of my mouth, half expecting to find loose teeth. I could taste blood. Then she flung her arms around me, squeezed, and began bawling on my shoulder—something Joe Louis wouldn't've done.

"Forgive me," she said. "I didn't mean to hit you."

In dead-ringer imitation of Father McGillick at Saint Brendan's, I said: "I absolve you, my daughter. Say ten Hail Mary's, and try'n behave yourself."

"Oh *do* shut up," she said. The words were mean
-spirited, but she was hiccupping and laughing when
she said them. "It's just that—oh, Thomas, what have
you done?" She looked around the cramped space. The
plane lurched, slamming her hard against the fuselage.
She gave me a friendly shove, like it was my fault. My
eardrums were popped in and out, but I heard her say,
"Golly, it's frightfully cold."

She wasn't joking. Being that the airline didn't
normally have living things in the cargo compartment,
they'd skimped on insulation. As the plane gained in el-
evation, the temperature turned Siberian. I felt around
and found a storage trunk with the lid right-side up. A
little key was hanging from the handle. I yanked it loose
and popped the locks. My fingers dug into the case and
hit on something warm and cozy. I tugged it out and
handed it over to Daphne.

"Mink," she said like a purr. "Come on over." I
snuggled up against her and she wrapped the fur coat
around both our shoulders. A kiss landed on my head.
"At least I know you're alive. You do know how to make
one mad with worry. My fingernails are down to the
quick and bleeding—that's how much I've been fretting.
First thing when we land in Lisbon, I'll ask the pilot to
take us back. And I'll beg him not to have you arrested
for trespassing."

"He wouldn't dare," I said.

"Now Jack, he wasn't in the least concerned. Which
is just like him, not a care in the world. He thinks it's a
lark, you constantly running off."

"He knows I'm tough."

"It's a simple fact that men haven't the maternal instinct."

"You don't say?"

"It's a scientific fact."

"Well, that's swell, Daphne. I mean, you having an instinct for me." I shimmied up a little closer, so her hair was blowing in my face. "What with my ma on the other side of the ocean and them German-U-boats in between, it gets lonesome. Lady Sop and Mrs. Balson have some of that maternal instinct for me, but I think you have the most…after Ma, that is."

Daphne pulled the mink over our heads and buttoned us inside. "Just remember," she growled, "some mothers eat their young."

CHAPTER SIX

THE PLANE LANDED WITH two bumps and a screeching halt. When we cracked open the cargo door sunlight flooded in and blinded us.

"That's one thing to be said for Portugal," said Daphne, as our eyes adjusted and she took the first peek. "Oh, my goodness," she said, slamming the door shut again. She burrowed her head into my shoulder. I hugged her to me.

"Why the waterworks?" I asked.

"We're...we're... Oh, my goodness gracious we're in Germany."

"How'd that happen?" I said, wide-eyed. I cracked the cargo door again and looked out. Right there next to the DC-3 was German airplane—a Siebel Si 204, to be exact—with *Deutsche Lufthansa* painted on its tail.

"Maybe the airliner was kidnapped," said Daphne, gnawing at her nails. "Or whatever they call it—*high-jacked*. We ought to get out of here before we're caught."

We rummaged around for my suitcase while I described it to Daphne, guessing at the measurements and not forgetting the V's and L's.

"Louis Vuitton," she said with a click of her tongue.

"You nicked a suitcase from the Sopwiths, didn't you?"

"Borrowed," I said, all indignant-like. "They have plenty more where that came from. Stacks and stacks of Louis Whatever-His-Name-Is."

Daphne spotted my suitcase first, wedged under a trunk. She threw it to the tarmac. Then, after taking off her shoes and putting one into each pocket, she jumped from the cargo hold. I did likewise, with nothing more than a twisted ankle to show for it. We inched to the tail section, keeping our eyes out for Nazis the whole time. That's when I noticed that Daphne had a pocketbook hanging from her elbow. She reached into it and took out a pistol. I gulped hard. It was a tiny thing, pearl-handled.

"Act like you belong here," she said. "Keep your back straight and your upper lip stiff. And better to not look anyone in the eye."

Two men stood guard next to the German plane. Both were dressed in black suits, with faces like pit bulls. They looked our way, focusing on Daphne's legs.

"*Guten Tag, Fräulein*," said the one.

Daphne had the pistol tucked in her coat pocket. That's when I realized she was still wearing the mink. She stuck her nose up in the air, like there was something nasty on the ground, something a dog left behind.

"No need to be like that, fräulein," said the second man. "Portugal is a neutral country. We're friends here."

I figured she was getting ready to plug them full of lead, but instead she marched off toward the terminal. One of the Germans yelled, "Come, come. We can be friends." She ignored him. I followed at her heels.

A sign over the terminal building welcomed us to Lisbon Portela Airport. Passengers were pushing to get a place on the line leading into the terminal. Daphne took a place at the end and I snuck up to the front to get an idea of what we were in for.

"*Passaporte, por favor,*" said a customs officer to a lady who answered back: "Do you mean passport, sir?"

I headed back to Daphne: "You got a passport?"

"As a matter of fact, yes."

"That's one of us," I said.

She reached into her pocketbook and found her passport and a fountain pen. "Turn around," she said, wanting to use my back for a desk. "You are now Thomas Clarke, a resident of Great Britain and my dependent." I spun around and looked at her passport. Inside the cover, she'd written my new name in a space for dependent minors.

"They won't believe I'm your son," I said. "No one has a baby when they're in kindergarten."

"We'll say you're my brother. Which is practically the truth." She bit her lip. "If they ask, we'll say our parents were killed in an avalanche and that now that I'm eighteen I've become your legal guardian."

"An avalanche where?"

"Tibet."

"Which mountain?" I said. She gave me the evil eye.

The line inched forward until we were next up.

"Best I do the talking," whispered Daphne. The customs officer smiled and Daphne gave him a Pepsodent grin, the one where her dimples showed. "Good afternoon, officer," she said. "Fine weather you're having in Lisbon."

"The sun is always shining in Portugal," he said, leaning in, "when there are beautiful women about." He clutched Daphne's elbow. His face was five inches from her nose. But she kept her cool, wiggling loose and then taking a step backwards. "This is my brother," she said, pushing me between her and the customs officer.

"I see," he said. "You have charge of the boy?"

"Ever since the tragic death of our beloved parents," she said.

I crossed myself and made my eyes water up. "Mountaineering accident on Mount Everest," slipped from my lips, "George Mallory was his name."

Daphne kicked me in the shin.

"But it says here that your family name is Clarke," said the customs officer, tapping his finger on the passport.

"We got adopted," I said. "By William Clarke, the great explorer. Then *he* died."

"No need to go on," said the customs officer, raising his palm. He flipped through Daphne's passport. "Where is your visa, *senhorita?*"

"Visa?" said Daphne.

"Visa."

"Well, surely it's in there somewhere."

"I'm afraid not, senhorita."

"Well, officer, we shan't be needing a visa because we have no intention of remaining in Portugal. Our plan is to book the next return flight. It's the experience of flying that we were after. A birthday gift for my daring little brother."

"Most irregular," he said. "I'll have to see your homebound tickets and you won't be permitted to step foot from the terminal. Please, senhorita. If you would wait for me in that office." He pointed to a glass-fronted door marked *Imigração*, and under that *Emigration*. "I will be but a few moments. Next!" he shouted, turning his attention to the passengers behind us.

"Come, Thomas," said Daphne, taking my hand and pulling me over to the BOAC ticket counter. A crowd of people were pushing and shoving and shouting to get the clerk's attention.

"There are no seats," yelled the clerk over the hub-bub. "We are fully booked on outbound flights!"

"This is outrageous," said an Englishman, twirling his mustache.

"Until which date?" yelled a lady with an accent I couldn't pin down. Black lace covered her face like a flamenco dancer.

"You must inquire at the city office," said the clerk. "Praça Marquês de Pombal, number 15." With that he pulled shut a curtain.

"Waste of time," said the Englishman throwing up his hands. "I've exhausted that avenue already. They claim to have no available seats until next month at the earliest. Unless you work for British Intelligence, I'm sure." He took a toothpick from his pocket and began chewing on it. Our eyes met and he shrugged his shoulders.

"Well, I suppose it's back to the roulette wheel for me," he said. "There are worse ways to spend the war. Good day to you, young man. And good luck." He tipped his hat and was off.

Everyone turned from the counter, but not Daphne. She kept on staring at the curtain like she was hypnotized. Her mouth hung open but she wasn't speaking. I set my suitcase down and motioned for her to take a load off.

"I'll go get you a cup of water from the cooler over there," I said, because sweat was beading on her forehead and she looked like she might faint. I bolted over to the cooler and filled two paper cups. I had to pour the water down her throat. This was when you needed brandy. Maybe the only time. There was rack of travel brochures and I used one to fan Daphne's face.

Finally she said something: "My sweet Jack. He was set on taking me dancing at the Savoy tonight. His first leave in weeks and I had to go and ruin it for him."

"You can blame me."

"I shall do just that." She snapped open her pocketbook and found a hankie. Wiping her forehead she said: "Crikey, it's hot in Portugal."

"It might help if you ditch the mink."

She jumped from the suitcase, tearing the coat from her body like it was on fire. "Stolen goods," she said, shooting guilty looks left and right.

Amateur, I thought.

I walked the mink over to the BOAC counter and stuffed it behind the curtain.

"We better bolt before that cop comes looking for you," I said, putting a tremor in my voice and making sure to knit my eyebrows and wring my hands.

The little pistol was still in her hand. She gasped and slipped it into her jacket pocket, grabbed my elbow and pulled me to the nearest exit.

CHAPTER SEVEN

WE PUSHED OUR WAY against a crowd of people, like salmon swimming upstream. Everybody was bug-eyed desperate to get out of Portugal. I worried we'd get trampled to death. Or worse, murdered by a Nazi. I bumped into a man wearing a little swastika pinned to his lapel, a Nazi party member, no doubt. Fast thinking had me slamming my foot down on his shoe. Meanwhile, Daphne was back to her old self, cool as cucumber. She walked ballerina-style, on the tips of her toes, so's she could see over the crowd and navigate for the both of us. We made it through with only a few scraps and bruises.

"Someone tried to rob me. Can you believe that?" she said, staring at her pocketbook. It hung open like a gaping mouth.

I patted my pockets. Everything was still right where I'd put it. In my front blue jean pockets: two marbles, a stone, a pack of chewing gum, my lucky four-leaf clover glued to a card, now with only one leaf. In my back pants pockets: assorted coins; a letter from my ma with a photograph of the family—everybody but my sister Mary, who I'd ripped off; and a German bullet Jack found lodged in his Spitfire's wing. In my jacket pocket:

a compass, a nail clipper, a buffalo head nickel, and lint.

Daphne riffled though her pocketbook, pushing things around until she found her lipstick and powder compact. She touched up her lips with a color exactly like maraschino cherries and mumbled, "It doesn't seem as if anything is missing, thank God."

"Funny you brought your passport along," I said.

"I was hoping for the best, whilst preparing for the worst."

A man called out: "Miss Daphne? Over here!" She snapped the compact shut and smiled wide.

"Dirk," she said. "What a surprise."

The Dutch airliner pilot was standing by the curb, surrounded by three stewardesses. He doffed his hat to Daphne. I looked down at their feet, expecting to see wood clogs, but the ladies were wearing matching blue shoes with silver buckles and stacked heels, and Captain Dirk de Koning was in lace-up oxfords. The tallest girl made eyes at me and reached over to pinch my cheek. I had to swat her hand away.

Captain Dirk, the pilot, was spitting out words like *wat, hoe,* and *oh mijn,* all with question marks and exclamation points at the end.

"I found him in the cargo compartment," said Daphne, introducing me with a flourish of her hand. "Meet Jack's brother."

Captain Dirk reached out his hand and we shook like two grown men, him almost crushing my fingers. "I'm suitably impressed," he said. "It's a wonder you didn't freeze to death."

"Aren't you a clever *jongen*," said one of the stewardesses.

"And your dashing fiancé?" said another stewardess, looking around and hoping to spot Jack. "Is he along too?"

"If he did follow us, he'll be AWOL: absent without leave," said Captain Dirk. "Why, that could have him court-martial, *ja*."

"Then let's hope he hadn't tried," said Daphne. "We're getting married soon and I can't have him in the brig. You're all invited to the wedding," she added, stretching out her arms to include everyone in the general vicinity.

"But how will you get back to England?" asked Captain Dirk, sucking in his lips before telling us the exact same thing as the ticket agent.

Daphne started explaining how she planned to go straight to the British Embassy and ask for advice. "Surely they'll think of some way to get us home."

Captain Dirk's lips said, "*Ik ben bang dat*," while his face said, "Keep dreaming."

A bus painted with the BOAC logo pulled up to the curb and the driver came around and started loading the crew's suitcases into the back. The stewardesses stepped into the bus and lowered down the windows, all of them ogling me. The driver got back into his seat and yelled out something in Portuguese. The captain answered him with a raised index finger.

"Lisbon is a disaster at the moment," he said, taking off his cap and raking his fingers through his blonde hair. "With the Germans now occupying the South of France, half of Europe is fleeing to Lisbon hoping to find a means of escape. Quite frankly, you might be stuck here for some time, *ja*. We're the only airline making the route and every flight back to England is full. People are willing to do anything short of selling their mothers to get a seat. I can't even count the number of times I've been offered bribes."

I wondered if he was hinting at something. For sure, I wasn't about to cough up a bribe. And Daphne was stone-broke. Every penny she possessed was going to fund her wedding.

Captain Dirk went on: "From what I hear there are more than a hundred thousand refugees in Lisbon and more pouring in every day. Meaning that every hotel is full to overflowing. It is really is an international crisis, *ja*. I hear that the Red Cross is setting up emergency shelters in rat-infested basements, but that is no place for you."

Daphne started biting her fingernails again.

"We can camp out in a park," I said. "They got something like Central Park?"

The captain sucked on his lips. I could tell he didn't like my camping idea. Looking at Daphne, he said, "I say, why don't you come with us and we'll sort something out at the hotel. The girls will make room for you on a foldout cot and the boy is welcomed to stay in my room. Jan, my co-pilot, usually bunks with me, although on this layover he's visiting a…a friend in Lisbon. We're laid over for two nights. But when we fly back to England, we can't have the two of you in the cargo bin again."

"That's terrifically kind of you," said Daphne, holding a hand to her heart.

"Good man, your Lieutenant Mooney," said Captain Dirk. "I enjoyed our conversation immensely. Without a doubt he would do the same for my girlfriend were the chairs turned. That's how the English expression goes...chairs turned?"

"Sure thing," I said, not wanting to embarrass Captain Dirk in front of the stewardesses. I'd tell him about turning tables when we were man-to-man.

He bowed and let us board the bus ahead of him.

CHAPTER EIGHT

THE STEWARDESSES were jabbering away in Dutch, leaving me in peace to do some sightseeing. Daphne sat up front talking to Captain Dirk, and I found a place at the end of the bus on a long bench seat, all to myself. Lisbon was mostly fields of short, knobby trees. I tapped a stewardess on the shoulder and asked her what kind they were. "Olive," she said and turned back to gab with her friend. Too bad, because I hated olives and, from the look of it, that's all they had in Portugal. Olives were good for nothing but martinis, a concoction grownups mix up at cocktail hour, the hour they tell the kids to get lost. I tried a martini once and that was the last time. The drink is liquid fire, with nothing left at the end but an olive on a toothpick. Now, compare the olive to the maraschino cherry. Both are about the same size and have pits. But the maraschino cherry is good in Cherry cokes, Roy Rogerses, and on top of banana splits. Give me the cherry any day.

We passed a golf course, and I seen a palm tree for the first time ever. I started counting them, but gave up after a hundred. The place looked exactly like Hollywood, not that I'd ever been.

The bus engine began straining as we got going uphill. We jerked forward whenever the driver shifted gears. Daphne turned around, making sure I was still on the bus.

The distant ocean was Technicolor blue. I should've brought along sunglasses and baby oil. I took my jacket off and stuck my arm out the window, thinking to get myself a burn; which, after peeling, might turn into a tan. Along the way, there were lots of billboards for politicians; every one of them hucksters had a pasted on grin. The letters were same as English, but in a totally different order. The Portuguese language had long words and would be hard to crack. I needed an English-to-Portuguese dictionary. There was probably one gathering dust in the Sopwith library. *Too late*, I thought.

When we got into the city, traffic slowed us down enough to get a good look at Portuguese people. Old ladies wore kerchiefs on their heads, and some of the old men had on straw hats. But the younger people might as well of bought their clothes from a Sears, Roebuck & Company catalog, they looked so American.

A bell rang and we pulled up next to a trolley car. For a second there, I thought I was in San Francisco, not that I'd been there either. But in a shoebox back home in East Hempstead, New York, I had a View-Master slide of the California city. From what I could tell, Lisbon was the spitting image: lots of hills, with colorful houses facing out on the sea. The only difference was Lisbon had a castle, which I already knew from my research in the Sopwith library. I scanned the horizon, on the lookout for its watchtower, meaning to pay the place a visit before heading to Paris.

The other thing I knew about Lisbon was that in 1492, Christopher Columbus sailed from the city headed to India. Turned out he went the wrong way and didn't know it. Because of him, every American kid got a day off from school in October. Anyone who got me out of Saint Brendan's Catholic School was a hero in my eyes, didn't matter if he had a lousy sense of direction.

The bus wound its way uphill, making hairpin turns that tossed us left and right. I reached out for a trolley going the other way and a little girl reached out her arm and our fingertips touched. We pulled over and the bus driver swung the door open. Daphne said, "Thomas, stay with me," and we waited until everybody else stepped off.

The hotel was called *Residential Estrela Dos Santos* and had two stars bolted under a brass plaque with an ashtray stand under it. A bellhop opened the door for us and Captain Dirk came in last, handing over a tip.

"Leave your suitcase here and the boy will carry it up," he said to me. This was the high-life. The bellhop was dressed like an organ grinder and should've had a chimpanzee on his shoulder. I felt sorry for him, having to wear that monkey suit and carry our suitcases besides. I gave him a stick of gum, thinking I better hold onto my coin. He nodded and got right to work chewing.

The lobby was small and crowded with us jammed into it. Good thing I wasn't claustrophobic. The chandelier needed a good cleaning and the wallpaper was coming down in strips. The ceiling was spotted with brown watermarks, probably where somebody let a tub overflow in the room upstairs. A roach shot across the tile floor, reminding me of New York City. The place smelled like a mushroom.

So this is what you get for two stars, I thought. *Interesting.*

"I'm bunking in the girl's room, and you'll be with the captain," said Daphne. "He's already on to you, so be on your best behavior."

Captain Dirk waved two keys with brass knockers hanging from them. He led the way to an elevator. "Three at a time," he said. "Ladies first." He swung open the gate and the three stewardesses crammed in. We watched as they rose from the ground and out of sight. While we waited, Captain Dirk said, "The place isn't much, but the location is primo."

"You won't hear any complaints from us," said Daphne, elbowing me. "We are ever so grateful for a roof over our heads."

"I thank you," I said. "My mother thanks you. Jesus, Mary, and Joseph thank you."

The elevator returned empty and we stepped in. Captain Dirk kept his finger pressed on a black button until we were up on the sixth floor. We stepped out into a dark hall with only a dead plant for decoration and a framed photograph of Lisbon, hanging crooked. A stewardess stepped out of a room at the end of the hall and waved for Daphne. Captain Dirk put his key in the opposite door and flicked a light switch.

"It's not the Taj Mahal, but strangely enough it always feels as though I'm coming home. Same room four nights a week. Same ugly wallpaper, same leaky toilet, same ashtray—hopefully different sheets. I often wonder who sleeps in the bed on the three nights I'm not here."

The bellhop came in right behind us and laid our two suitcases next to the radiator. "Welcome back to the Residential Estrela Dos Santos, sir."

"See what I mean?" said Captain Dirk.

The bellhop reached down and turned a knob on the radiator. The thing began to rattle and hiss. Then he pulled open the curtains and I seen we had double doors leading out to a balcony with a twisty-curly iron railing.

"Can I?" I said, pointing to the balcony.

"Don't jump," said Captain Dirk. "I'm calling down for a drink. Anything I can get you?"

"Seriously, sir?" I said. "Do they have Coca-Cola with maraschino cherries?"

"No harm in asking."

Captain Dirk dialed a phone, which was placed on a night table. At the same time, he loosened his tie and shimmed out of his pilot's jacket. I stepped out on the balcony and looked down. Except for the observatory deck on top of the Empire State Building, and the Eiffel Tower, this was the highest I'd ever been above a street. From up there, people looked like ants. It would be a great place to launch paper airplanes.

Captain Dirk hung up the phone and said: "You're in luck. I ordered appetizers, in case the cherries weren't enough. I realize that you missed our outstanding cabin service."

"You're A-Okay, Captain." My stomach rumbled. My last meal was the Cadbury bar.

He told me to take the bed closest to the balcony, laying down on the other one and kicking off his shoes. "Beware of the spring that sticks up near your kidney."

"What's it like to be from Holland?" I asked. He was the first person I'd ever met from the place. Everything I knew about it included tulips, windmills, and wooden clogs.

"At the moment, lonely," he said. "But much better than being *in* Holland. We escaped when most weren't so lucky. My family is still in Amsterdam."

"Your wife and kids?"

"Mother, father, and two sisters. So far, I've avoided matrimony."

Three knocks on the door and I ran to open it. The bellhop balanced a tray on one hand. A metal platter was topped with a lid. Two bottles of Coca-Cola jiggled against a bottle of whiskey and glasses full of ice. My heart started racing. I stepped aside and let the bellhop enter. He placed the tray on a desk and opened the lids with a can opener he kept chained to his belt. "Will that be all, *Capitão?*"

Captain Dirk sat up and forked over another tip. I got a close look at the food: Mussels cracked open with wedges of lemon, black shriveled olives, and shrimps with the heads still attached, their beady eyes staring at me. A basket full of bread came with little pats of butter wrapped in foil. The label said *manteiga*, but under that was the French: *beurre*. Real butter. Wait'll I told Mrs. Balson.

"Mind if I show Daphne?" I said, because it was one of the strangest meals I ever seen.

"Take the tray with you. I'm not much hungry. Only, leave the whiskey and a glass." Captain Dirk yawned. He needed a nap after dodging Messerschmitts all the way from England. I set the booze on the night table next to him. "Thanks buddy," he said with his eyes closed. "Is that what you Americans say...*buddy?*"

"Exactly right."

I gripped the tray with both hands and shut the door behind me, using my foot. Daphne and the ladies started squealing when they got a look at what I'd brought them. Two of the stewardesses were already changed into bathrobes and had their hair down. By mistake my eye caught the refection of the third stewardess, standing in front of the bathroom mirror wearing nothing but a brassiere and slip.

"I'm Anke." It was the tall one, now a little shorter in her stocking feet.

"Cookie," said the other.

"No cookies—just shrimps and mussels," I said.

"Not cookie," said Daphne. "Cokkie. That's her name. I made the same mistake. She's Cokkie with one O and two K's."

They started gorging themselves, picking the mussels from the shells with a little two-pronged fork. I'd had plenty of mussels before. And clams—caught with my toes in the Long Island Sound. But I planned to stay clear of the shrimps. I let the ladies have one of the bottles of cola, but hoarded the cherries.

Anke told me their big plans for the evening: they were going gambling. "We're taking a taxi to the Palacio Estoril," she said. "It's about 25 kilometers outside of Lisbon, on the ocean. Swank isn't the word." She described the place: baroque curtains, gilded furniture, red plush carpets everywhere you stepped.

"We're looking for rich husbands," said Cokke, without even blushing. "The men playing at the roulette wheels are dripping with money. Really, Daphne—you can have your Spitfire pilot. I'm not planning to be a glorified waitress for the rest of my life. It's only a means to an end."

"One must be careful, though," said Anke. "I hear tell there are Nazi secret agents at the Palacio Estoril, pretending to be exiled Frenchmen. I've no intention of ending up in lederhosen, rolling out apple strudel and pickling sauerkraut."

"Oh, but one can always tell them apart. Gestapo agents have dark suntans," said Cokke.

This was the first I'd heard it. I listened with both ears.

"It's true," said Anke, gluing on fake eyelashes. "They say that Gestapo agents spend their free time sunning in the Alps, or on the French Riviera now that the Germans are occupying the South of France."

"Are there rich Germans at the casino?" I asked. "Germans who want a bargain on a diamond tiara?

Maybe half-blind Germans?" *Who*, I could've added, *don't know the difference between paste and real diamonds.*

"Oh, you wouldn't believe it," said Anke, "but outside the casino one will often find refugees selling off their valuables"—she made a sad face—"so that they can buy their way to freedom."

"Or Jewish refugees hoping for passage to Palestine," said Cokke. "It's true."

"Oh, that's *too* tragic," said Daphne, who was half-Jewish on her mother's side.

"One can pick up lovely things for a fraction of their value," said Anke. "Swiss watches and Austrian crystal, silverware and pearls. As for me, I wouldn't touch the stuff. It breaks my heart seeing it. I imagine my family back home having to sell off our treasured heirlooms only to buy bread. I hate the Nazis and what they've made of our lives. Heartbreaking. It would be immoral to take advantage of someone else's misfortune."

"You're doing them a favor," said Cokke. "One can't eat a Swiss watch."

Daphne was going to flip when she realized I'd taken a tiara off Lady Sopwith, but she'd come around once the mussels and olives were finished and she started to get hungry again. Back in the other room, I found Captain Dirk sound asleep. I took the glass out of his hand so's he wouldn't roll over and break it. The floorboards creaked and I tiptoed to my suitcase and back out the door carrying it.

"Don't tell me you're moving in with us?" said Daphne when she saw me.

"No way," I said. "But I figure I'll tag along to the casino tonight. I got a little something to sell. To someone with a suntan."

"You will not. Not if I have anything to say about it."

"Daphne, you're good at picking locks," I said when I seen the latches on both sides of the handle wouldn't budge. Funny, because I didn't remember locking the suitcase. I brought it over to the bed, laying it flat on the coverlet.

"What? You lost the key?" asked Daphne.

"The thing is, I never had a key. I could'a sworn it was open."

She took a hairpin from her hairdo and got straight to work, popping one lock straight off but having trouble with the other. I watched closely, trying to learn the tricks of the trade. That's when I noticed that the four gold letters were missing. "Move over," I said, rubbing my fingers over the place where Lord Sopwith's initials should've been. Somebody, somewheres in Lisbon, was about to find themselves the lucky owner of a fake tiara. "It's not my suitcase," I said.

"I know that," said Daphne.

"It's not Lord Sopwith's, neither."

Daphne's hand went to her mouth and she backed away from the suitcase like it had a bomb inside.

"Stop stalling," I said. "Pick the lock and let's see what we got stuck with.

CHAPTER NINE

THE LADIES NEEDED PRIVACY, so I took the suitcase back to Captain Dirk's room, moping all the way down the hall. The suitcase had nothing but farmer's overalls with the dirt still on them, an old moth-eaten felt hat, socks with holes in the toes, and a pair of work boots. The only thing worth keeping was a set of binoculars. I stood on Captain Dirk's balcony and focused on the store across the street. The lenses were so sharp, I could read the label on a cigar box. In a window down the street, I seen dribble coming from a sleeping man's mouth. At a grocer a block away, I made out a lemon and an orange.

I tried on the boots, which were dirty but brand spanking new. They were a little big in the toes—nothing a wad of toilet paper wouldn't fix. The rest of the clothes were worthless, so I threw them in the trash can.

I'd seen Captain Dirk's shoes sitting outside the door. He must've put them there so's somebody would come along and give them a good spit shine. I decided to put the boots next to his shoes, figuring they could use a polish too. As I walked them to the hall, I looked a little closer, thinking it was odd that the boots were so new when the clothes were rags. That's when I noticed something funny on the inside of the tongues, which were now hanging down over the laces. Somebody had removed the labels. I could see little threads sticking out where the label had once been sewn in. That got my attention, so I went back and took the clothes out of the trash. The labels were gone from them too.

Captain Dirk rolled on his back and started snoring. The suitcase was laying empty on the floor with the lid open. No wonder we'd gotten the wrong one. It was the twin of Lord Sopwith's. I got down on my knees to take a closer look. It had the same little yellow L's and V's embossed in the leather, the same brass latches with built-in locks, and the same handle. There were satin pockets inside the lid. I found a comb, a shaving brush and razor, a bar of soap, and boxer shorts. Then I checked the pockets along the sides and found nothing but men's handkerchiefs and an empty flask.

My back was leaned against the bed while I let the wheels in my head spin, keeping my eyes on the suitcase the whole time. The suspicion came to me slow but steady.

I remembered packing Lord Sopwith's suitcase. That tiara had a tall peak and it was a squeeze to get the lid closed. But the tiara wouldn't've fit in this suitcase, even though from the outside it was identical to the other one. It wasn't my imagination: Lord Sopwith's case was deeper inside by a couple inches.

I went back to the other room and made sure to knock before entering. Cokke yelled that it was safe to enter. The stewardesses were now dressed up in their Sunday-best clothes, with their hair rolled up and their cheeks and lips painted. They had on plenty of jewelry—what you call *costume*, not *paste*.

"Let's go explore the city, Thomas," said Daphne. "We'll find a coffee shop and get a sandwich. I'm sure the man at the front desk will exchange pounds for the local currency." She opened her change purse, a little thing that couldn't hold more than a day's wages. Her finger moved coins around, while her mouth drooped at the corners.

"Cool your heels a minute," I said, going for the little two-pronged fork.

Back in Captain Dirk's room I used the fork to pry the bottom from the inside of the suitcase. It pulled apart without much trouble. "Holy macaroni!" I shouted when I seen the secret compartment.

"*Wat?*" said Captain Dirk, sitting up and rubbing sleep from his eyes.

"There's something here you better see, sir."

He threw his feet onto the floor and stood up stretching and yawning. I explained about us taking the wrong suitcase from the airplane. That woke him up and he came over and took a look inside the hidden compartment. There were canisters of film—I counted 36—and the smallest camera I'd ever seen. It made a Kodak Brownie look like a tank.

"Leica," said Captain Dirk, tumbling it in his hands. "German made." I gave him the binoculars. "Same," he said, going to the balcony and trying them out for himself.

"They wouldn't fit in the secret compartment," I

said. "That was their mistake."

We found nautical maps with all sorts of scribbles made along the coast of England: "German writing," I said.

"Absolutely," said Captain Dirk. "I believe you've stumbled upon a German spy. Good work, my boy." He slapped my back so hard the air came out of my lungs. Then he shook my hand. This time I was ready and it didn't hurt half as much. "Of course, we've long suspected that German agents make their way back and forth from England on the BOAC flight. Military intelligence has even begun making spot checks, hoping to uncover just this sort of thing."

"I betcha the photographs are of military targets and landing points, so the Luftwaffe could know where to drop bombs and tell the Wehrmacht where to land an invading army."

"You'd make a good spy yourself, Thomas. I'm sure you're not far off the mark." He found a thick leather billfold in the compartment, opened it and whistled. "Reichsmarks, Portuguese escudo, French francs, and Spanish pesetas. Not to mention the British Pounds Sterling."

Daphne knocked on the door in her ladylike style, more of a tap than a knock. She was bowled over when we shown her what I'd found. "Jolly good work," she said, kissing my cheek. "You've likely saved lives, Thomas."

"You're the one who took the wrong suitcase, Daphne. Feel free to take a bow yourself. Do you think the king'll give us the Victory Cross?"

She made a deep curtsy, then got up on her toes and twirled around, making her skirt fly up above her knees. "This is ever so thrilling!" she said. "Imagine us uncovering a ring of spies. Us!"

"I say we take these Reichsmarks and trade them in for a nice dinner," said Captain Dirk. "As it happens, I'm acquainted with a café owner who runs a little black market currency exchange on the side. He also happens to make the perfect grilled ribeye."

"Oh, let's," said Daphne. "And how delicious that Adolf Hitler will be footing the bill."

"My thoughts exactly," said Captain Dirk. "And we shall order a very good vintage of wine to toast to the downfall of the Third Reich."

"And a very good bottle of Coca-Cola for me, to let him know the Americans are coming," I said.

"The very best vintage of cola, Thomas," said Daphne.

"1942 will do fine," I said. "Any older and it will be flat."

CHAPTER TEN

THE RESTAURANT WAS ONE of them dark, smoky places—down a few steps and with a low ceiling, made lower by things hanging from it: baskets and wine bottles wrapped in straw, copper pots, and lanterns. Captain Dirk had to duck. As soon as we got to our booth, the waiter started decorating it. First came a white tablecloth, smelling of starch. Then he brung over an electric lamp made to look like a candle, dripping wax and all. I volunteered to crawl under the table and plug it into the socket. Next he brung a vase of flowers. It reminded me of Lady Sop. She always had flowers on the table, even at breakfast. Only she would've said *brought* instead of *brung*, and she wouldn't've let the word *vase* rhyme with *lace*.

The waiter was giving us the full treatment. He put empty plates in front of us only to take them away as soon as we ordered. He opened up cotton napkins and put them in our laps. Those were the only napkins we were gonna get too, because there wasn't a napkin dispenser in the whole joint. I counted three kinds of forks and two spoons. All that fuss and he forgot to bring the ketchup and mustard bottles.

I looked around for a juke box, thinking this might be the kind of place to have one. But they had live music instead. Gypsy music. A whole band came to our table and played us a tune with violins and guitars. Captain Dirk bought a rose for Daphne from an old lady with missing teeth.

They were going to have to roll me back to the hotel. Since the *Abwehr*—German Intelligence—was paying, I ordered two *entrées* and three deserts. Turned out the Portuguese had egg pudding to beat all. While I stuffed myself, Daphne picked Captain Dirk's brain about transportation to Paris. I was glad to see that she was warming up to my plan. Maybe we'd rescue Sophie after all.

"I'm not happy about this," said Captain Dirk, wiping egg pudding from his mouth. "I strongly advise against making the journey. But if you're determined to go to Paris, I can't see that I can stop you."

"Duly noted," said Daphne. She hadn't touched her dessert. I stared at it until she pushed it my way.

Captain Dirk took a sip of his Port wine, a Portuguese specialty. "One thing I'll say in your favor is that it might be easier getting into France than getting back home to England. Not many people are making the trip in that direction, and for good reason."

I was thinking about Daphne, Jack, and me—how we hiked over the Pyrenees Mountains, making an escape from France. We had a Basque guide and the Belgian Resistance helping out. By the end of the hike, I was ready to drop dead from exhaustion and Jack had to carry me on his back. I didn't want to do that hike again any time soon.

"We can't trek over the Pyrenees Mountains," said Daphne. "It's getting to be winter and the higher passes will be treacherous, not to mention freezing cold. I'm not prepared to do it."

Captain Dirk suggested we ask refugees who'd just escaped from France. "I've seen them standing in an endless queue outside the American Embassy," he said, burping. It was exactly what I wanted to do, and so I let one loose myself.

"Goodness gracious," said Daphne. "The both of you have no table manners."

CHAPTER ELEVEN

5000 feet above Portugal

As the crew prepares the BOAC evening flight for landing, a stewardess bends at the waist, placing a napkin on a tray table.

"Can I get you anything else, sir?" she says, lifting a penciled eyebrow. "And, I do mean *anything*. It gets awfully lonely on layovers in Lisbon."

"Just get me a Pimm's and ginger ale. And be fast about it," says the man, refusing to meet the stewardess's eye.

She heads straight for the galley. "That one in 2B...," she says to the steward, switching to Dutch. "You don't think he's one of those Nazi spies, do you?"

The steward turns casually, narrowing his eyes as he examines the passenger in 2B. "We can never be too careful," he says, thinking about the posters plastered around England. He brings up an image of one particularly effective poster: a Nazi, half his body in plainclothes, the other half in an Waffen-SS uniform. He mouths the slogan: *Talk less...you never know.* He puts his mouth near the stewardess's ear:

"What makes you suspicious, Katja?"

"I don't know exactly," says the stewardess. "He's so terribly cold, *ja*. Gives me heart palpitations just hearing his voice. He's not British, I'm certain of it. He's got a very odd accent, and…" She pauses to think and then decides, "It's his cleft chin, and the way his eyebrows are nearly joined together in the middle. Some girls might call that handsome, but *not* me."

"I don't know…he's handsome enough," says the steward.

"Incidentally, he asked for a Pimm's and ginger ale."

"The Germans train their spies to know the habits of Englishmen. Makes sense that he'd ask for a Pimm's and ginger ale."

"Let's wait and see if he asks for lime juice, too."

"If he knows what he's about, he will. It's frightening how well the Abwehr train their spies. Last week they rounded up a whole cell of them living in Cornwall and pretending to be with the Local Defense Volunteers. On the lookout for German planes, or so they said. No one batted an eyelash when they pulled out their binoculars and spyglasses."

"Spyglasses. Can you imagine that?" says the stewardess with a shiver. "And all the time they were reporting back to Berlin with military positions, using their long-range ham radios, *ja*. Exactly why the Luftwaffe is so accurate on their bomb raids. My flatmate's boyfriend died in the Blitz. And then there was the stewardess who worked for Air France, Édith was her name. She escaped France only to be killed by a falling chimney."

The steward pours Pimm's into a glass and then flips the cap on a bottle of ginger ale. He spits into the glass. "We're not giving him lime. No we're not. Tell him we've run short. Blame it on rationing."

The stewardess takes the glass and sighs. "At least we're safe from the Luftwaffe this time, because I'm sure that he radioed ahead telling them his flight plan. I've been losing sleep worried that they'll shoot us down. Look at the bags under my eyes. No amount of concealer can cover them."

"I'll have a word with Captain Tepas. He'll alert the authorities as soon as we touch ground," says the steward. "Probably won't do any good, but it will delay 2B an hour or two. By the way. Did you notice who we've got in 4A?"

The stewardess cranes her head over the steward's shoulder. She pulls a pair of eyeglasses from her apron pocket, setting them on the bridge of her nose. As she folds them away again, she says, "You know I'm blind as a bat. Why didn't you point him out sooner, Pieter?"

"Saving him for myself," says the steward with a wink.

"And me who's seen *Gone With The Wind* a dozen times. But he looks so different out of uniform, so *completely* different."

A minute later, she says to the passenger sitting in 4A, "Can I get you anything, Mr. Howard? And I do mean *anything*..."

CHAPTER TWELVE

THE NEXT MORNING, after sleeping like a rock, I found Captain Dirk already awake. He was sitting by the double doors leading out to the balcony, reading a newspaper and drinking orange juice and coffee at the same time.

"Rest day for me," he said. "Might go on a stroll later, but nothing more taxing than that." He reached in his pocket and handed me money: "The change from last night. You deserve it. Buy yourself and Daphne a hardy breakfast. Might want to sample the Portuguese pastries. Much better than the English fare."

"Aye, aye, Cap'n," I said.

Daphne was dressed and rip-roaring to go. We got back in the elevator and I pushed the button. The man at the front desk recommended a café around the corner. The way he went on about it, I knew it was probably owned by a relative. He lent us a map after circling the café, and then the American Embassy after we asked him to.

"Can we take one of them cable cars to get there?" I asked. I was a jumping bean with excitement. Yesterday I had my first airplane ride and today it would be a tram.

We found the café easy enough. The owner was standing outside, a carbon copy of the hotel man. Racks were stuffed full of pastries in all kinds of shapes: rectangles, triangles, towers and twists; some were filled with cheese and some with meat. Daphne let drop that we were staying at the Residential Estrela Dos Santos and the man showed us to a table with a view of the street. She ordered a double espresso and an orange juice for me, claiming that too much cola would rot my teeth. "And you've lost your toothbrush," she said, thinking that I'd packed one in Lord Sopwith's suitcase.

I picked the pastries. While we ate, Daphne scanned a French newspaper. "*Havas News Agency*," she said. "It's in both Portuguese and French. Oh my!" A hand flew to her mouth. "North Africa is heating up. I'm afraid the news isn't good. You know that Jack wanted to volunteer to go to Malta, but I put my foot down."

"I heard Sel Edner went. And the Number 601 squadron is in Egypt. Jack should've volunteered to go there."

"Jack's not leaving England until I have a wedding ring on my finger."

"He flies to France and Belgium every day, remember?"

"Doesn't count if he doesn't land the Spitfire."

I paid the bill and we found the cable car stop without a problem. There was a line of people waiting and two cars filled up before there was room for us. Luckily we were at the front of the line by then and got the seat behind the driver, one with a panoramic view. A route map was pasted to the wall and I seen that the cable car went around in a loop.

"What's to stop us from staying on and looping around a few times?" I asked Daphne.

"Nothing but a need to get off and carry on with one's business," Daphne said.

I was sitting at the window and caught sight of the castle, hanging over the sea, looking like it might tumble in. "Nothing beats this but the roller coaster at Coney Island," I said. "Let's stay on if they let us."

"And meanwhile, whilst we go around in circles, my best friend in the world is having her fingernails torn out by the Gestapo."

Daphne was finally getting into the swing of things.

We got off by a statue of a conquistador riding a stallion. I checked to see if it was Christopher Columbus, but it wasn't. We climbed up a thirty-degree staircase and came to a square with a church on one corner. Daphne consulted the map.

"This isn't the right place at *tall*," she said. "Why I believe this is an American travel agency, not the embassy. How very frustrating."

Turned out we had to take two more tram rides, which was fine by me. We saw the sea, even got a look at cruise ships.

The American Embassy was in a fancy-schmancy mansion surrounded by gardens. This way refugees would be fooled into thinking that all Americans were rich. It's what my ma and da thought before they came over from

Ireland: *Street paved with gold*. Boy, oh boy, were they in for a let down.

Hordes of people crowded outside the embassy. An American flag flapped above the front door. I put my hand on my heart and recited the Pledge of Allegiance.

We got up closer and I seen two American soldiers blocking the entrance. People were waving papers in their faces. The soldiers had to put their rifles up against their chest just to keep from being crushed.

I noticed a lady turning back. She had a face that might've been pretty if only she'd smile. A boy and two small girls huddled up against her. They had faces like poor kids who'd just looked into a candy store. The family walked past us, dragging their feet. I heard them speaking German.

"It's no use," the lady said. "We will try again tomorrow."

"They're letting Germans go to America?" I whispered to Daphne.

"It *tis* odd," she said. "Unless...perhaps...they're Jews who have managed to escape Nazi occupation."

The boy overheard us talking and said in English: "You are correct in thinking we have escaped, although we aren't German. We are Austrian, from Linz."

"Isn't that where Hitler was born?" I said.

"That's right," said the boy. He reached his hand out to me: "I'm Jacob Hershberg. This is my mother and these are my sisters. They don't speak English."

"Where's your father," I asked.

"He's waiting for us in Brooklyn, New York. He

went ahead to secure a job, and a flat for us to live in. And yet, even so, the Americans are slow to endorse our visas. And with so many people after the same thing, it's become impossible to get into the door."

Jacob's mother said something to him and he asked us where we were from. Her eyes lit up when she heard I was from New York.

"My mother has a million questions for you," said Jacob. "May we buy you a cup of coffee?"

Daphne said yes really fast, even when I knew she'd just had a double shot of espresso. This was our chance to get the information we needed. If Jacob and his family didn't know a way into France, we'd return to the embassy and try again with someone else. I had a good feeling about Jacob. For one thing, he was about my age. And his English was better than mine—more Shakespearian, that is.

"We know a coffee shop with free refills," said Jacob. "And it's warm inside."

Mrs. Hershberg said something again. I got the idea that she could understand a lot of what was being said.

"My mother prefers this place because the owner doesn't mind that we sit there for hours on end. It's around the corner," said Jacob. He started walking down an alley and we followed. Daphne took Mrs. Hershberg's elbow, glad to have a friend. As it turned out, they both knew French. Before long they were chattering away.

We came to learn that the Hershbergs had been stuck in Lisbon for more than a month. Every day, they went to the American Embassy with proof that Mr.

Hershberg was living in New York on a proper visa. On top of that, they had a letter from his boss, a tailor out on Flatbush Avenue with glowing things to say about his newest employee. Jacob showed me the letters and they seemed legit. If it was up to me, I'd let them go to America and I told him so.

"We've already had an interview with the American Embassy," he said. "The problem is that when we inquire about the status of our visas, we are told to come back the next day. They're overwhelmed." He sighed. "Every day another tragic story comes to their door. Some people sleep on the street just to be first in line. Or perhaps they have no other option. We are fortunate to have found a small room. Today we arrived at the Embassy before the sun had come up and already there were many people in line ahead of us."

"I figure that me being American gives me the right to cut in front of everyone else." I said.

Jacob agreed.

Coffee was brought to the table, along with hot cocoa. Mine came with extra whipped cream. This was the good life, being in a country without rationing.

Meanwhile Jacob told me how they'd escaped from Austria. It was back before the war started. The Nazis annexed Austria and began roughhousing the Jews. Jacob's family hightailed it out of there, and good riddance to Hitler. They went to Paris, figuring that their troubles were over. But in 1940 they had to flee to the South of France. Jacob went on: "We moved to Marseilles, staying with my uncle's in-laws. My father anticipated the worst, worried that the Vichy government would turn on our people sooner or later. Six months ago he left for America, hoping to find work and earn enough for our tickets. He did that within no time, working around the clock until his eyes were throbbing, *Baruch Ha Shem*, we left a fortnight before the South of France was occupied by the Germans. We have a booking on an ocean liner departing in two day's time."

"Then you're set," I said, a little jealous if the truth be told.

"But without a proper visa to America we will not be permitted onboard the ship."

"Seems simple enough," I said. "I'm gonna march up to the soldiers singing 'The Star Spangled Banner.' Them doors will fly open for us."

"I should have thought of that," said Jacob. "Only I've never heard the song."

"I'll teach you. It's something you're gonna have to know if you ever want to see the Brooklyn Dodgers play at Ebbets field"—Jacob looked confused—"I'm talking about baseball."

"I've heard of that sport! It requires a bat and a ball, if I'm not mistaken."

"Promise me you won't become a Yankee fan and I'll help you get that visa."

"I hate the Yankees already," he said.

Meanwhile Daphne was pumping the mother for information. When Mrs. Hershberg went to powder her nose, Daphne told me everything she'd learned. Seemed there *was* a train between Spain and France. I was amazed that the Germans allowed the line to stay open. Rumors were flying, it seemed. The Nazis were using the train to transport gold into Spain and onward to Portugal. "Lisbon is an ideal place to launder gold," said Daphne.

"They can't wash it in Germany?" I asked, a bit confused.

"No, silly. Money laundering is a process whereby one takes ill-gotten gains and trades it for ready money. So you see, money that was considered dirty, because it was stolen or gained through criminal activity is, *presto*, clean."

"Oh, I get it. The Mafia in New York does that using ice cream trucks. Ma makes me get my ice cream bars from Good Humor 'cause she says they're on the up and up. Mr. Frosty has soft-serve, but she says they're in the racket."

"Very clever, the Mafia," said Daphne. "And *do* let's try and help these darling people. Their story is so tragic and they've lost nearly everything. Oh, how I hate Hitler and his Fascist lot."

After that, Jacob and me made a plan and everyone fell in line. We marched back to the embassy, me leading the way. I had to yell over the crowd to get a soldier's attention.

"Hey Bud, over here," I shouted with my New York accent, so's there was no mistaking me for a refugee. "Let us Yanks in, would ya?"

One of the soldiers parted the crowd for us. "Quickly now or there'll be a stampede," he said, pointing to a door with U.S. CITIZEN SERVICES painted on the glass.

"Yankee-doodle dandy," I said to a lady sitting behind a desk. "Any way to get a visa around here?"

"Come in, please," she said.

On the wall behind the desk was a framed photograph of President Roosevelt, which I dutifully saluted. Jacob's mother took a seat next to me and Daphne and the rest of them stood, keeping their mouths shut like I'd told them to. On the desk was a plaque that read B. J. Shaw. B. J. had yellow pencils lined up on the desk, each with a razor-sharp point. There was an "In" and "Out" tray, and forms with carbon paper stuck between the sheets.

"You're American, are you?" she asked, glancing at each one of us.

"My ma came through Ellis Island in 1916," I said, warming her up. I was about to employ my gift of gab. Ma said that when you want something, all you had to do was talk non-stop. I seen her do it at the butcher shop, where she always got the best cut of meat. Without missing a beat, I said: "Da came to America in 1914. Him and my ma, they met at a church dance. I think it was called Saint Columbo, over on the Lower West Side."

"It's a busy day for—" said B. J.

"I'm American on account of my being born at Mercy Hospital in Rockville Centre," I said. "You heard of the place?"

"No, I'm from Virginia."

"I know about Virginia. That's where they got Appomattox, that place where Lee surrendered to Grant. Not that I want to rub that in your face. See, I know my American History. I got a B+ in American History, I swear'ta God. Got it for making a diorama of George Washington crossing over the river from Staten Island. I used cotton balls for the waves, ice cream sticks for his boat. Had to eat a bunch of ice pops to do it. The nun said it was the best thing she ever laid eyes on. Her name is Sister Aloysius, you can ask her yourself."

"Wha—?" said B. J.

"Never been to Virginia myself, but I'm dying to go to Monticello. Everyone's gotta see the Jefferson place, they say."

Jacob shook his head in agreement, even though I'm sure he didn't have a clue what I was talking about.

I rattled on: "That Jefferson place was built by slaves. That's the bad part."

Sooner or later, B. J. would give me whatever I wanted just to get rid of me. I gave a blow-by-blow description of the White House and the Capitol building. Whenever she tried to get a word in edgewise, I piped in with another tidbit about America: The Grand Canyon, Brooklyn Bridge, Mount Rushmore; even the geyser at Yellowstone got a plug. I racked my brain trying to remember my View-Master slides. I threw in something about bears.

B. J.'s eyes rolled around in the sockets, she nodded off once or twice. Finally, she said, "And how *exactly* can

I be of help?"

I lowered my voice to a whisper. "Don't make a liar out of me. I promised these swell people to help them get a foot in the door."

"Did you? You mean to say this isn't your family?" She narrowed her eyes and looked back and forth between Jacob and me, trying to catch our differences.

"Look," I said, "I told these people about the Statue of Liberty: 'Give me your dog-tired, your dirt-poor, your huddled masses dying to breathe free.'"

"It's *yearning* to breathe free," said B. J.

"—them miserable refuge of your teeming shore. Send them homeless—"

"Stop already," she said. "Give me their documents and I'll see what I can do."

Jacob ripped the papers from his coat pocket and slapped them on the desk. B. J. looked them over. "Wait here," she said, making her way out the door. Then she looked at Daphne. "What about you, miss? I don't see your papers amongst the others."

"Ah, I'm set," said Daphne. "I'm about to marry an American Spitfire pilot. This blabber mouth's brother, in fact."

"Well, congratulations," said B. J. "I hope your fiancé is the silent type."

We waited a long time for her to return. Daphne kept biting her nails. Jacob's mother prayed by rocking her body back and forth.

Daphne said, "Here she comes, at last."

"Happy face or mean face?" I asked.

"Deadpan, leaning towards trepidation."

B. J. took her seat again. She found a stamp and an ink-pad in her drawer. If I'd known it was there, we could've saved ourselves a lot of trouble. She stamped a bunch of forms and put her signature everywhere, even inside the passports. "*Bon Voyage*," she said, handing everything to Mrs. Hershberg. To me she said: "Don't let me see your face around here again. I mean it."

Mrs. Hershberg hugged me so tight I thought my guts would spill out. The girls made me dance around in a circle with them. Jacob reached out a hand.

"I don't know how to thank you, Tommy. I hope that you get back to America soon. We can go to a Dodgers game together."

"I'd like nothing better," I said. "But first I need to rescue our friend Sophie from the Nazis."

Jacob's face fell: "That will put you terrible danger. Where is your friend?"

"Paris, we think. At least, that's where she lived before she went missing. Your ma told Daphne we could get a train from the north of Spain."

"Yes, that's how we came." He scratched his head. "They'll check your papers at the border. It won't be safe for an American and British citizen. The Nazis might arrest you. We were lucky. The French Resistance provided us with Spanish passports."

Jacob's mother spoke in German too rapid for me to catch. She opened her pocketbook and found an envelope. Inside were four passports. She handed two to

Daphne.

"We won't be needing these, thanks to you," said Jacob. "Spanish passports with French and Portuguese visas. Entirely forged, but excellent forgeries. You can use mine and Daphne can use my mother's. The photographs won't match, though. Take a night train over the border and look for a dim place to sit. Daphne can cover her face with a *mantilla*. She can buy one in Spain. You speak Spanish I hope?"

"I know a few words," said Daphne.

"And I can speak German," I said.

"Then you should be in good stead. Speak as little as possible. Not like at the embassy."

Everyone laughed, even though I could tell that the Hershbergs were worried about us.

Jacob said, "The Nazis aren't manning the borders as tightly as did the Vichy government. Everything is chaos at the moment and they haven't managed to make order yet. Between Canfranc, France, and Bedous, Spain, we sat up front with the locomotive driver—the Resistance arranged for this. The locomotive cabin isn't usually checked at the border."

Jacob tapped his mouth. "That gives me an idea. The driver was a man named Arnaud. See if you can find him, pay a small bribe if need be. It will be safer than sitting in a passenger cabin. I suspect that Arnaud is accustomed to stowing contraband."

"Thanks for the heads-up. And for the passports," I said.

"It was a fair exchange," said Jacob.

I wrote my address in East Hempstead inside Jacob's notebook, and then the Hershberg family were off to the shipping company. Jacob's mother promised to pray for us every morning. I gave Jacob an American nickel and told him to buy a Hershey bar when he got to New York. I asked him to drop a line to my ma, too.

"We can meet at Ebbets Field," I said.

"You'll take us to see the Statue of Liberty?" asked Jacob.

"Sure thing, my pleasure."

"When next we met, we will no longer be *yearning* to be free."

" 'Cause we'll *be* free," I said.

We waved until the Hershberg family turned a corner. Daphne was weepy, like she was saying goodbye to family.

CHAPTER THIRTEEN

DAPHNE WENT SHOPPING for essential ladies' things: an extra pair of underwear and nylon stockings if she could find them. She'd be going to the train station to get us tickets for Madrid, too. No mention of visiting the British Embassy or the downtown BOAC office. Now that we were halfway to Paris, she wasn't looking back. She pretended not to be worried about Sophie, but I seen through it. I caught her mumbling to herself, saying, "Oh, don't be daft, Daphne...Sophie is per*rrrr*fectly fine...Right as rain...Tip-top," just before swallowing back tears. When she seen I was watching, she said in a high-pitched voice, faster and louder than normal, "Tommy, won't it be a hoot when we show up and find out it was all a joke?" She laughed like Bette Davis—my least favorite actress—sounding shrill and borderline insane. But soon as my back was turned she let her face crumble, wrung her hands, and sighed. I watched her reflection in the window glass—a backwards image, but there was still no fooling me. Only time I seen her this troubled was when Jack was missing in action.

Captain Dirk was sitting in the same place where I'd left

him. He laid his book down and said, "Not bad. It's by Helen MacInnes, a Scottish author. Spy genre. Not bad at all."

"Are you finished with it?" I asked. My books were lost with Lord Sopwith's suitcase. And I loved a good spy yarn. They helped with my espionage training. I already had a foot in the door with MI5—the British Security Service—after uncovering a cell of Nazi spies working undercover as WAAF plotters and RAF navigators. Everything I knew about espionage came from movies, paperbacks, and personal experience. *The 39 Steps* was my favorite so far, the Hitchcock version that is.

"Keep it," said Captain Dirk, tossing the book to me.

I leafed through *Above Suspicion*, then I got cozy on the bed, fluffing the pillows first. Captain Dirk called down for two colas with ice.

What would we do without Captain Dirk? I wondered.

Daphne didn't get back until I'd finished three chapters.

"We're set," she said, waving tickets in my face. "There's a night train and I managed to get us a place in second class. It's not the sleeper car, but the seats fold down. I couldn't afford the sleeper. . ."

"What's in that shopping bag?" I asked.

"None of your business."

The bag had the word *lingerie* printed on it, so I didn't push.

"I've been thinking," said Captain Dirk, reaching

for the leather billfold we'd found in the Nazi spy suit-case. "You ought to take this. You'll be needing it. And besides, if I hand it over to British Intelligence, along with the rest of what we found, it will likely end up in a file cabinet until the war is over."

"Are you quite certain it will be permissible?" asked Daphne.

"I'm the captain of the ship, supreme commander," said Captain Dirk. "We found it on my flight and so it's up to me to decided what happens with it. I'll take the billfold, though. It might provide evidence."

"Fingerprints," I said. Only Captain Dirk had his fingertips all over the billfold.

Meanwhile Daphne was flipping through the money. "This will come in handy. But it's an awful lot. More than we'll need."

"Whatever is left over, give to the French Resistance," said Captain Dirk. "And by the way, when I went to trade the Reichsmarks last night I learned that they are quite useless in Portugal. I had to pay the restaurant bill with Portuguese currency. But the Reichsmarks should be useful in France. The Germans print currency without gold to back it, so once they're defeated it won't be worth the paper it's printed on. Spend it fast."

The captain winked.

Our train didn't leave until ten o'clock that night, but the book kept me occupied until suppertime, when Captain Dirk ordered room service again. Afterwards, the three of us walked over to the castle. Spotlights lit the place up.

That was the funny thing about Lisbon, how bright it was at night. They didn't have the blackout like in England. Daphne said she needed sunglasses because she wasn't used to them neon lights glaring in her eyes. We walked by a movie theater so bright you could've seen it from the moon. For the first time in months, I could peek into people's windows. Luckily, I'd brought along the German binoculars. The lenses were so good, I could see the lighthouse on the tip of Long Island. Could've sworn it.

"Impossible," said Daphne. "The curve of the earth would prevent one from seeing across an ocean. The world is round, after all."

"Try and tell Christopher Columbus that," I said.

Cannons were mounted to the rapports and I scrabbled out onto the end of one, hanging over the edge with a hundred foot drop below me. Daphne started yelling for me to come down. On the way back to the hotel, I spotted a rack of postcards. We picked out one showing the castle and bought a Portuguese stamp, too.

"We really shouldn't have written from Portugal," said Daphne, after we put the postcard in a mailbox. "Your mother has enough to worry about."

After that, we said our goodbyes to Captain Dirk and the stewardesses. One of them gave Daphne her suitcase, packed with frilly things. Another stewardess gave Daphne a lipstick and a pot of rouge. In exchange, Daphne promised to bring back French perfume. The dames squealed with joy. I had to put my hands over my ears.

We got to the train station with time to spare. The place was made of bathroom tiles, floor to ceiling, same as most of Lisbon. Sometimes the tiles fit together into a picture. Daphne said they were "smashing." She'd know, being an artist.

Our train pulled in right on the stroke of ten. We were in a cabin with four other passengers. We made the seats flat and then laid down like sardines in a can.

I took the place near the door.

Daphne was out before her head hit the cushion. I fished through her pocketbook, took the Portuguese money, and went exploring. Three cars up I found the restaurant car and ordered a cocoa and a piece of cake. It came with pineapple on top. I had my book, *Above Suspicion*, along.

The heroes in the story were two spies, an Oxford don and his wife, pretending to be on a hiking trip to the German Alps in 1936. They were trying to locate a missing agent. I was riveted and didn't sleep a wink, interrupted only once when a Spanish policeman came around wanting a look at my passport. Luckily, he didn't want *too* close a look.

Come daylight, I woke Daphne and said, "Welcome to Spain!" and then showed her the way to the restaurant car. We ordered another piece of pineapple upside-down cake, coffee, and toast. Before long we were pulling into Madrid. It would've been nice to sightsee, maybe take in a bullfight, but the connection to Canfranc was leaving right then. We ran full-speed to the train. A conductor had to hold the door open for us. By the time we found our seats we were both gasping for air.

We got off in Canfranc and hung out near the end of the platform, waiting for a train to pull in and hoping that Arnaud was the locomotive driver.

But the driver turned out to be another fella. Daphne told him how much I wanted a ride in the locomotive compartment and even volunteered me for shoveling coal. But he was onto the fact that we were sneaking into France spy-style. After Daphne slipped him a Spanish bill, he welcomed us into the compartment.

Good thing too.

Because when we crossed over into France, there were Nazi soldiers waiting on the track. They had rifles and German Shepherds. I spotted a Gestapo agent, dressed in a long black trench coat. The locomotive driver stood in the snow outside the locomotive, blocking the door and smoking a cigarette. Daphne and me hid behind the coal bin. For two minutes there, I regretted coming to France—the time it took for one of them Nazis to questioned the locomotive driver. It took everything not to wet my pants.

We were almost to the next station when the locomotive driver stopped the train and told us to get down. "Best you walk to town," he said. "There you can hire a taxi to the Sarrance station. You want to avoid Bedous. This is where the Germans inspect baggage and ask probing questions."

I wasn't happy about walking, but at least it was downhill. Along the way, we stopped in a village and got us some hot drinks. From there we hitched a ride to Sarrance. The train to Paris didn't leave until later that day. We had to look inconspicuous, which was impossible in Converse sneakers. Daphne asked around and found a man selling used clothes.

"Your blue jeans scream American, Thomas. Thankfully, these used clothes are clean enough. Think of it as a disguise," she added, knowing just what to say.

Before long, she had me in wool trousers and a vest/jacket combo, with suspenders instead of a belt. I switched into the work boots, leaving my sneakers behind: a crying shame. To finish the getup, Daphne picked out a sweater with patches on the elbows, a scratchy scarf, gloves to match, and a tweed cap. When I pulled the brim down over my eyes, she said I looked like a Parisian street urchin.

"What I need is one of them paste-on mustaches," I said.

There weren't many Germans around. For one thing, it was freezing cold up in the Pyrenees Mountains. Nazis, I'd heard said, preferred the Riviera. Daphne started shivering and I figured it was payback time. I made her try on an ugly red coat lined in matted rabbit fur.

"It's so out of fashion," she said, looking at herself in a mirror.

"Think of it as a disguise," I said.

The shopkeeper threw in a Swiss Army blanket and we huddled together on a bench with it wrapped around us. To get our minds off the fact that our toes were getting frostbit, I brought Daphne up to speed on *Above*

Suspicion. We began reading along together, with her looking over my shoulder.

"But is it a good idea to be sitting in German-occupied France reading a book about English spies?" she said. She had a point.

People began straggling into the station. A man came along selling newspapers, magazines, and sandwiches on French *baguettes.* Daphne bought a fashion magazine for herself and a comic for me. I slipped *Above Suspicion* into our suitcase, deep into one of the side pockets.

A whistle blew and a train came chugging into the station. The car numbers were chalked on the side of each carriage and some of the numbers had rubbed off. We ran down the track trying to find our car. Finally, Daphne hired a porter just to show us the way, even when we didn't really need him to carry our one suitcase.

We were on our way back to Paris.

For most of the trip we had swell cabin mates: a lady who shared apples with us, a man who let me smell his cigar, and a mother with twins. But at the Tours station, a group of *Sturmabteilung* soldiers boarded our cabin. "Brownshirts," you call them, or storm troopers—take your pick. My shoulder brushed up against a swastika armband. I was about to start slugging, until Daphne began making bug-eyes at me. We closed our eyes and pretended to be asleep, but neither of us could do it until after the SS vacated our cabin. We were in Orleans when they got off, home of the Louisiana pioneers.

After that, we were dead to the world until a conductor came down the corridor yelling, "*Gare d'Auster-litz! Gare d'Austerlitz!*"

"Paris, oh, how I love Paris," said Daphne, taking her suitcase from the rack.

CHAPTER FOURTEEN

THIS WAS MY SECOND trip to Paris and it felt like a homecoming. I could barely remember my real home in East Hempstead, New York. When I tried to picture my school, Saint Brendan's, all I saw was something like a heat wave. Even the soda fountain on Jerusalem Avenue was like a mirage. But Paris was an old friend—a snotty friend, but a friend just the same.

Right off, I noticed there weren't as many Nazis loitering about. At first I figured they were having a rally. Nazis like to gather in packs, sorta like rabid dogs. But then Daphne said it was because they were spread thin, what with occupying all of France. On top of that, they were shipping soldiers off to Northern Africa. "Where the Americans will show Rommel what a breakfast of Wheaties can do," I bragged.

When Daphne and me was in Paris last time, it was summer. Now it was nasty cold, the kinda cold that freezes the hairs in your nostrils. Cold that has you coughing up green phlegm before long.

The French ladies looked fatter, too. Not that they were, only a lot of them were wearing fur coats. I got of whiff of mothballs every time we passed one of them dames.

We stepped out of the station and got hit with sleet and freezing rain. A hail ball hit my cheek and left a mark. Daphne ducked into a store and bought an umbrella and one of them waterproof kerchiefs to protect her hat. The hat was useless. It looked like a pincushion and didn't even cover the tips of her ears. Next she bought herself rubber galoshes. Luckily I had the work boots. In my opinion, galoshes are for little kids and old ladies.

It was morning in Paris and the smell of croissants filled the air. We let our noses lead us to the source. A sign in the window said, "No Jews Admitted," in both French and German. Daphne was fuming mad.

" 'Cause you're half-Jewish?" I whispered. "How're they gonna know, what with your Spanish passport?"

"It's the principle," she said.

We found another place, this one without croissants. They had stale rolls, which we couldn't even buy without a ration coupon. No cola either, only Fanta. The tables were the size of a cake platter. We had to squeeze into our chairs they were so close together. A lady gave me a dirty look when I pushed my chair back an inch. I said, *"Excusez-moi, mademoiselle,"* with a dead-on imitation of Charles de Gaulle. The lady smiled and slid her chair in. Not because I said, *excuse me,* but because I called her a young lady. In actuality, she had one foot in the grave.

"Pardon-moi," she giggled. I swear, she was flirting with me.

Daphne snapped a finger and shouted, "*Garçon!*," and a waiter came running over. "It's lovely to be back in Paris," she said after we'd ordered. "I only wish there wasn't a war on. I miss the days when my only worry was getting to art class on time, or remembering which day the Louvre was open and which day it closed. Now it's closed seven days a week and only heaven knows what's become of the paintings. They were shipped to the south, is what I heard." She wiped a tear from the corner of her eye. "Hitler will want to get his hands on the whole collection, especially the *Mona Lisa*. He'll burn anything he doesn't fancy."

I was no artist, finger painting was about it, but I'd been to the Metropolitan Museum of Art. My sister Nancy lured me with promises of cat mummies, when all along she meant to show me what she called "fine art."

Fine, I'll say.

Paintings of totally naked ladies.

So I asked Daphne to fill me in on what kind of art the Nazis fancied and what they didn't. Turned out that back when the Germans first took Paris, they made a bonfire out of paintings and books. But later on, when they figured out what them paintings were worth, they started selling them instead. Daphne began listing the artists that Hitler didn't like: "Cézanne, Dalí, Picasso, Van Gogh, Miró, Morandi, Braque, Klee—"

"Who are they?

"Painters of 'Degenerate Art,' according to Hitler."

"You mean paintings of naked ladies?"

"No. As a matter of fact, most are paintings of ordinary people, or flowers, or fruit, or plain old bottles. But they're too modern for Hitler's taste. He hates modern art. You see, before he was a fascist megalomaniac dictator, he was a realist painter."

"They the ones painting naked ladies?"

"Yes, as a matter of fact."

"Figures then that Hitler did that. *He's* the degenerate."

"You're missing the point," said Daphne. She called for the waiter and ordered another espresso. It came in a doll's cup, so she needed more than one. She complained, "It's not even coffee. Toasted barley with chicory would be my guess."

"There's no time to waste," I said, sucking up my Fanta and suggesting we take a cab to Sophie's apartment building.

Daphne tried to smile. "I'm sure that by now Sophie is safely home. Won't she laugh her head off when she sees we've come all this way simply because of a letter written with vinegar? The very idea of it. This is obviously Juliette's idea of a lark. You know how young girls can be."

"Not really," I said. "They're a mystery. If it weren't for them paintings of naked ladies and the Sears, Roebuck catalog, I'd know practically nothing."

"What's a Sears, Roebuck catalog?"

"They sell everything under the sun, which includes garter belts and brassieres."

"You didn't!"

"I was looking for model airplanes."

Daphne did a tut-tut. "An accident, I'm sure. Well,

what I'm trying to say is that girls Juliette's age enjoy a lark. My, my, aren't we going to have a laugh."

"Only one way to find out," I said.

Our cabbie took turns like he was in the Grand Prix. I loved it, but Daphne gripped the seatback for dear life. She screamed once or *thrice*, as Lady Sop would say.

"Give him a good tip," I said, when we arrived.

"I will not," said Daphne, huffing. "I have a mind to report him to the police."

We pressed the bell for the Doumer apartment and I stepped out to the sidewalk, looking up at the fifth floor. Before long, a window swung open and Juliette hung half her body out and yelled: "*Vache sacrée!*" Which means "holy cow."

She shut the window again and we waited.

Juliette was six months older than me and about three inches taller. The men in my family are average height until we hit the eighth grade, when we shoot up like sunflowers in July. My brother Jack hit six-feet by the time he was seventeen. I wasn't worried. Any day now and I'd tower over Juliette. My new boots had one-inch heels, which would make up some of the difference.

The front door swung open and Juliette flew at me like a tornado. Before I could put up the storm shutters, she'd thrown her arms around me.

"I knew you'd come," she said. "I knew it. My only worry was that my letter wouldn't get through. I entrusted it to a friend whose family was moving to Provence. What luck!" She put a finger to her lips and we followed her up to the apartment. There was no sign of Sophie and that had me worried.

"Can you turn the heat up?" I said. It was colder in the apartment than outside.

"We haven't money for coal," said Juliette. "*Maman* has been using our coal money to bribe officials, and to no purpose. We still have had no word about Sophie. They are only good at making up excuses."

"Where is your ma?" I asked. "I mean ya maman."

"Working. She's taken another job besides the one at the hat shop. With the extra money we'll hire a private detective."

"Like Sherlock Holmes," I said.

"Oh, can you recommend him? Is he here in Paris?"

"Yes," said Daphne. "In a bookshop."

Juliette laughed. "A fictional detective, you mean? Like Hercule Poirot or Jules Maigret."

She went into the tiny kitchen and put a kettle on the gas stove. The kitchen was so small they had to hang the pots from the ceiling. A gas burner sat on the counter and there was no oven, which meant that cakes had to be store-bought. Juliette opened the cupboards and showed us how empty they were. I was sorry to see they'd fallen on hard times, but even sorrier that there were no cookies.

"We're loaded with cash," I said. "Reichsmarks, francs, you name it. Point me in the direction of a sweet shop."

Juliette licked her lips. I could tell she was thinking about the pastry shop around the corner, famous for their world's best chocolate éclairs.

"Food has become so scarce," she told us, "that people are breeding guinea pigs in their apartments to add into stews. The authorities sent around a bulletin warning that cat meat is unhealthy. You won't believe, but I was sitting in the Luxembourg Gardens and I saw a man hunting pigeons. He come with a net. He broke their little necks. It was impossible to keep watching. People have begun making trips to the country for hunting. The problem is, we don't own a gun. Not even a bow and arrow."

I didn't mention Daphne's pistol, but if we got hungry enough…

"What about the black market?" asked Daphne. "Surely that's still going strong."

"Oh yes, strong as ever," said Juliette. "Go into a butcher or a baker and you will see the maids of rich people walking into the back and coming out with a basketful of goodies. Meanwhile the shelves are bare. We wait in line all day to get a loaf of bread or a can of beans."

"Just like the depression we had in America," I said. "People ate their leather shoes."

The kettle started hooting and we drank weak tea with no sugar. Daphne asked about Sophie, and Juliette shook her head and looked like she'd bust out crying. "She warned us that she might be forced into hiding. We didn't believe her, of course."

"Is she working for the Resistance?" I asked.

"I wouldn't think so," said Juliette. "Not that Sophie

isn't a patriot, only she's not very brave. She won't go to the cinema if the film has violence, and she won't read detective novels because she says they scare her. After reading the *Hunchback of Notre Dame*, she was afraid to attend Mass. And what use would she be to the Resistance? Her only real skill is painting."

Daphne asked if there was a boyfriend in the picture. The obvious answer was that Sophie eloped.

"Maybe he was someone your ma wouldn't approve of," I said. "A Protestant, for example." I looked at Daphne, "Sorry. I don't mean to bring up a sore point. But you know how my ma was against Jack marrying you, you not being Roman Catholic."

"Sophie would have told me if she had a beau," said Juliette. "Whenever she is fond of a boy, she talks about him nonstop."

We sat dead-silent, each of us trying to think what might've happened to Sophie. I was coming up blank.

"Maman should be home for a lunch break soon," said Juliette. "She will be so glad you've arrived. We've been at our wit's end trying to think what to do."

"Why'd you tell us to keep quiet in the hallway?" I asked.

Juliette lowed her voice. "We're afraid of collaborators." She told us about weasels who went running to the Gestapo hoping to get extra ration cards in exchange for information. People who'd rat on their own mothers for a leg of lamb. "We haven't told anyone in the building that Sophie is missing, especially not the old woman who lives in 2C. We suspect that she was the one who reported Monsieur Kline. He lived next-door to her in 2D. He had a cat she didn't like. And a better view, too."

"What happened to Mr. Kline?"

"One night the police took him away. The very next day, that wicked woman moved into his apartment. The Germans had already taken anything of value, but she kept a set of Louis XV chairs. She lied to the Germans, claiming that they were hers. Whenever we come and go, she sneaks a look from behind the door. She would love to see us go. We are on a higher floor, and with a view of the Eiffel Tower." Juliette took us to a bedroom window to showed us the view. You had to be double-jointed to see it.

"What happened to Mr. Kline's cat?" I asked.

Juliette left the room and came back with a big ball of fluff. "Meet Antoinette," she said. "We saved her from the guillotine."

"Or a pot of stew," I said.

CHAPTER FIFTEEN

THERE WAS A KNOCK on the door. Juliette shot us a look.

Daphne kneeled behind the couch and I got behind a curtain. I had a good view through a rip in the fabric.

Two men were at the door. It might've scared most girls, but Juliette was a cool character. She was talking French, but I caught the meaning. Turned out they were looking for Sophie, too.

Juliette said: "My sister is away on holiday. We've explained this to you already."

One of the men handed Juliette a card. When they left, she wedged a chair under the door handle. Then she stood on the chair and looked through a one-way peephole. She signaled for us to come out.

"They show up almost every day looking for Sophie," she said.

"Who are they?" asked Daphne.

"They never say." She handed me the card. It had nothing on it but a phone number, no name or address. "They have yet to explain why they're looking for my sister. The first time, they rushed in and ransacked the apartment. I was home alone. I shook in my boots, not that I was wearing boots. I was wearing my *très élégante* ballet slippers. My mother went to the police and complained."

"That mightn't have been wise," said Daphne. "The police are in cahoots with the Nazis."

I wanted a detailed description of each man, and the blow-by-blow on everything they'd said and done.

"The only thing they took was a collection of my sister's rough sketches," said Juliette.

"You mean doodles?" I asked, thinking that was a funny thing to take.

"Yes, just a few pencil drawings. There are more if you'd like to see. They are drawings of a man looking at a globe."

"Is the man dressed?" I asked.

"Yes. In a robe."

"A bathrobe?"

"Something like that," she said.

We followed Juliette into the bedroom she usually shared with Sophie. Since we'd last been in the apartment, the room had been turned into an art studio. Now I understood why there was an extra bed squeezed next to Madame Doumer's double.

Juliette pulled up a carpet and removed a pile of drawings, setting them on a table full of paint tubes and coffee cans, some with paintbrushes sticking out of them. The drawings were crumpled.

"I found these in the trash bin a week or two before she went missing. It's my chore to take the rubbish out. The sketches were so pretty, I couldn't bear to see them thrown away. I didn't want Sophie to get angry and so I hid them. The men took drawings similar to these. But I'd already hidden these under the carpet. Clever, no?"

We crowded around to get a good look. I wasn't much of a judge, but they seemed pretty good to me. It was strange that Sophie would throw them out. One was of a hand, another of a face. It looked like an ugly lady, but Juliette said it was a man. I took another look:

"Why the long hair and earring then?" I asked.

"Maybe he's a bohemian," said Juliette.

"I think it's a Renaissance man," said Daphne. "I'm almost certain. And the window—it's a window I've seen before, if my memory is serving me right."

I compared it to the windows in the apartment, but they weren't the same. The windows in the drawing had little panes.

Juliette told us that a month before she went missing, Sophie asked if they could bunk in one room so she could turn the other bedroom into an art studio. She made up a cockamamie story about having to use powdered lead.

"It's true that lead can be dangerous to breathe," said Daphne. "Especially in powder form. The artist Chardon went blind from lead paint, and Édouard Manet was deathly sick. Goya died from lead poisoning, they say."

"Should we even be in this room?" asked Juliette.

"Why would Sophie need powdered lead?" I asked.

"It could be that she was grinding her own oil paints," said Daphne. She looked around on the table and found a big glass paperweight. "This is called a muller. It's used to grind pigment into oil. Lead is used to make white paint mostly, although it's also in some yellows—Naples yellow, for instance."

I was sure glad Daphne was along.

She went on: "Lead can also be used for primer, the white base applied to the canvas before painting." Her eyes scanned over the tabletop. She took a paintbrush from one of the cans. "This is peculiar," she said.

Juliette and me went, "Why?" Although hers came out *que?*

"There's paint dried on the brushes," said Daphne. "They're ruined. Sophie would never have left the brushes without cleaning them first. Sable brushes are so dear." She felt the end of the brush. "Cerulean blue, and as hard as a rock." An oval board had globs of paint stuck around the edges, a rainbow of colors. "Just look at her palette!" Daphne went on. "She's left the paint to dry. It's her habit to keep the palette in the icebox."

"That's true," said Juliette. "The palette is usually kept on the top rack, right above the ice cube tray."

"Sophie left in a hurry," said Daphne. "And whatever she was running from, or towards, must have been important to her. More important than her precious sable brushes."

I shook Daphne's hand. "Brilliant deduction, Holmes."

Daphne opened a closet door and started going through Sophie's clothes, looking for other clues. A black trench coat caught her eye.

"Find anything interesting?" I asked.

"Yes, if you must know. Something a bit more stylish that that red monstrosity. Sophie and I are always swapping clothing. She won't mind my borrowing this." Daphne reached into the pockets coming up with nothing but a crumpled hankie, a movie ticket stub, and a scrap of paper with some scribble on it. "BU 8-0555," she read, shrugging a shoulder. "A phone number?"

"Or a license plate?" said Juliette.

"Maybe an airplane number," I said.

We heard the front door open and Daphne and me ducked into the closet. Juliette slid the drawings under the carpet. A minute later, she called for us to come out.

Madame Doumer was shocked to see us. She dropped her pocketbook and string bag, and put a hand on her heart. Juliette brought over a chair. We told her the whole story, starting with the letter written with invisible ink.

"You are Sophie's truest friend," she told Daphne, "I shouldn't be surprised that you'd come immediately you heard the news."

"It was my idea," I said. "Daphne came kicking and screaming."

"Sweet child, but it's not safe for you to be here. There have been men coming around and asking questions. Do you have proper papers? They'll want to see them."

"Spanish," I said. "Very improper."

"What are your names?" said Juliette, her eyes popping open.

"I'm Diego and she's Maria," I said, and Daphne

showed them our passports. Madame Doumer was the first to notice that the photographs weren't ours. "The snaps are of a Jewish boy named Jacob Hershberg and his mother," I told her.

"Then it's really not safe for you here," said Madame Doumer. "What if these men *are* with the Gestapo? For all we know, the building is being watched. You can't remain here in the apartment." She tapped a finger on her mouth. "I have an idea."

"Lay it on us," I said.

"A friend of ours is caretaking a houseboat. Its owner fled to the South of France and left the key so that my friend could water the plants and see that no one breaks in. That's been happening in abandoned flats, you know. Refugees, with nowhere to live, look for abandoned apartments. Who can blame them? Then there are others who use the opportunity to steal and loot. The war has brought out the best and worst in people. The houseboat sits on the Seine River, not far from here. My friend—I only tell you this because I know you can be trusted—my friend uses the boat to hide people."

"People the Nazis are looking for?" I asked.

"*Exactement.* I can ask if the boat is presently unoccupied. It will be safer for you there."

This was a swell turn of events. Much better than sleeping on the lumpy couch at the Doumer's apartment. Madame Doumer promised to visit her friend after work. Daphne gave her some of the money we had, seeing that there wasn't enough food in the cupboards to feed an ant. Madame Doumer hated to buy food from the black market, but hunger won out. She returned after work with her string bags full.

She had the key for the houseboat, too.

The houseboat was more of a barge—low and squat, with a room sticking out of the top. Fog kicked up, thick as oatmeal without enough milk. I gave the ladies a hand so's they wouldn't trip getting on. The deck creaked, but otherwise the boat was rock-solid. From the rust on the chain that held it to the pier, I could tell the boat hadn't been moved in years.

"I don't like this fog in the least," said Daphne, shivering. "Someone might be following us, and we shan't know it."

I said, "Villains pick foggy nights to stalk their victims. Think of Jack the Ripper. He killed eleven dames that way. London is spooky, what with the fog."

"There's a charming view of the Eiffel Tower, over there," said Madame Doumer, trying to change the subject. She waved a hand toward a bank of fog. Then she fished around in her pocket for the key.

"Do you see that?" said Daphne, pointing to the padlock, which was hanging open. "I don't like the look of this. The lock has been forced open."

"There could be a hobo in there," I said. "Or a fugitive from justice or —"

Daphne took off a glove and knocked with her knuckles. "Is anyone home?" she shouted. But there wasn't a peep from inside.

Madame Doumer lit a match and went in first.

Climbing down into the cabin, she searched for a kerosene lantern. Her matches were damp and they kept going out. Meanwhile, we stood in pitch-dark, breathing heavy.

Somebody grabbed my hand, me hoping it was Daphne's. It's one thing for a future sister-in-law, six whole year's older, to hold your hand; another thing for a girl your own age to do it. Frenchies, I knew, are notoriously romantic. I was having none of *that*. I pulled my hand away.

Finally, the lantern flared up and we got a look at our new home. I felt like Jim Hawkins just then—the hero of *Treasure Island*, my favorite book. Only it was Nazis I was going to have to fight off the boat, not pirates.

The place smelled like a terrarium. White powdery mold grew on the wood cabinets. It was set up with a little kitchenette area, a dinette table, a wrap around couch, bunk beds, and a door leading into the back. Two bicycles were blocking the way, but I managed to crack the door open. It was a bathroom: toilet, overhead shower, and a sink big enough to wash one hand at a time. Whatever went down that toilet fell straight into the river.

Note to self: No swimming in the Seine.

A little potbelly stove had wood stacked next to it. Madame Doumer handed over the matches and I got to work. In no time, we were warm and cozy. Madame Doumer found a bottle of wine under the sink. Daphne found a corkscrew. After they opened the bottle, I slipped the corkscrew into my pocket. Madame Doumer wiped four glasses with the hem of her dress and poured wine into them, with two of the glasses half full.

"None for me, thanks," I said. "Plenty in my family got drinking problems, my da for one. I'm not starting down that road."

Daphne got the gas stove working. Before long, we were sitting down to a supper of meat stew with (too many) potatoes, carrots, and turnips. I didn't ask what kind of meat it was.

"This is a treat," said Juliette. "If only Sophie were here with us."

"*Elle adore le ragoût,*" said Madame Doumer, as if to herself.

While we ate, they brought us up to speed:

Before she went missing, Sophie worked at an art gallery. At night, she'd come home and paint, always making sure to lock the door to the art studio whenever she went out. Juliette figured that Sophie was painting something for their mother's birthday, wanting it to be a surprise. Then the birthday came around and Sophie gave her mother a hand-knit scarf. Madame Doumer had it wrapped around her neck and pulled at the fringe. "Something was bothering her," she said. "My normally sweet daughter was sulky, snapping at the slightest thing. That isn't like Sophie." Madame Doumer began crying and Daphne put an arm over her shoulder.

"The gallery where she worked had been a museum before the Occupation," said Juliette. "Sophie was so excited when she won the job. A dream come true."

Daphne said: "Which museum?"

"*Galerie Nationale du Jeu de Paume*," said Madame Doumer.

We decided to snoop around at the gallery the next day. Madame Doumer let Juliette stay with us for the night, even though she wasn't thrilled about it. After she left, we latched the door.

The girls were taking the bunks. Daphne put the pistol under her pillow, first checking to see that the safety was on. I took the couch, which was next to the door. If anyone tried and break in, I'd know straight off. I slipped the corkscrew under my moldy pillow. Then I decided to put an ice chest against the door and pile pots and pans on top of it. But I couldn't sleep with the sneezing I was doing. I ditched the pillow and laid flat on my back, so both ears would work to the maximum.

Next thing I knew, pots and pans were banging. Lighting fast, I was off the couch with the corkscrew in my hand.

"Sorry," said Daphne. "No tomato sauce, worse luck." My eyes adjusted to the light and I seen she was standing at the stove with an apron around her waist, frying up potatoes with enough garlic to drive off a horde of vampires. She had that chirpy morning face that was hard to take before breakfast.

"*Bonjour,*" said Juliette, who was sitting at the dinette table with half her head braided, both hands working the other side. "Did you notice, Daphne, how wavy my hair was when I let it down? It's the reason I keep it braided. It's impossible to have one's hair permed. The

Germans use the chemicals to make weapons, awful weapons like the ones they used on our soldiers during the last war."

"You have lovely hair," said Daphne. "That shade of auburn is simply stunning. Alizarin crimson with a touch of cadmium yellow."

"Do you agree, Tommy?" said Juliette.

"Leave me out of it," I said.

"The place is nicely decorated, wouldn't you agree?" said Daphne, not letting up. She waved her hand around the space. Juliette laughed. I looked around. It seemed the same as last night: a dump. The curtains were brown and pink checked. A ratty carpet covered a scuffed linoleum floor.

"What's so special?" I asked.

They rolled their eyes.

Obviously, I was missing something.

"You've never been much of an art connoisseur," said Daphne.

"I wouldn't even know what one was," I said.

That's when I seen it, hung from a hook inside of the bathroom door, now swung open. I threw the covers from me and ran to it. Daphne and Juliette were right behind me.

"What is it?" I asked. "I mean, who is it?"

"Vermeer," said Daphne. "I knew something was familiar about Sophie's drawings. Notice the window?" She touched the left side of the painting, where yellow light streamed through a paned window. "I've never seen this particular painting before. Although, the artist used the same window in other works."

"Is it good art or degenerate?" I said.

"Vermeer is one of the Masters," said Daphne.

"As good as that Rockwell fella who does the covers of *Boy's Life?*"

Daphne laughed. "I'd say Vermeer is right up there with Norman Rockwell. You can be sure of it."

"Is it worth anything?" I asked, thinking we could sell it and use the money to buy chocolate éclairs, maybe crème brulee, the French version of vanilla pudding.

"It's worth a small fortune," said Daphne. "Vermeer is one of the most sought-after of Northern Renaissance painters. There was one of his works at the National Galley in London before it was moved for safekeeping. It's titled, *A Young Woman Standing at a Virginal.*"

"A *virginal?*" I said, almost afraid to ask.

"It's a type of harpsichord. I've drawn that painting many times, both in pencil and charcoal. I'd begun copying it in oils just before it was removed to a bomb shelter."

I wanted to know if she was talking about forgeries. Maybe Daphne had a dark side none of us had seen before now.

Daphne said, "Heaven forbid, Thomas. Copying a masterpiece is a time-honored way for a student artist to learn—we call it *transcription.*"

"And the picture hanging in the bathroom?" I let my eyes drift that way. "Is it the real McCoy or what you call a transcription?"

Daphne cocked her head, bit her lip, and hohummed, all the time her nose almost touched the painting.

Meanwhile, Juliette was pointing to a carpetbag the size of a army-issue duffel, laying on one of the bunks. It wasn't there the night before, I was sure of it. Juliette said she'd discovered it when she went to use the toilet. "It's my mother's sack, but inside we found Sophie's things." She smiled like someone who'd found a treasure chest.

I went to take a look.

"I'm warning you—there's ladies' undergarments in there," said Daphne.

I backed away fast.

"Sophie's makeup kit is in the bag. She'd never go a day without having her face on." Daphne bit the wicks of her fingernails for a minute and then added: "It can only mean she left the boat expecting to return."

"And now my sister is forced to go without lipstick and rouge," said Juliette.

"Even worse, she's wearing dirty underwear," I said.

While we ate, Daphne showed me the new padlock she'd bought. It came with three keys and she gave one to me and hid one under a tarp. Then we made our way to the Metro station. Seven stops and we got off the train. We came out at the edge of a park, where people were walking their dogs. We had to step around dog-doo. Juliette pointed to a stone building that looked like a train station:

"*Galerie Nationale du Jeu de Paume*," she said.

"Funny looking art gallery," I said.

There was a Panzer tank parked in front, with two

German soldiers standing on top, rifles strapped around their chests. I didn't like it, not any of it. A big swastika flag was hanging above the door. Two more soldiers stood on either side of the entrance.

"This was originally Napoleon III's tennis court. That's what the name means," said Juliette.

"I've been inside," said Daphne. "Before the war it exhibited contemporary art. Sophie and I came to see the Picassos, which was quite a treat."

"Why are the Nazis guarding it?" Juliette asked.

There was only one way to find out: I walked over to the Panzer tank and said, "*Guten Morgen.*" One of the soldiers told me to get my hands off the tank. Then he asked me for cigarettes. "*Nicht,*" I said, and he told me to get lost. When I asked what they were guarding, he answered by pointed a rifle at my chest.

I did an about face.

"Did you learn anything?" asked Daphne.

"*Nicht.* I think you should give it a whirl."

"Okay, here goes. Wish me luck." She walked over to the tank swaying her hips. The soldiers tipped their helmets and smiled big. They didn't bat an eyelid when she put her hand on the tank. One of them offered a cigarette, but she turned it down.

Before long, she was back. "Idiots, the both of them. They don't know what's in there. They say it's a repository for crates, but they haven't a clue what's inside the crates. Their only interest is in dancing."

"Dancing?" I said.

"Taking *me* dancing," she said. "Braggarts—telling

me that the Germans have taken over the best dance halls and that the only way for me to enter is on the arm of one of them. I'd never! Rather that I never danced a step again than dance with their likes. And you know how much I adore dancing."

We walked around the place, looking for a way in. The entrances were being guarded, even the back ones. Daphne had the idea to watch the front entrance. We couldn't think of anything better to do, so that's what we did. Luckily, there was a bench across the way.

A couple of hours went by. The tank guards switched shifts. Lunchtime rolled around and people came flooding out. A woman walked over to our bench and we squeezed over to give her space. She reached into her lunch sack and started eating a sandwich: French baguette and canned ham, from the looks of it.

Daphne said, "Like your job? I've longed to work in an art gallery."

The lady grunted and went on eating her sandwich. She slid away from us, to the edge of the bench. Daphne tried again with the chit-chat, but got the same snub. The lady stood up and shook crumbs from her skirt before marching back to the building without so much as an *au revoir.*

We were about to take off when a man sat down on the bench. He was skinny as a toothpick and had no lunch. Funny thing was that he was staring at Juliette and ignoring Daphne.

"Don't I know you?" he said, finally. In French, of course.

"Do you?" said Juliette with a puzzled look.

"I remember," said the man, snapping his finger. "Aren't you Sophie Doumer's little sister? I've seen you together."

"When was that?"

"Must have been when you met up with your sister after work. I'm Jean-Michel." He nodded his head in the direction of the gallery. "I'm also employed at the Jeu de Paume. I should tell you, rumors are flying." He took a cigarette case from his inside pocket. He stuck a cigarette into his mouth without lighting it.

Daphne squinted one eye: "What sort of rumors?"

"People are saying that Sophie stole a painting, a *very* valuable painting."

"She'd never!" I said. "Not Sophie, no siree."

The Germans—the ones from the first shift—came strolling back to the tank. But when they spotted Daphne, they beelined to her. Jean-Michel saw them coming and jumped from the bench. "Look," he whispered, "We need to talk."

Then he vanished.

I seen he'd left a matchbook laying on the bench. I flipped it open, wondering if he'd left a message. No such luck. On the cover was a drawing of a piano, musical notes, and the name of a nightclub in cursive script. I slipped the matchbook into my pocket, thinking we might need the matches for the kerosene lamp.

Daphne grabbed onto our hands and rushed us from the place.

I looked back and saw one of the Germans raise a fist.

CHAPTER SIXTEEN

Somewhere in Paris

A BELL TINKLES AS A CAFÉ door swings open, letting in a gust of frigid air. The café owner says, "*Entrez!*" while worrying about the scarcity of oil. A woman enters, tugging at a leash. A schnauzer plants his bottom and refuses to move. The woman bends and wags her finger near the dog's nose. She says affectionately, "*Schnucki.*" The café owner switches to German, "*Guten Tag, Fräulein.*"

A patron seated near the front window tightens a silk scarf around his neck, shivers, and takes a sip of coffee, which he suspects is mostly crushed acorns. *At least it's hot*, he thinks. He keeps his eyes on the street. The German woman takes a seat at the table next to him. He can feel the chill bouncing off of her chinchilla coat. All the while, she's complaining to the owner, asking him to turn up the heat. She clears her throat, trying to get the man's attention. *Not now*, he thinks, without diverting his gaze.

"*Excusez mein français, s'il vous plaît,*" she says, apologizing for her French.

The man is forced to interrupt his surveillance. He

answers in her language, "*Kein Problem, Fräulein.*" No problem. He offers a mock salute.

"Oh, how nice," she says, daintily removing her gloves, one finger at a time, before placing them in her snap-top handbag. "One is made to feel so at home here in Paris. Everyone makes the effort to speak our language." She bats her eyelashes, circles a leg over her knee and hitches her skirt hem so that a hint of garter belt shows. "And where are you from, may I ask?"

"Berlin," he says. The dog begins growling and takes a nip at his ankle.

"*Schnuckiputzi!*" says the woman, giggling.

The man kicks the dog away with his boot. *Such a perfect vantage point, too*, he thinks, taking one last look out the picture window to the apartment building across the street. He stands, reaches into his trouser pocket, and throws a few coins on the table.

"You aren't running off, are you?" says the woman.

"I'm afraid I must, fräulein. Duty calls."

There's a gust of frigid air as the man exits the café.

CHAPTER SEVENTEEN

As we made our way back to the Metro station, Daphne kept looking behind us, turning corners and jumping into shops where I knew she wasn't interested in the merchandise: a tobacconist, a barber, then a men's haberdashery. We were standing in a hardware store, behind a rack of pipes, when she said, "I'm certain that we're being followed." The hairs on my arms stood up.

"You think maybe it's Jean-Michel following us?" I asked.

"Could it be Sophie?" said Juliette.

"I'm probably imagining it," said Daphne. "Call it women's intuition if you must. It's just that once when I turned my head, I could have sworn I saw a man jump behind a parked car." She took in a lungful of air, like she was getting ready to jump off a diving board. I picked up a copper pipe, keeping my eyes glued to the door. A salesman asked if we needed assistance and Daphne said, "Directions to a back exit would be appreciated." He pointed to a curtain and we made our way through a storeroom full of sinks, toilets, and spanking new garbage cans. In the alley, two tomcats jumped out of an old can, puffed up, and hissed.

Across the alleyway, a door stood wide-open. We walked through and into the back of a stationery store and straight out to a wide boulevard.

"Where to now?" I said. "Back to the boat?"

A green and white bus stopped at the curb and Daphne said, "Hop on!" She didn't even care which direction it was headed. After handing over money to the driver, we found a spot to stand in the back. A gentleman offered Daphne his seat and she took it. Juliette sat on her lap with her arm strung around Daphne's shoulder. The bus screeched to a stop after a couple blocks. People opened windows and craned their necks out, trying to see what the hold up was. I heard a tuba, then a trumpet. Up ahead a troop of German soldiers marched across the road, having themselves a parade.

"They think it will increase our morale," said Juliette.

Two Germans at the front of the bus started singing "Deutschland, Deutschland," giving it the vigor. I'd take the Saint Paddy's Day parade over this, any day.

"Let's step down," said Daphne. We elbowed our way to the door and had to push out against people trying to squeeze in. Daphne headed into a café and found a table near the front window.

"This is a nice change, going from café to café," said Juliette, using her chair like a trampoline. "May we order something to eat this time?" She rubbed her tummy.

Daphne waved her hand and a waiter came running. After putting in our order she went to powder her nose. Juliette said: "I'm sure she's only imagining someone following us. Everyone thought the same when the Occupation first began, terrified night and day, thinking we were being watched constantly. Eventually, one gets used to the Nazis being here. But at first it's *très* unnerving."

"*Très*," I said, watching an Waffen-SS major take a seat near us. His skull ring was meant to scare you, and it worked. A French lady returned from the ladies' room and kissed him on the lips, right there in broad daylight. He had a lipstick stain on the side of his mouth.

"She's probably a lady of the night," whispered Juliette, giving the traitor the evil eye. "He must keep her in silk stockings, eating chocolate bonbons and wearing expensive perfume. She has no shame." I took a big whiff and looked at the lady's legs. It was true what Juliette said.

Daphne returned and told us she'd been thinking: "It's not safe to remain on the boat. For one thing, we know someone has already broken in. It might have been Sophie, but we can't be certain. And obviously she was afraid to return, for whatever reason, or she wouldn't have left the painting behind. Besides, I wasn't able to sleep a wink last night. Every creaking board or lap of water against the boat woke me in a fright." She said the last word like "fooooo-right," yawning at the same time. "I suggest that we return to the houseboat, take our things, and go elsewhere."

"Back to the apartment?" asked Juliette, bouncing in the chair again.

Daphne put a hand on Juliette's shoulder. "We shall

return you home, darling, before Thomas and I check into a hotel."

"How about the Crillon?" I said, knowing it was the snazziest joint in town. Rumor was they had chandeliers in the public restrooms and steamed washcloths for when you finished up at the urinal. A dish was there so's rich people could tip, but poor folks didn't have to. They gave you the washcloth anyways.

"I know of a hotel a tad more affordable," said Daphne.

"A dive, in other words," I said.

"My parents stayed there when they came to visit me while I was studying art. They were invited to stay with my aunt Dalia and me, only my father doesn't like sleeping on a pullout cot. The hotel is simple but clean, with a shared toilet and bath down the corridor. Not *ensuite*, it's true." She sighed. Even to her mind the place wasn't stacking up to the Crillon. "Still, we ought to be careful with our money, not knowing how long we'll be in Paris. Airline tickets must be frightfully expensive and we might have to resort to bribing officials and whatnot."

"*Excuse moi*," said a woman with her hand on our spare chair. "May I sit with you?"

It was a strange request, what with empty tables all over the place. Daphne patted the spare chair, motioning for the stranger to join us.

The lady said, "It invites suspicion, my always sitting alone. I overheard you speaking English and knew that you'd be sympathetic to my plight." A coat was hanging over her arm. She looked both ways before showing us the yellow star sewn to the breast pocket. "I'm on the run, you see."

"She's a U-Boat," whispered Juliette. "This is what the Gestapo call them. We must help her, Daphne."

Daphne took off Sophie's black trench coat and laid it in the lady's lap. "You'd best take my coat," she said.

The lady looked like she'd start bawling: "You are so very kind. I knew when I saw you sitting with these sweet children that you were a compassionate woman. Not like others in this city, who turn their eyes and pretend not to see."

Daphne waved her arm again and ordered the lady a sandwich and coffee, saying, "I wish we could do more."

"If only I could rest," said the lady, her eyelids drooping shut. "An hour or two would make a difference."

"Have you nowhere to stay?" asked Juliette.

"Nowhere."

The lady ate faster than me, which was saying something. She slipped Sophie's coat over her shoulders and we skirted past the Nazi, who wouldn't pull his legs in. Each one of us was forced to step over his jackboots. Rude is what you call it.

After two Metro connections we were back where we'd started. We stood back from the boat, making sure the coast was clear. Once we were onboard, Daphne said, "We know of a dress shop used by members of the Belgian Resistance. They helped us to escape France recently. I think they'd help you, too."

"Do you? Oh, I hope so," said the lady.

The place warmed up after I lit the potbelly stove. The lady slipped off the black trench coat and rolled up the sleeves of her dress. It was a nice dress, something they might sell in a store like Les Misérables, where our Belgian Resistance friends were holed up. Daphne took the trench coat, along with the yellow star coat, and hanged them from a hook on the back of the door.

I racked my brain trying to remember the way we'd been told to signal to the Resistance, coming up with a picture of the mint pastille tin—*pastilles* being scrumptious sugar-coated candies, it wasn't too hard to remember. Daphne sat down again and closed her eyes, like she was thinking hard and trying to come up with a plan. I started to say the name of the mint company: "Le Re—"

Daphne reached under the table and squeezed my knee. She said, "The place is called Le Fille, don't you remember? It's over on Rue du Renard. Or was that Rue Beaubourg? It's near to where the street changes names, anyway." Lying through her teeth, but I knew there must be a good reason.

"Rue Beaubourg," I said. "Definitely and without a doubt one-hundred percent."

Daphne raised her voice in the direction of the visitor, "Come lay down on one of the bunk beds," she said, fluffing a pillow and turning down the edge of the blanket.

"You're so kind," said the lady with her eyes half closed.

Daphne took the carpetbag into the bathroom,

while the lady settled in for a long snooze.

A few minutes ticked by and Daphne came out again. She spoke to us using hand signals. I lifted our suitcase and Juliette took the trench coat from the hook, leaving the other one behind. We jumped from the boat and Daphne snapped the padlock shut.

The lady started banging on the inside of the door. She yelled out French curse words. She shouted, "We'll find that painting!"

The three of us hightailed it out of there.

CHAPTER EIGHTEEN

"How'd you know she wasn't legit?" I asked.

We were back on the Metro.

"It was the size of her coat that tipped me off. I noticed whilst hanging it on the hook. Size 32 would *never* have fit that large a woman. She was at least a size 44. Didn't you notice that she never put on the black trench coat? She kept it hanging from her shoulders. If you recall, we never actually saw the woman wearing the coat with the star sewn to the pocket. And yet the café was ever so cold. One would have thought she'd have kept it on, buttoned up to the chin. I believe she stole that coat and then used it to—"

"Sucker us," I said. "Thunderation! We almost blew the cover off the Belgian Resistance."

"Yes, we were fools. Never again, do you hear? No matter how desperate someone seems."

"Do you suppose she was a Nazi?" said Juliette.

"Either that or someone from the gallery looking for the painting," said Daphne. "We can't be certain of anything. And yet she seemed so sincere. So convincing."

"Do you think she was an actress before the war?" asked Juliette. "It's very difficult to find roles now that the Nazis control our film industry. So many of our best actresses have fled the country." She tried for a pin-up girl pose but didn't exactly pull it off. "I'd make a fine actress, don't you think Daphne?"

"You're the very image of Elizabeth Taylor in *National Velvet*," said Daphne.

We dropped Juliette home, backtracking to the hotel. The place had seen better days, but I liked it from the get-go. For one thing, in the lobby they had a mannequin wearing knight's armor. I looked close and seen that it was a dame, with red-painted lips and false eyelashes. She held a genuine sword in her hand. Paintings of Joan of Arc lined the walls. Made sense seeing that they'd named the joint after her. The staircase was lined with black and white photographs. A lady came from behind the counter and pointed to one, saying, "That's the opera *Jeanne D'Arc Au Bûcher*. It opened in 1939." She pointed to another: "And that, of course, is Renée Jeanne Falconetti playing Saint Jeanne in the film version. Here's another with Simone Genevois, the great actress."

Being Catholic, I knew all about Saint Jeanne, but she'd always be Joan to me. The hotel lady was wearing a Joan of Arc medallion around her neck. I showed her the one I had of Saint Christopher, the patron saint of travelers. I told her how I'd picked it up cheap in London.

Daphne gave me the evil eye.

"I'll have to see your identity papers," the lady said.

"Just a formality."

Daphne handed over the passports. I turned my back, pretending to be interested in the knight's armor.

The lady said, "Spanish? Why, I took you for English." I didn't dare turn my back, but I could tell she was on to us by the way she was hemming and hawing.

Daphne said, "*Originalmente.*"

To my relief, the lady said, "Mademoiselle, the photograph doesn't do you justice. But then again, passports rarely do." I spun around and saw her handing the passports back and winking as she did it. She gave us a key and asked for pardon because there was no one to help with the bags and the room was on the third floor.

Daphne flicked her wrist and said, "*No hay problema.*"

A bellhop would have carried our suitcase at the Crillon, that's for sure. There was no elevator at the Hôtel Joan de Arc, and we lugged up five floors—this being Europe and the ground floor not numbered—me carrying the suitcase. A brass plaque pointed left to the A-F rooms, the G-L rooms were to the right. Daphne looked at the key and turned left. Pictures of Joan of Arc lined the hallway. At the end stood a plaster sculpture, Joan with her nose broke off.

"They sure do have a thing for Joan of Arc," I said.

"Obviously. Even the keychain is engraved with her image."

"She fought against the English, didn't she?"

"That's right, in the Hundred Years' War."

"I know about it from reading *Henry V* with the

Sopwiths. Let's hope this war ends faster."

"Here, here," said Daphne.

We stepped into the room. I flicked the light switch but the electric was out. Daphne opened the blinds to a view of a church across the side street. We were level with another sculpture of a saint, this one holding a book.

"I wonder who he's supposed to be," I said.

"Oh, look," said Daphne, standing next to an open door. "We have our very own toilet. And it's not one of the hole-in-the-floor types one usually finds in cheap Parisian hotels." She pulled the chain she was so excited. The flush sounded like Niagara Falls and gave me a scare. "And look here! Our own little sink." The sink was inside the room, near a beat-up dresser. "I suppose the bath is down the corridor, yet isn't this divine?" I looked into the bathroom. The toilet had rust stains, no seat, and brown rings where the water leveled off. Divine wasn't the word I'd've used. The Crillon would've had a toilet seat, I betcha, along with one of them French contraptions called a *bidet*, used for washing the *derrière*.

"No phone," I said. I opened a drawer under the night table. "And no menu either. Means we can't order room service like in Lisbon. But they have a card with a picture of Saint Joan on one side and a prayer on the other side. They must want you to read it before you go to sleep. It's in French, or maybe I would'a."

"I'd be happy to translate it for you."

"That's okay," I said. "I'll stick with the one my ma taught me in the cradle. Is breakfast included in the deal?" Pulling back the bedcovers, I looked for fleas. A few black hairs stuck to the pillow. Under the bed I found a 20-centimes coin and a comb full of gray hair.

"Before we speak of breakfast, we ought to consider dinner," said Daphne. "Personally, I wouldn't mind running out to a market and bringing back things to nibble on. I'm all in, and it would be lovely to put my feet up and read a good book." She took her shoe off and rubbed her foot, groaning so's I get the point. I opened our suitcase and found *Above Suspicion*. Using the corkscrew I cut the spine in two, throwing the first half to Daphne, who said: "Don't give away the ending if you should get there first."

"Obviously, I'm gonna get there first. I've got the back half of the book." My stomach started sounding like a cement mixer just then. "Where's those snacks you promised?" I said.

"If you insist," she moaned, putting her shoes back on. "Stay put and don't open the door for anyone but *moi*."

"Even if it's the Gestapo?"

"Especially if it's the Gestapo."

We agreed that she'd knock twice, wait two beats, and knock again three times. Before long she was back with hard bread, smelly cheese, two apples with worm holes, and an orange Fanta for me. "You won't believe the queues," she said. "If there's one thing to be said for the black market, it's the fast service." She took a bite of her apple: "Although, I've never paid more for a worse apple."

"I like mine candied. You know, coated in caramel or with that hard red sugar-coating with nuts stuck to it. You don't even notice if the apple is rotten."

"In that case, we shall buy nothing but candied apples in future," said Daphne. She examined her apple, skewed her mouth, and then tossed it into the trash can.

CHAPTER NINETEEN

Hôtel Saint Jeanne d'Arc, Paris

A BELL JINGLES ABOVE a poster for an opera featuring Joan of Arc.

"*Guten abend*," says a man, who enters without removing his hat.

The receptionist's head snaps toward the door. She responds in French, but without much welcome in her voice. She notes that the man is in civilian clothes, which only slightly diminishes her anxiety. As the man casts his gaze around the small lobby, she mouths a prayer to Saint Joan.

Stepping to the counter, he looks at the cubbyhole rack attached to the wall. Only a few keys are missing from the pegs.

"I would like to view the ledger book, please," he says in broken French.

The receptionist hands him the ledger, taking a step backwards even though the counter is between them. The man opens to the last page and scans down the entries. His finger stops on the last line, seeing that these guest are in room 4/C. He glances back to the cubbyholes and notes that the keys for room A, B, D, and E are resting in their slots.

"Are any of the rooms on the fourth floor adjoining?" he asks.

"Only room C with E," she says. She examines the cubbyholes and adds, "I could give you two adjoining rooms on the second floor. Is it two rooms that you'll be wanting? Will there be more in your party?"

"I'm alone," he says. "I'll take room E on the fourth floor. There's sure to be a better view."

The woman thinks for a moment: "Actually, that room has a view of a brick wall. I could give you room number…"

"The brick wall will be fine," he says, interrupting her.

"I'll have to see your papers, monsieur," she says.

"That won't be necessary." He reaches under his shirt collar for a chain fastened around his neck. Hanging from the chain is a small disk. One side is engraved with *Geheime Staatspolizei* and a number. Gestapo.

"Is there any trouble?" asks the woman, clutching the edge of the counter top.

"No trouble at all," says the man, winking. "Assuming you keep your mouth shut."

CHAPTER TWENTY

IN THE DREAM, I was sleeping in a canopy bed at the Crillon, on a feather mattress. With my x-ray vision I was able to see through the door. A waiter dressed in knight's armor stood in the hall, waiting to serve me breakfast in bed. Balanced on top of his shield was a bowl of cornflakes covered in powdered sugar and topped with a maraschino cherry. Next to that was two bottles of Fanta and a banana split. He knocked on the door with his metal plated knuckle. I yelled, "Come in!" He kept on knocking. "*Entrez vous*," I shouted, in case he didn't know English. I yelled even louder, just in case his metal helmet was making him hard of hearing.

Daphne said, "There's no one there, Thomas. And if there were, the proper address would be simply: *Entrez.* Not *Entrez vous*."

Opening my eyes, I seen her sitting cross-legged on the floor with a shoe in her hand. She had a painting laid out on the floor, upside down. Another painting, this one smaller, was wedged into the back of the bigger one. She was using her shoe like a hammer, bending a nail so it would hold the two paintings together. I asked what she was doing.

"Hiding the Vermeer," she said, showing me how she'd stashed Sophie's painting behind one of Joan of Arc being burnt at the stake. "Now we've only to hang it back in the hall and no one shall be the wiser. Just a precaution, in case someone comes snooping around our room looking for the painting whilst we're out."

"Hidden right under their noses," I said.

"Right under *her* nose," said Daphne, rubbing Joan's nose. Leaning the painting against her bed, she stood near mine. "Now get up, would you? It's noon and I want to return to the Galerie Nationale and look for that Frenchman. He seemed anxious to help." She bit the wick off the side of her thumb and then added, "I wish we'd taken his telephone number."

"What if we run into that lady again?"

"Which lady?"

"The one we locked in the boat."

Daphne chewed the side of her pinkie nail. Her fingers were swollen and bleeding. She couldn't wear nail lacquer without getting poisoned, but her toes were lacquered pink. Them she couldn't reach with her teeth. "You have a point," she said. "It's likely that woman works at the gallery. I'll confess, I'm at a loss as to what to do next." She looked like a kid who just found out she'd have to do summer school.

The matchbook was still in my pocket. Luckily I slept in my clothes, saving valuable time. I said: "Gotta hunch he hobnobs at this joint." I tossed the matchbook to Daphne. "How's about we ask around for him there?"

Daphne fingered the matchbook. "You haven't

started smoking, have you?"

"Where would I get cigarettes? You need rations coupons for them." It was true. Ever since the war started, cigarettes were scarcer than undiscovered Egyptian pharaoh tombs. Besides, I tried smoking once and it made me wheezy.

"It's worth a try," she said, flipping the matchbook over. "Although he might have picked these up anywhere. Did he look the jazz type to you?"

I brought up an image of the fella: "Big shoulder pads, thin necktie decorated with palm trees, pointy shoes, pinkie ring, Brylcreem in his hair. Is that the jazz type?"

"Sounds about right."

"And another thing. There was an initial on the pinkie ring." I racked my brain for a second. "The letter A."

"That's odd. Hadn't he said his name was Jean-Michel?" She bit her lip. "I suppose it might have been his girlfriend's ring and that's why he wears it on his pinkie finger: Adalie, Agathe, Angelique, Adrianne, Alixandra—"

"Antoinette." I pictured Jean-Michel with a girl wearing a towering, white wig.

I followed Daphne out to the hallway, her with the concealed painting. A picture hook stuck from the wall between the two rooms across from ours. She bent the wire attached to the back of the picture frame, so's it would catch better on the hook.

"Tell me if it's straight," she said.

The rest of the paintings were lopsided. "Not *too*

straight or it will draw attention," I said.

We heard the door in the room next to ours clicking shut. Someone'd been spying on us. Daphne put a chewed-up finger to her mouth and took the painting down again. Next, she slid her shoes off and tiptoed to the end of the hallway, replacing a painting—this one of a battle scene from the Hundred Years' War—with the hidden Vermeer. The whole time, I stood in front of the room next to ours, keeping my hand over the keyhole.

Now Daphne was carrying the Hundred Year' War painting to its new location. It was too heavy for her, what with the frame and all, and I watched in horror as she stumbled backwards. The painting bumped against the statue of Joan, almost toppling it. I ran over, and together we managed to get the painting hung.

"Gruesome," she said, standing back and looking at the battle scene: Englishmen getting slaughtered; dead bodies piled up on both sides of the picture, missing limbs, swords sticking from their stomachs. In the center, Joan of Arc was on horseback—a halo over her head—trampling some fella. The look on his face... Now that was art.

I pointed out the fact that the picture was a different shape than the one that'd been hanging there before. A rectangle of bright wallpaper showed above and below the frame.

Daphne had the perfect solution. "Give me a lift," she said, and I joined my fingers together so's she could use them for a step ladder. A second later she had the lightbulb unscrewed.

CHAPTER TWENTY-ONE

THE SAME LADY WAS still at the reception counter. I wondered if she owned the place.

"Beware," she whispered. "Keep your eyes open."

"She seems spooked," I said when we got out to the sidewalk.

It was pouring rain, cold rain mixed with sleet. "I'm going to ask if she'll lend us a brolly," said Daphne. A *brolly*, I knew could mean an umbrella or a parachute.

I waited under the awning. It was ripped in places and water streamed down. A cold wind whipped up and I flung the scarf around my neck and pulled my socks up. My trousers were for a shorter man.

Up came a bicycle taxi, inviting me to step in. "*Non merci beaucoup*," I said, waving him off. He stood on the pedals and flashed me a dirty look, like it was my fault he stopped in the first place.

Another taxi pulled up, this one the motor variety. The driver stretched across the seat, rolled down his window and snapped a finger. I looked behind me, thinking he was calling for the bellhop. Then I realized he thought *I* was the bellhop. A lady slid out of the back seat, petting the fox fur wrapped around her neck. She pulled on a black leather glove before pointing to suitcases, sticking from the half-opened trunk. She mumbled something in French, then wobbled up to the stairs. Once at the top, she stood towering over me like the Queen of England, stiff-lipped and expecting me to open the door.

What the hey? I thought, expecting a tip. But when I opened the door, she pushed right past me. The taxi driver snapped his finger again, but I wasn't getting the suitcases, no siree. Daphne walked out just then and saved me a confrontation.

"Come along, Thomas," she said, opening an umbrella and looping her elbow through mine. We veered to a side street and into a store where she whispered into the shopkeeper's ear. His eyebrows went up when Daphne slipped him money. He scanned the store looking for tattletales, then slipped the money into his apron pocket.

So this was the black market. And all along I pictured it being in a big black tent.

Before long we were eating little pies wrapped in greasy newspaper. Daphne called them *quiches*: scrambled eggs in piecrust. We passed by wet park benches, eating with our fingers as we went. According to the greasy newspaper, the Germans were winning the war. "Lies and more lies," said Daphne, crumbling the paper and throwing it into the gutter.

The club was called *Le Chat*, which Daphne said meant "The Cat." It was located in a basement. The sign in the window said it was closed, but we stepped down and put our noses to the glass door. Inside, a man was mopping the floor in big sweeps. When Daphne rattled the door handle, he put his mop in a bucket.

"*Fermé*," he said. Closed. But he cracked the door open anyway.

The place resembled a cave, brick-arched, the only light coming in through the glass door. Chairs were placed upside down on top of little round tables. The stone floor was slippery with soapy water, cigarette butts floated to the surface. Daphne started jabbering away in French. Meanwhile, I scouted the place out.

A platform took up the back of the nightclub. On it stood three microphone stands. I counted five music stands and the stools to go with them. At the front they had a wood lectern, like you see in a Catholic Church, but instead of a Bible it had a reservation book. I looked it over and didn't see anybody named Jean-Michel on the list. I'd never been in a nightclub, not even during the day. The closest I'd come was crashing the high school junior prom, where I polished off a bowl of fruit punch. There was the Coldstream Pub, where my da spent most of his time, but this place was nothing like it.

Daphne was still chatting it up with the janitor. I spotted peppermints sitting in a glass bowl. *Toot-sweet,* I stuffed them peppermints into my pockets. They also had toothpicks. And since I didn't have a toothbrush, I took a few of those too.

I glanced over at Daphne, who was pointing to an invisible ring on her pinkie finger. The janitor shook his head, then walked her to a door I'd failed to notice until then. A plaque on the door said *bureau*. Quick thinking told me it was an office.

Daphne made her way over to the door, with me right behind her. The door was half open. She knocked and said, "*Bonjour.*"

A gravelly voice said rudely, "*Mademoiselle, Puis-je vous aider?*" I figured meant, "Whatta you want?" But then he got a good look at Daphne and his voice switched to a purr, repeating them very same words only turning them into a welcome.

I stepped around Daphne. It was an office, sure enough, but unlike any I'd laid eyes on before. Framed photographs filled the walls; just like at the hotel, but without a saint in one of them. More like sinners, I'd've said. Girls with dresses slit up to their waists, bosoms overflowing, bare-backed. Other pictures showed people holding up shot glasses filled with booze, drunk as skunks.

This place, I realized in a flash of clarity, was as far as you could get from the Coldstream Pub. At the East Hempstead joint, kids ate pizza at horseshoe-shaped booths. It's where I tasted my first maraschino cherry, bobbing on the top of a cherry coke. We never saw the drunks. They were hidden behind a red velvet curtain that separated the pizzeria from the bar. But a few times when my ma sent me to fetch Da for supper, I'd gotten a peek behind the curtain. There sat my da, on a stool at the bar, drinking a Budweiser and bragging to the bartender about his son, the Spitfire pilot.

This Paris joint was on a different level: black tie and tails, martinis instead of Budweiser, wingtips versus steel-toed work boots.

The nightclub owner, if that's what he was, came around the desk to land a sloppy kiss on Daphne's hand. His suit was shiny. A rumpled bow tie hung loose around his neck. Lace ran up and down both sides of his pearl-buttoned shirt. If it weren't that we was in France, I'd say he was Mafia.

After taking a stack of receipts from a chair, he offered it to Daphne. Me he left standing. Daphne started describing Jean-Michel. The nightclub owner pushed back his chair, putting his feet on the desk.

"This Jean-Michel," he said. "He used to fill in on the drum kit now and again, although not for some time now. There were accusations made, you see. Too much trouble. Disturbs the patrons. And, if I'm honest, not very skilled on the drum. His type we don't need around here." He took his feet off the desk and opened a side drawer, removing a bottle of whiskey and offering some to Daphne. She refused, of course. We watched as he knocked back one drink and filled the glass again.

"What type would that be? The Jean-Michel type, I mean," asked Daphne.

"A communist," said the nightclub owner. "We have certain…certain patrons, you understand, who objected to his political rhetoric. He caused an ugly scene one evening. The police had to be called in, and the Gestapo. We never like when that happens. Even though—" he laughed—"we are *above* the law here. Your Jean-Michel, he slipped out the storage room window and hasn't been seen since."

"What type of patrons objected?" I asked.

"Our guests, the Germans." He threw up a hand. "What to do? These are difficult times for everyone. One must survive." Reichsmarks were stacked up on the desk. From the look of it, he was doing more than surviving. He licked his fingers and began counting the bills.

Collaborator, I thought, growling under my breath.

Daphne stood up and I did likewise. "Where might we find Jean-Michel?" she asked.

"I've seen him around Montparnasse with that artist, Picasso, also a Bolshevik from what I hear. Try Le Dôme. A bit passé, but still a haunt for the starving artists types. Now, if you'll excuse me, mademoiselle. It's been a long night and I've yet to go to bed. Of course, you are welcomed to return tonight when we open."

"I wouldn't be caught dead in the company of Nazis," said Daphne.

"As you like," said the nightclub owner.

Daphne stomped to the door. I took one last look at the nightclub owner and wagged my finger.

He spun his chair around so's his back faced me.

CHAPTER TWENTY-TWO

THE METRO DELIVERED US to Montparnasse, smack in front of a graveyard. I ran straight through the gates, wanting to get a look at the tombstones. When Daphne caught up, she told me that famous people were buried there. Most of the graves were above ground and some looked like miniature houses. There were plenty of statues, some of them heartbreaking. Like the one of a naked lady falling down weeping. One was downright funny: a man and his wife chatting in bed, with the husband under the covers but still wearing his business suit.

"There lies William-Adolphe Bouguereau," said Daphne, pointing her finger to one of the graves.

"Priest?" I asked. A giant cross was carved on his marble sarcophagus.

"19th century painter. And somewhere here, they've buried Henri Fantin-Latour. His floral still lifes send chills up my spine—they're *that* good."

"Bella Lugosi movies send chills up my spine," I said. "Have you seen *Son of Frankenstein*, Daphne, with Boris Karloff?"

"I abhor horror films. And cemeteries, for that matter."

Daphne didn't see the man walk up behind her, carrying a rake. He tapped her shoulder and she shrieked, jumping three feet and hugging me for dear life. "*Mon Dieu!*" she said with a hand flying to her heart. The caretaker—because that's what he was—offered us a tour. He said we could pay whatever we thought was fair. I was game, but Daphne said she'd had enough. I looked up at the sky. A few spots of blue were showing through the gray. Rain turned to drizzle. Daphne closed the umbrella. "Just look at my hair," she said.

It looked fine to me, maybe a little frizzy is all. The caretaker followed us, begging us to take the tour, telling us about his six kids needing food. Daphne handed him change just so's he'd stop bugging us.

We looped around to a guard's hut set next to monstrous iron gates, and crossed the street. Daphne began looking in the windows of cafés and bars. All the time I thought we were looking for Jean-Michel, but then she asked me to keep my eyes peeled for a short, bald guy with a big nose. Picasso was his name.

We turned a corner and spotted the joint called Le Dôme. On the red awning was the word *BRASSERIE*: French for grub. My stomach growled so loud even Daphne heard it. "Let's pretend we've come for a bite to eat," she said. "It's a warm spot with a good vantage point."

We took a seat inside. They were saving money by keeping the lights dim. Daphne said the place had *ambiance* because of the wicker chairs, glass-topped tables, a red carpet runner, brass spittoons, and posters hanging on the walls. The place was empty, except for a few people sipping coffee while reading newspapers or tiny books. Poetry would be my guess. Daphne excused herself to visit the ladies' room. A waiter came to take our order and said they were out of everything but onion soup and baguettes with ham, onion soup being another one of them wartime concoctions. Before the war it was called beef soup, now it was only onions. "Spam?" I asked, wanting to know more about the sandwich. They probably called it something else in France, but canned ham was canned ham was canned ham.

The waiter said, "*Pardon?*" Meaning canned.

"Hitler's probably eating sirloin steak," I said.

"You are mistaken," said the waiter, throwing up a hand. "The man is a vegetarian."

Daphne came out with her lips repainted and her hair tied back. She started gabbing to the waiter, holding up the delivery of our sandwiches, asking if he knew Jean-Michel. He nodded in the direction of a man who was sitting near the window reading a newspaper. Daphne caught the man's eye and was invited to take a seat at his table.

He was older than Jack, younger than Da. He had a bald patch at the back of his head. A hat was placed on the chair next to him. A silk scarf was tied around his neck. He had gold cufflinks shaped like horse's heads, and a knit vest under his tweed jacket. Except for his scuffed work boots, he looked sharp. When he folded his newspaper into quarters and stuffed it into his coat pocket, I seen he was wearing a pinkie ring, just like

Jean-Michel. Daphne waved me over and I came running. The man stood and introduced himself.

"Charles Delaunay," he said, bowing and inviting me to sit. "My friends call me Charlie. Daphne tells me she is the fiancée of your older brother. Pity." He turned his attention back to her. "I might know the man you are seeking, Jean-Michel, the drummer and percussionist. A very talented musician. That is, if we are talking about the same Jean-Michel." He sat down and draped a napkin over his lap. I noticed a stain on his fly, onion soup probably. "He comes occasionally to a club I'm a part of. I'm one of the founders, in fact. We meet to discuss jazz music, swing and blues, that sort of thing." He called the waiter over and ordered an espresso, asking if we wanted one too. Since he was offering to pay, I asked for a Fanta.

"Where's this club of yours?" I said.

"We meet here and there, often at my flat. You are a jazz fan?"

"I'm a sucker for Glenn Miller. Is that jazz?"

"Some might call it such," said Charlie. "I'd say it was big band or swing."

"I'm from New York and we've got Harlem. My brother went to the Cotton Club right before it closed. He took the subway from Penn Station to the last stop. Jack said the joint was hopping. That's how I know about jazz. Jack bought a Duke Ellington record and we played it until the needle broke."

"Your brother is a fortunate man," said Charlie, moving his eyes up and down Daphne's legs. "We don't have anything on par with the Cotton Club. Not when

Dr. Goebbels and his Ministry of Propaganda are calling the shots. They have chosen to label jazz as—" His fingers signaled quotation marks. "—nigger, kike, *jungle* music." He groaned. "Wagner is more to Hitler's taste. And yet, I'll tell you a secret."

I leaned in.

"There is a club called the Place Blanche Café, opposite the Moulin Rouge. I went once, but wasn't permitted to enter. Only Germans are allowed entrance. From the street, I heard jazz music! Nazi-sanctioned jazz, that is." He shuddered. "Many of our best musicians fled to New York before the Germans arrived. Of course, one of our best, Django Reinhardt, the guitarist, is still in the city. Being of Roma Gypsy origin, this puts him in a rather dangerous position. You'll have to hear him play, Daphne."

"I'd like that. Perhaps we might join one of your gatherings?" she said.

"You'd be welcomed. Maybe you'll bump into your friend Jean-Michel. Come by tonight. Here, let me write the address." He tore off a piece of his newspaper and scribbled the address. He didn't exactly invite me, but there was no way I was letting Daphne go by herself. I just hoped she wouldn't make me wear a tie.

Or dance.

The Fanta arrived, along with the spam sandwiches. Charlie footed the bill and even left a tip. "Tonight, then," he said. "I shall look forward to it." He put his hat on, only to doff it to Daphne. Then his eyes landed beyond us, on a short man who was taking a seat about five from ours. "*Buenas tardes*," said Charlie, calling to the newcomer in Spanish. Being a Spaniard myself—Diego, according to the passport in my pocket—helped me peg the newcomer as a compatriot. The balding Spaniard with the big schnozzle was staring straight at Daphne in a way that had me squirming. He was old enough to be her grandfather, but his roving eyes were anything but grandfatherly.

"Could it be—?" said Daphne, her hand flying to her mouth.

Charlie leaned down and spoke in her ear. Daphne started giggling, her face turning a shade of maraschino cherry. She whispered, "Me? His muse? Surely you jest, Charlie. I appreciate the warning however." She turned her eyes away from the old man, saying, "For one thing, I've found my soul mate. It's true that my Jack can't draw a stick figure, but I'll stick with him anyway. No matter how esteemed his rival."

After Charlie left, Daphne made me switch chairs so that her back was to the Spaniard, giving him the cold shoulder, in other words. Me giving him the evil eye so's he'd know to keep his distance. I watched as he removed a book from his pocket, and a pencil. I figured him for a poet, but then he began sketching Daphne's back, moving his glance back and forth between the little black book and her. I decided not to say anything, but if he tried to make a move I'd whack him with the plate.

I made a move to examine the tip, but Daphne slapped my hand away. The waiter saw the whole thing, swooping over before I could make a second attempt.

"Just checking to see the dates on the coins," I said.

"A coin collector now, are you?" said Daphne.

"Laugh all you want but a kid in Hempstead found a rusty can full of gold dollars buried in his backyard. Found them when his father was digging a new septic tank. Now he's got himself a brand new Packard with the extra chrome package. I'm on the lookout for a 1776 Silver Continental dollar. Ben Franklin made them and everybody knows he lived in Paris."

"Really, Thomas. You're incorrigible. And what made you order these dreadful sandwiches?" She looked like she'd swallowed a bug. I took the sandwich from her hand. It wasn't half bad washed down with the Fanta. We weren't eating enough and I could see that Daphne was losing weight. My brother wouldn't like it. He said her figure was perfect. And on top of that, her wedding dress wasn't gonna fit. It was made from the silk of a German parachute her ma fought the whole block to get her hands on. Between sips of espresso, Daphne said, "Let's call around to the Doumers'. With any luck, Sophie will have returned home and that shall be the end of this nightmare. Then we'll return to England." She started biting the side of her thumb, thinking how difficult that might be.

"Good thinking," I said. "Juliette is probably worried stiff about us. And besides, they got that swell black market bakery around the corner."

"Is food the only thing you ever think about?"

"Juliette says that's the only thing anybody thinks about in Paris. So I fit right in."

"A real Parisian." She licked her lips. "I could do with a croissant or two. With orange marmalade and gobs of butter."

"Now you're talking," I said.

As we exited the restaurant, I got a glimpse of the Spaniard's drawing. Sure enough, his sketch of Daphne looked like an alien. Like every other artist in Paris, he was imitating that Picasso fella.

CHAPTER TWENTY-THREE

JULIETTE BEGGED to be taken along to the jazz club. Before long she was decked out in a white lace number along the lines of a communion dress. Daphne raided Sophie's closet again, landing on a dress that reminded me of a cupcake. Against my will, I took a bath (in cold water, insult to injury). Daphne, meanwhile, was scheming to get me into Mr. Doumer's church suit, but it turned out that moths got to it first. Mr. Doumer was no worse for it, being that he was a machinist forced to work at a factory in Germany.

Daphne draped a bow tie around my neck. "Now, hold still," she said, pulling a comb through the knots in my hair and then tying another knot in the bow tie. "Aren't *you* debonair? And here… A finishing touch." She pulled a silk flower from one of Sophie's hats and pinned it to my lapel.

Meanwhile, Juliette was puckering her lips. "Something must be done about those *très* awful boots," she said, running to the kitchen and returning with a can of shoe polish and a bristle brush. I'd watched O'Reilly go at Lord Sopwith's shoes enough times to know that the secret was spit, and plenty of it. I watered up my mouth and let a glob land on my left boot. After a few minutes, I could see my reflection in the leather. General Eisenhower would be proud of them boots.

I figured we were finished, but Daphne grabbed my hand and said: "Where's that nail clipper of yours?"

"Lost," I said. I'd had enough sprucing up.

We took the Metro back to Montparnasse but got off a stop before the cemetery. It was raining again and we'd forgotten the umbrella. Daphne bought a newspaper and gave us each a section to hold over our heads. It was pouring so hard the ink stained our hands. We ran from awning to awning, jumped around rain gutters, and got splashed by passing cars. Juliette talked my ear off, all perky because this was her first grown-up party.

"Perhaps Sophie will be there," she said. "She loves music almost as much as art. If she couldn't be a painter, she wanted to be a composer. But not like Chopin, more like Gershwin." She took my hand every time we came to a puddle. "Tommy, have you ever heard *An American in Paris?*" she said. "It's by George Gershwin."

"Never heard it," I said. "But I'd probably like *An American in Paris*. I guess that would me *moi*."

We turned into a narrow street and stood in front of Charlie's building. From the look of it, the place was rat and roach infested. I told Juliette about how roaches ate wallpaper paste because it was made with flour, and that peeling wallpaper was a sure sign of an infestation. But she kept talking about Gershwin.

"He's wonderful! Sophie has the record. When we return home, I'll play it for you. We really ought to have taken it along to the party. They'll likely have a record player. I might have danced to it with a real American. *Parfait!*"

"I don't dance," I said. "The Irish jig on Saint Patty's day, that's it."

Charlie was standing on a fire escape, talking with a skinny blonde. He let down the ladder and we climbed up.

"It's rusty," said Daphne, gathering up her skirt. "Be careful or we could get tetanus." She let us go first.

We climbed into the open window, into a smoke-filled room packed with Bohemian types: lots of feather boas, bead necklaces, berets, and goatees. No one seemed to mind that two kids just come in the window. One lady said something that meant, *Aren't they simply darlings?*

I found a dark corner. From my lookout behind a Chinese screen, carved with dragons, I took in the whole scene. There were instruments hanging from the walls: violins, tin-whistles, and a trombone. In the corner they had a grand piano, angled so's it faced the crowd. A half-dressed lady was sprawled on top of it, making snake moves and hissing at passing men. I'd steer clear of the piano.

Now I knew why Charlie made us use the fire escape. People were jamming up the stairwell and hallway, the kind of bottleneck you get on a New York City subway during rush hour. Juliette threw herself smack into the center of things, kissing everybody's cheeks and asking if they'd heard of Gershwin.

One man claimed to *be* Gershwin.

"He's jesting," said a lady wearing a Japanese kimono. "Georgie is two heads taller and better looking."

Charlie handed Daphne a glass of bubbly. He laid his hand on the small of her back. Through the fog of cigarette smoke, I seen a man come up behind them. He lit a match and for a split second I could see his face. If I didn't know better, I'd've said he was my brother. I inched around the screen, but by then he was gone.

My eyes were playing tricks on me, that much was obvious. Might've been on account of the smoke, or the fact that the only light came from an oriental lamp with a red shade; or it could be that jazz music confused the brain. Because a minute later I seen a man who looked like Jean-Michel, but who turned out to be somebody else.

He was sitting on a love seat next to a dame dressed up like a man: top hat and tails, and smoking a cigar. No mistake about it, she was going for a Marlene Dietrich impersonation. The man was licking the lady's fingers, one by one. I walked right up and put out my hand for a shake.

"Hi, Jean," I said. "Just the man we're looking for."

He laughed and took my hand. His palm was slippery and made me think of baloney. Now that I was closer, I seen there was something about his eyes that were different from Jean-Michel's. The black frame glasses with bottle-thick lenses made them look like a horsefly's.

"Charmed, I'm sure," he said. "Although my name is Antoine, not Jean."

"My mistake," I said, focusing on his nose. *Did Jean-Michel have a bump on his nose?* I didn't think so. And this man had pockmarks from scratching his face when he was a kid with chickenpox.

The lady made space for me on the love seat, patting the velvet seat cushion. "I adore younger men," she said.

I didn't want to squeeze in between them, but it would've been rude to refuse.

Daphne came over just then and made the same mistake as me. "It's Antoine," said the man correcting her. "Charmed. Are you a member of this little coterie? First time for me." He took Daphne's hand and was getting ready to lick it when a glass of red wine dropped onto his white jacket. Daphne and me jumped away in the nick of time. Splashes of wine landed on Antoine's white trousers, too. He looked like a murder victim.

The lady yelled, "Klutz!" shooting daggers behind her, looking for the culprit who'd dropped the glass, all the while jabbing her cigar in the air. She glared at Daphne, even though there was no way it was her fault.

"Really, my dear," said Antoine. "No need to make a fuss." He patted his jacket with a napkin and the stains turned pink. I was embarrassed for him.

"We need club soda," said Daphne, running to the kitchen. She returned with a bottle and can opener.

"That won't work, you damned fool!" said the lady. "Club soda works on grease, not wine. For wine stains one needs salt and boiling water."

"My mistake," said Daphne, who sounded like she was about to cry. I took her hand in mine and squeezed hard.

I heard a whack and looked up to see the tuxedo lady's hand fly to her cheek. "Who slapped me? The nerve!" she yelled. She got up from the love seat and began pushing her way through the crowd, turning back only once to say, "Are you coming Antoine?"

"*Oui, oui, mon chérie*," he said.

Charlie came over to see what the fuss was about. By then Antoine and his date were gone. Charlie went to the kitchen and returned with a broom and pan, swept up the glass, and mopped up wine with a rag. "I apologize for my guests," he said, putting his hand on Daphne's waist. "But I've good news for you." He handed her a piece of paper. On it was an address. "Your friend Jean-Michel. I had a time finding it, but there it is."

"I'm ever so grateful," said Daphne, inching away until Charlie's hand dropped to his side. Someone holding a guitar whispered in his ear. He nodded his head, raising his voice so's it could be heard over the crowd.

"*Attention, s'il vous plaît!*" he said, clapping his hands.

The show was about to begin. People started cramming into the apartment, sitting on each other's laps, cross-legged on the floor, crammed up against the furniture. It was getting hard to breathe. Daphne pulled me in the direction of the fire escape. "Time to go. Have you seen Juliette?" she asked.

I spotted Juliette sitting on an ottoman, facing an old man with a goatee. Her hands were palm up, resting in his. I wondered if he was telling her fortune, *palm reading*, it's called. But when I got closer, I seen she was crying, saying, "*C'est pas possible! C'est pas possible!*"

"Time to beat it," I said. "Daphne's waiting on the fire escape."

Juliette kissed the man's cheeks, both of them. He said something by way of an apology, shaking his head. Juliette answered in French, which I might've understood if it weren't for the jazz music in the background. She flung herself at me, weeping on my shoulder and saying over and over, "*C'est pas possible!*"

We heard a needle scratch against a jazz record. The room got quiet. People started talking in a hush, with every eye glued on the man with the guitar, even though all he was doing was tuning up. I whispered, "What's the matter, Juliette?" She was crying so hard, snot was flowing from her nose.

She put her mouth to my ear: "Tommy, that man swears that Sophie is a—must be a—claims she's a—" She couldn't say it.

"Spit it out, Juliette. Must be what?" I said.

"A Nazi," she said, choking back tears.

CHAPTER TWENTY-FOUR

WE WENT STRAIGHT BACK to the hotel, keeping to dark alleyways so's we wouldn't get caught breaking the curfew.

Daphne phoned Madame Doumer from the front desk, which took forever since there was no telephone in the Doumer apartment. Daphne had to call a downstairs neighbor, who hoofed it up three flights to bring Madame Doumer to the phone.

Meanwhile, me and Juliette went up to room. I checked on the painting of Joan slaying the Englishmen. Everything looked copacetic. Daphne came up and told Juliette, "Your mother agrees it will be better if you stay with us tonight rather than risk being caught breaking the curfew. But she's very unhappy about it. And now, why the tears?"

Juliette launched into her story:

"I was making enquiries around the party...That's how you say it, *enquiries?* Enquiries, yes, hoping to find someone who might know Sophie. That's how I was introduced to Monsieur Vittet. He said he was an art collector, mostly of modernist painters. Henri Matisse is a favorite of his."

"I never cared for Matisse," said Daphne.

"Most of his paintings were bought from a man named Paul Rosenberg," said Juliette, "who owned an art gallery on the Rue La Boétie. That was before the Nazis confiscated Monsieur Rosenberg's collection and drove him from the city, forcing him to escape through Portugal."

"Portugal," I said, thinking about grilled steak.

"He managed to escape to New York."

"Lucky fella," I said.

"Not so lucky," said Juliette, "because the Nazis had taken so many of his lovely paintings. The Reichsleiter Rosenberg Taskforce, they are the villains in the story."

"Pirates," I said.

"Monsieur Vittet, having become a good friend of Monsieur Rosenberg's, tried to learn what had become of the collection. He traced the paintings to the Galerie Nationale du Jeu de Paume, the same gallery where Sophie was working."

She started bawling again, like only a girl can. Daphne found a hankie and helped Juliette blow her nose. I poured her a glass of water from a pitcher, then gave her a peppermint.

"Monsieur Vittet is certain that the Jeu de Paume is being used as a clearinghouse for things that the Nazis steal. The Reichsleiter Rosenberg Taskforce, he told me, is the group that finds and steals the paintings, mostly those belonging to Jewish families. Then they bring them to the gallery for cataloging. From there they are shipped off to Germany. So you see, don't you, that it makes sense what he said? Anyone working at the gallery must be a Nazi collaborator."

A dead silence filled the room. Daphne jumped up from the bed and paced from one end of the room to the other. "It's impossible," she said.

"That is what I said," said Juliette. "*C'est pas possible.* Those very words."

"If she wasn't a collaborator, then what was she doing working for them?" I asked. I didn't know Sophie that well, and was okay playing the devil's advocate. Plenty of people were collaborating with the Nazis, people who had sisters and best friends willing to stick up for them.

Daphne was about to hit me, so I said fast, "*C'est pas possible!*"

"And there's another thing," said Juliette, who was sucking her lip.

"Worse than being a Nazi?" I said.

"It's about the painting, our painting. Mind you, I didn't let on to Monsieur Vittet that we knew anything about it. But it came up in our conversation, when he mentioned another collector who had paintings confiscated by the Reichsleiter Rosenberg Taskforce: Édouard de Rothschild. The painting is called *The Astronomer* and it was stolen from the sitting room where Monsieur de Rothschild had it hung. Monsieur Vittet was certain that the painting had made its way to Germany by now. He told me that Vermeer was a favorite of Hitler's."

"But the painting's still here in Paris," said Daphne.

We both turned our heads in the direction of the hallway. I had a terrible feeling that the Gestapo would break the door down and haul us away. We had something that Adolf Hitler wanted, and he wasn't gonna let two girls and a boy stop him. My hands started shaking and I had to clinch my teeth to stop them from chattering. But I put on a brave face, a stiff upper lip. I puffed out my chest. I pounded a fist into my palm, hoping it would make the girls feel safer. But deep inside I knew I was no match for the Gestapo.

"We must return the painting to Monsieur de Rothschild, it's only right," said Daphne.

"There'll probably be a reward," I said, cheering up a bit.

"Did Monsieur Vittet mention de Rothschild's address?" asked Daphne.

"He lives now in New York City," said Juliette.

I clapped my hands and said: "Then it's a job for me. I know the place like the back of my hand. Why, I've got an uncle living on the Lower East Side."

"If you recall," said Daphne, "it's quite difficult to cross the Atlantic at the moment. Isn't that why you are still in Europe?" She looked up at the ceiling, then back toward the hallway where the painting was hanging. "No, we must hide the painting until the war is over. Or, at the very least, bring it to London for safekeeping. My father works at the National Gallery and he'll know the right people to be in touch with. Our national treasures have been shipped off to Wales to protect them from bombings. So that's the solution. The Vermeer shall go to Wales for the duration."

Somehow in all the talk about the painting, we'd

forgot about Sophie. An idea hit me, so I ran it by them: "What if Sophie had the same idea? Maybe she was only working at that joint so's she could save the painting from Hitler."

"Now that sounds exactly like something she would do," said Daphne, smiling so's her dimples showed. This new idea of mine sat better with her, better than the one where Sophie was a lowlife traitor. Juliette was smiling too. It was swell while it lasted, but I was about to wipe the grins off their faces.

"The only problem," I said, "is that means Sophie might'a been taken by the Gestapo, after all. That is, if they suspected her of taking the painting. I'm darn tooting sure they don't want to get on Hitler's bad side." We all exhaled at the same time.

"You've a point," said Daphne. "Which leads us back to Jean-Michel. He's really our only lead. Perhaps he's heard rumors about where they'd taken her. It shan't hurt to speak with him again." She rummaged through her pocketbook and found the slip of paper with his address. "Tomorrow, first thing," she said.

"But if he works at the gallery, wouldn't that make him a collaborator, too," I said.

"You've made another good point, two in a row," said Daphne. "We mustn't tell him that we have the painting in our possession. We have to keep mum about that."

"We better take along the heat," I said.

"Heat?" said Juliette.

"Gangster slang for pistol."

Juliette's eyes opened wide, super impressed with my vocabulary.

Daphne and Juliette shared a bed, with Juliette sleeping in one of the nighties Daphne lifted from Sophie's dresser. I had trouble falling asleep, thinking that every passing car was a Gestapo paddy wagon. And it turned out that Juliette talked in her sleep, odd bits of French that I couldn't make out. I decided to stuff a sock in my ear, but the smell, so close to my nose, kept me awake some more. And the bed was lumpy, with springs poking my side. That would've never happened at the Crillon.

I was kept awake by the idea that I might never see my ma again, that I might be a casualty of war like so many other sorry souls. I made up my mind to go back to England, keeping the painting right where it was. If the Hôtel Jeanne d'Arc survived the war and I got back to New York, I'd pay Mr. de Rothschild a visit and give him the good news. But I wasn't risking my neck for fine art—no way. With that thought in mind, I fell into a tortured sleep.

Daphne and Juliette woke me by waving a French baguette under my nose. They brought me a piece of cheese, too. *Parmesan* it was called, so hard it almost broke a tooth. When I asked what they'd had for breakfast, both of them started giggling. I figured it was éclairs. I said, "Tonight, I'm stuffing socks in your mouth, Juliette. It's not right, keeping me up half the night and then me missing out on the éclairs."

"Oh, Tommy," she said. "There were none. The bakery shelves were empty, the saddest sight on earth. We had the same breakfast as you, only with make-believe coffee, what we call *ersatz* coffee, which isn't coffee at all." She let her shoulders droop. "What with the shortages, white flour and sugar are going to the Germans. And chocolate. The best chocolate used to come from Belgium, but the Germans are occupying that country also."

I told her I'd been to Belgium and she was wrong. The best chocolate came from Hershey, Pennsylvania. It came wrapped in brown paper and silver foil. This had Juliette licking her lips. Meanwhile, Daphne was pinning up her hair, using the window glass for a mirror. At the Crillon she would've had a gold-gilded mirror, one that'd belonged to Marie Antoinette.

I heard steps outside our door and put a finger to my lips. Daphne peeked out, making sure to keep the chain on the lock. "It's only the maid," she said turning her head to us. "Here to make the beds." To the maid she said something French. Then she put the "*NE PAS DE-RANGER*" sign on the outside doorknob, meaning we didn't want to be disturbed. Once the door was closed, she whispered, "We can't trust anyone."

"I'm sure they have a skeleton key," I said, "One that works on every door."

Daphne took a pin from her hair. "I can jam the lock easily enough." She reached for her hem, pulling at a stray thread until she had a piece about two inches long. "And this will tell us if someone comes snooping. Let's not forget to check it when we return tonight."

CHAPTER TWENTY-FIVE

JEAN-MICHEL LIVED NEAR a place called the Marché aux Puces, a giant flea market. On Long Island, when people want to get rid of their junk, they have a yard sale. They find cardboard and markers, make a few signs, and nail them up on telephone poles. Next thing you know, suckers come flocking to buy your trash. In Paris people don't have yards, so they bring their junk to the Marché aux Puces instead. I wanted to look for treasure, but we were on a mission. Daphne told us to watch for pickpockets. She clutched her pocketbook under an armpit. This was the last place I'd come if I was a thief. Head for the Crillon is what I'd do.

At Jean-Michel's building the front door was hanging from rusty hinges and the lock was already broken. The hallway smelled like a urinal. Every lightbulb was burnt out, or maybe somebody forgot to pay the electric bill. Either way, it was dark. Daphne said not to touch the railing. Suddenly, Juliette wanted to go home, whimpering, "I'm scared."

The only light came from a skylight, up above the top landing. I was leading the way. Somebody left a baby carriage in the hallway and I slammed right into it. From one apartment we heard voices, which turned out to be a radio tuned to the news. Music came from the apartment next door. Clothes were hung up to dry in the hallway, what with the rain we'd been getting. Ladies brassieres were right out in plain sight.

On the Lower East Side, where my Uncle Jimmy lives, they call places like this *tenements*. Dirt-poor immigrants live in them. When Ma arrived from Ireland, she lived in one of them tenements and the memory still gave her the willies: three families jammed into one apartment, an airshaft for ventilation, no heat in the winter, and a hotplate instead of a proper kitchen.

A man with a scruffy beard answered Jean-Michel's door. I could tell from his white teeth that he was younger than he looked. He invited us in.

The place was a dump. The man had me sit in chair with three legs, with books making the fourth. Daphne and Juliette sat on a couch with feathers spilling out from rips. I seen Daphne flick a flea off her arm.

"Must've escaped from the flea market," I said, and everyone agreed.

Jean-Michel was still sleeping and the man went to wake him. We sat there quiet, staring at our feet until a lady dressed in nothing but a slip came into the room. There were black circles under her eyes; from stale makeup was my guess. Her hair was a mess. *The bride of Frankenstein,* I thought. On top of that, she had a leather belt strapped around her arm for some reason I couldn't figure.

"Are you the new recruits?" she said, half-asleep.

Turned out she was searching for a spoon. The bearded man came back and shoved the lady into a bedroom, slamming the door behind her and turning the key. She started kicking from the inside and he yelled in French, "*La junkie!*"

I was scared out of my wits. Daphne signaled for us to leave, but a cat jumped up on my lap wanting petting. The bearded man sat in a chair across from me. "Hey, English," he said. "You like cats?"

"Love them," I said.

"Take him then. We don't have the money to feed him."

The lady yelled through the door: "*Mon chat!*"

He shouted back: "*Ta gueule!*"

"Really? I can have him for free?" I said. I wanted a cat bad, but my sister Mary was allergic. She was three thousand miles away and this was my chance.

"*Sans frais,*" he said, making a zero sign with his fingers.

"*Non merci,*" said Daphne.

Jean-Michel was still nowhere in sight. Daphne explained that we'd wait in a café down the street. She made out like she was starving, so's the man wouldn't get offended. He didn't care one way or another and seemed glad to see us go. The cat bit my hand and I decided not to take him. The three of us bolted for the door, Juliette getting there first.

About an hour later, Jean-Michel came walking into the café, scanning the place and looking for a familiar face. He spotted Daphne and smiled so big his gums showed.

"*Excusez moi,*" he said to her. "You are the English girl, the friend of Sophie?" He noticed Juliette. "But, of course." He whacked his forehead. "I apologize for my friend Claude. He has no manners, no class whatsoever. He is a guest in my home, too. Sleeping on the sofa. One would have expected more gratitude, but no. He has overstayed his welcome." He brushed the air, ending the topic of 'Claude The Ingrate.'

"Forgive me for forgetting," he continued, "but did we have an appointment?"

"Oh no, there was no appointment," said Daphne. "And we've had a dickens of a time tracking you down. Our apologies for showing up unannounced. We had only your address and no telephone number. A letter would have taken too long. You see, we're desperate for news of Sophie."

He waved a menu in the air, getting the waiter's attention. I could tell he was stalling for time, trying to decide what to tell us and what to hold back. The waiter stuck his jaw out and Jean-Michel asked for an ashtray and matches. When he finally started talking, his eyes darted around the café but never landed on us.

"I have no idea where she is," he said. "But trouble is coming, and I don't mind telling you that she's to blame."

"What kind of trouble? The Gestapo?" I asked.

"Worse yet. Hermann Göring."

"Head of the German Luftwaffe?" I asked. "*Reichsmarschall* Hermann Göring?"

"The very same. And he's after that painting—the one that's gone missing."

I guess we looked a little confused, because he said: "Look, I suppose I'd better explain the situation." He lowered his voice. We pushed our chairs closer. "About a month ago, a painting was discovered by the *Möbel-Aktion*. This is the German agency responsible for the systematic plundering of furniture, mostly from the homes of those who have fled, or those who have been taken into German custody."

"You mean Jewish families?" said Daphne.

"Jews, communists, homosexuals. And people who have been caught working for the Resistance. The Nazis take anything of value, whole households in fact. Everything is sorted at a warehouse located on the outskirts of Paris. Valuable items are shipped to Germany or used to furnish the homes of high-level Germans living here in Paris. The rest is either sold at auction or destroyed."

"What does this have to do with the Nationale du Jeu de Paume?" asked Daphne.

"Not much. Until a month ago. That was when the Möbel-Aktion brought in an armoire, 15th century, I believe. While examining it, a tube was found. Inside the tube was a painting. Vermeer's *Astronomer*."

"Never heard of it," I said, and Daphne blew me a kiss.

"Well, believe me, everyone at the Jeu de Paume had. Because they'd sent the identical painting to Germany in 1940, cleared through the gallery and earmarked for Hitler's Führermuseum." He swung his head around and then continued. "The first thing to do was to bring in experts, to examine the new find, determine if it was the original or a copy. If it was the original, there'd be trouble with the Germans. It would mean that one of our art historians had misattributed the painting in 1940. If it was a copy, well—*c'est la vie.*"

"But it *was* the original?" asked Juliette.

"Some said yes, some said no, others said *peut-être*...maybe. If it was a copy, it was an awfully good one, a contemporary of the original. We were waiting for the premier German art historian to arrive from Bonn, a man who'd worked at restoring Dutch Renaissance paintings, a Vermeer scholar who would know a copy when he saw one."

I tried to put the pieces together. Two paintings: one the original, one a fake. I wondered which one was hanging at the Hôtel Jeanne d'Arc. Or was there a third painting?

"And the painting found by the Möbel-Aktion..." said Daphne.

"It vanished. Along with your friend, Sophie. No one thinks it's a coincidence."

The waiter interrupted by pointing to a chalkboard with most of the dishes crossed off.

"*Ersatz café, pour moi,*" said Daphne.

Jean-Michel pulled out the lining of his pocket.

"*Deux,*" said Daphne, raising two fingers.

I pulled out the lining of my pockets, but she waved the waiter away. Jean-Michel scanned the café again. We moved our chairs closer to him and leaned in to listen.

"Sophie loathed the idea of a genuine Vermeer going to Germany, if that indeed is what it was. There were some of us at the gallery who agreed with her. We drove ourselves crazy trying to come up with an idea. Sophie suggested that we copy the painting. It was as simple as the German expert arriving to find a modern copy—*fini*, end of story. He'd think we were fools, that would be the worst of it. Hitler would rest assured that the original was safe in his hands. Sophie volunteered to make the copy."

"She's very talented," said Daphne. "She might have pulled it off."

"Transcription," I said, and even Jean-Michel was impressed.

He went on with the story: "Mademoiselle Villand, who oversees the gallery, hadn't liked the idea. Too risky, she thought. By then word had reached Germany and we were told that Hermann Göring himself was determined to view the painting. He fancies himself an art expert." Jean-Michel laughed. "The man's a neophyte, doesn't know the first thing about art. He only wants to line his pockets. It won't be the first time he's visited the gallery. And each time paintings fly out of France."

"He's got the airplanes to do it," I said.

"He has an arrangement with Hitler. The boss gets first pick, Göring is next in line. The rest are sold through Swiss dealers to fund German armaments."

"*Ma brave sœur!*" said Juliette, clapping her fingers. "My brave sister has saved the painting."

"And the rest of us will be lined up against a wall

and shot," said Jean-Michel. "Think. Do you imagine for one moment that Hitler will allow an eighteen-year-old girl to run off with his favorite painting? They will hunt her down until they find her. In the meantime, there'll be the rest of us to suffer the consequences." He motioned toward Juliette, "Do you think your own family will be spared?"

Daphne closed her eyes, concentrating. The rest of us sat quiet, but I'm sure we were thinking the same thing: if that painting wasn't returned before Hermann Göring showed up, heads would roll. I pictured a guillotine with Juliette's head under the falling blade. I remembered driving through the town of Arras on my first trip to France, where 240 French Resistance members were executed in the citadel. In broad daylight the Nazis lined them up against the church wall and shot them one by one. Their horrified families stood on watching, waiting to collect the bodies.

"When is Göring coming?" I asked.

"Saturday next. There isn't much time," said Jean-Michel.

CHAPTER TWENTY-SIX

FROM WHERE I WAS SITTING, I had a view of the cash register, soda dispenser, a rack of wine bottles, a menu board, and a mirror with *Punchs Cocktail Exotique* written on it. My eye followed a piece of chocolate layer cake, being delivered to a customer by the front door.

In walked two men wearing plainclothes. They had that look that spells trouble: hats pulled down over their eyes, dark glasses, and bulges under their trench coats. They walked stiffly, as if they had no knees. They might as well've worn a sign around their necks: GESTAPO. Their heads stayed dead still, but I knew they were scoping out the café. One of the men jutted his chin in our direction.

"We've got visitors," I said.

Jean-Michel's head spun around. He jumped from his chair and made a beeline for the kitchen, knocking into the elbow of a lady and causing her to spill coffee.

Gestapo agent #1 chased after Jean-Michel. His Luger pistol was now in plain sight. Gestapo agent #2 grabbed Daphne, dragging her through to the kitchen. She was kicking and screaming and trying to scratch his eyes out. Impossible without fingernails.

They ignored Juliette and me.

Juliette snapped to action first, hightailing it to the kitchen. I followed close behind, stepping by accident on the back of her shoe. Meanwhile, a dishwasher was waving us away. "*Pardon*, Juliette," I said, running in front of her. Once in the alleyway, I seen the Gestapo agents tossing Daphne into the back seat of a black Renault Nervasport.

The car starting pulling away. Luckily for me, the back windows had been blacked out. I jumped on the bumper and climbed onto the roof, being sure to make myself flat as a pancake. With my head twisted backwards I seen Juliette wave goodbye. Tears were streaming from her eyes.

The car picked up speed, racing across Paris. There wasn't much traffic except for bicycles, gasoline being scarcer than éclairs. I got my bearings by looking around for the Eiffel Tower.

We headed north.

By the time the car slowed, I was so frozen my fingertips were turning black. The car turned into a dead-end street and I slid to the road, scraping my knees something bad. I gave myself a second to thaw and then walked, easy-going, down the street—whistling so's I wouldn't seem a threat. Ducking behind a newspaper kiosk, I had a view of the courtyard where the Renault came to a screeching stop. We weren't at the dreaded Fresnes Prison, and for that much I said two Hail Mary's.

A gray Volkswagen Kübelwagen was parked outside the gate, and a swastika flag flopped wet and heavy from a pole. The newspaper kiosk was, give or take an inch, twenty feet from the gate. It wasn't one of them grand boulevards, but just a cobblestone side street. I watched as a canvas-top truck backed out, swiping the paint off a parked car. It blocked my view for a minute. Once it passed I seen three German soldiers posted next to the VW, armed to the hilt.

The newsstand was closed, it being Sunday. That reminded me about Mass, which once again I'd skipped. If Ma knew, she'd say I was doomed. And from the look of it, she might be right.

I found a loose brick and broke the padlock on the newsstand, entered the cramped space and sat on stacks of magazines. I wedged open the window and here's what I seen: Daphne being manhandled to the front door. Jean-Michel was nowhere in sight and I figured he got away.

What with them soldiers guarding the entrance, no one was sneaking in that way. I ran through a list of possible commando moves, none that would end well. For a minute there I panicked, thinking I'd never see Daphne alive again and knowing it was my fault for dragging her back to Paris. Hives broke out on my arms, which only happened once before when I ate shrimp cocktail.

Would Jack ever forgive me?

I watched in horror as one of the guards walked over to the newsstand and knocked on the wooden shutter. I froze like a Popsicle.

"*Cigarettes, s'il vous plaît, Gitanes,*" he said.

My God, he wanted me to sell him cigarettes at a

time like this. I looked around the cramped space and spotted the brand he wanted, slapped the pack on the ledge, and threw in a box of matchsticks. Coins dropped onto a brass dish. He said, "*Danke*," and walked back to his post. Sweat was beading down my forehead and stinging my eyes. I forgot about the coins, that's how shook-up I was.

Obviously, the newsstand wasn't a safe place. Besides, I wasn't helping Daphne none by staying there. *Maybe there's a fire escape at the back of the building*, I thought. It might be a long stakeout so I took a comic book with me.

Circling around the block, I found the backyard. It was fenced in, one of them black iron jobs easy enough to squeeze through if your head isn't full-grown. On the other side was a garden with boxwood bushes, trimmed razor-sharp. I laid flat on the ground and peeked under a shrub. That's when I seen a door leading into a kitchen. It was just about lunchtime and I could hear pots and pans being banged around.

I noticed a white curtain, blowing from a room on the second floor. One dimensional trees grew up the side of the building, almost like they'd been flattened by a steamroller. Upon closer inspection, I seen they were attached to wires, screwed into the wall at one-foot intervals.

Parfait! I thought, perfect.

Before long I was swinging my foot over a windowsill. It knocked over a chair, but the room was carpeted and it didn't make a sound. The whole time, Adolf Hitler glared at me from a portrait hung over a fireplace. I grabbed a poker and jabbed it through his nose.

Applying my extra-sensitive hearing, I made my way to the door, opening it in slow motion. The parquet floorboards creaked with each step down the long hallway leading to a circular staircase. Crawling on my hands and knees, I wiggled to the railing, so low to the ground I got a splinter in my stomach.

Two men were shooting the breeze at the bottom of the staircase.

Germans. No surprise there.

Over the edge of the rail, I spied the soldiers guarding a room with double doors, both shut. One of the soldiers took a cigarette from a case and asked his skinny friend for a light. I knew his brand: Gitanes. Luckily I understood enough German to get the gist of what they said:

"We'll be here awhile." That from the scarecrow. "The *Sturmhauptführer* is in a fine mood. That one's as yummy as a *bethmännchen*." A bethmännchen, I knew, was the German version of an éclair. Only it was filled with marzipan instead of crème and wasn't iced with chocolate. After comparing Daphne to a pastry, he moved on to the main course. "Ha!" he said, "When he's finished with her, she'll be a mincemeat pie."

To my shock and amazement, Gitanes wasn't going for it. He shook his head and said, "She's only a girl," and then looked at the double doors shaking his head again. He was one of those Germans Lord Sopwith once told me about—*conflicted*, was the word he used. If only I could get his name, MI5 might be able to turn him.

I wanted to challenge Scarecrow to a duel, right then and there. But he had a rifle slug across his shoulders. I'd never get close enough to use the poker.

Create a diversion. That's what was needed.

I crawled back to the bedroom and out the window, down the wires, and back to the garden. That's when I seen a breezeway, with bicycles stacked up against the wall so's they wouldn't get rusty. The breezeway led back to the front courtyard.

The Renault was parked at the perfect angle. I waited until the soldiers went into the building and then dashed for the car. The key was still in the ignition.

The fools! I thought.

That's when I seen a lady sitting in a Mercedes coupé parked across in the street. She was holding a French poodle. The French lady was wearing a hat that looked like a fruit bowl. The poodle had a ridiculous pink bow on its head.

I moved the gear stick around just the way Jack shown me back in East Hempstead when he taught me to drive his old Ford pick-up. The courtyard was on a slope. With the gear in neutral, the Renault rolled backwards in the direction of the street. Good thing the gate was opened.

I aimed for the Mercedes.

The Renault weighed at least a ton and it picked up speed crossing the street. In a crash, you want to be in a Renault Nervasport. The Mercedes coupé was like crumb cake. The door flew from its hinges. The French lady gasped in horror, clutching the poodle to her chest. She got out of the coupe and came around to my door, opened it, and grabbed me by my shirtsleeve.

I'd been hoping the crash would get everyone out of the building for a look-see, but my hopes were dashed.

Time for Plan B.

I pointed to the Gestapo building and yelled, "*Mon père! Mon père!*" which translated meant, "My da, my da." The lady dragged me to the front entrance, barging right up to the front door. She banged her closed fist against it and then hit me on the head. The door swung open and there stood Scarecrow. The lady hammered him in a mix of French and German, slapping him with a leather glove.

Her husband was now at the scene of the crime, mourning for his Mercedes. He joined his wife on the front steps, pushing the soldier against a potted tree. Scarecrow reached for his rifle. Gitane came to the door, throwing his cigarette on the stoop and grinding it with the heel of his boot.

Everything was going according to plan.

From the stoop, I had a view into the foyer. I seen the double doors open. The Gestapo agent appeared, the one who'd nabbed Daphne, wanting to know what the ruckus was about. He stepped toward the entrance. The French lady began shouting at him, thinking that he was my *père*. She was still holding my shirtsleeve, but I managed to bite her hand and run for the double doors, which I bolted behind me.

That's when I seen Daphne, in what I knew then

was a library. She was seated in a straight-back chair with her hands and feet tied. There were scrapes on her cheeks; she'd have a nasty shiner before long. The sight made my hands shake while I untied her.

The Nazis were banging on the library door, yelling "*Öffnen!*"

The Frenchies screamed insults at the Germans, shouting *Vichy* this and *Vichy* that—claiming to be in tight with Marshal Petain, who I knew was head of the French Vichy government.

Collaborators, I thought. Figured that they had a German car.

I heard the poodle whine.

I considered the windows, but they faced the front courtyard. There was only one way out. I pointed to it. At the same time, I grabbed a hammer that was sitting on a table with other instruments of torture: brass knuckles and something that looked like a rubber-topped bludgeon. From previous experience, I knew I'd be needing the hammer. Daphne grabbed a picture that was propped on the mantle, clutching the frame under her armpit. Both her passports were sitting on an end table and she stuffed them into her pocketbook, along with her pearl-handled pistol. Then she looped the pocketbook over one elbow, put a big smile on her face, and leaned over to kiss my cheek.

I motioned in the direction of our escape route. Up the fireplace we went, using the chimney sweep handholds. I used the hammer to bust open the chimney cap. In seconds we were jumping down to the slate roof and climbing to the ridge that ran from one edge of the building to the other. Daphne balanced on one foot and handed me the picture. "I'm glad for my ballet training," she said, twirling around and making my stomach jump.

The Nazis were now in the courtyard, trying to get into the windows. They saw us on the roof and the Gestapo agent took aim with his Luger pistol. It didn't worry me a bit because we were out of range. I seen Gitane, who I had a sneaking feeling was a sharpshooter, aim his rifle about ten feet below us, hitting the gutter pipe. But then Scarecrow joined the action. Now I knew what a duck feels like when a shooting party shows up.

A bullet hit the roof, sending slate raining down on their heads. We ran to the neighbor's roof—flat and a four-foot jump down. Soon, we were climbing down a fire escape and leaping into an alleyway.

"Oh, my dear," said Daphne, taking the picture from me once we'd landed. Her hand brushed the surface. "The Klee is covered in soot."

"That's the least of our problems, don't you think?"

"And blood, covered in blood."

It was true. Red blood ran across the picture glass. Daphne's eyes rolled around in their sockets. The picture dropped to the ground and bounced against a garbage can, sending glass shards flying. Daphne flopped to the ground like a popped helium balloon.

It was hard to see where the blood was coming from—a trickle ran from her hand, that's all. I looked at her shoulder, thinking that's always where the good guys get hit, but the fabric was bone-dry. If there was a gunshot wound, I couldn't find it. Then I realized, with a shudder, that she might've been shot in the back.

A man wearing a bloody apron and holding a cleaver came out a back door.

"Help!" I shouted. "The Nazis shot her."

Gitane appeared at the opening of the alleyway, looking behind him and then at the butcher, swinging his rifle from Daphne to the open door but not shooting. He spun his head around and shouted, "*Nicht hier!*" Not here. Right then, I wanted to buy him a carton of cigarettes.

The butcher snapped into action, running over and lifting Daphne in his arms. He carried her into the shop, to a room where skinned animals hung from meat hooks. He tilted her, this way and that, hoping to find the bullet hole. His wife peeked her head in and said, "Oh, la, la." She was back in a flash with a bottle, forcing booze down Daphne's throat. Daphne made sputtering sounds, like a car out of gas.

"*Je vais appeler un médecin*," said the butcher's wife.

I shrugged my shoulders, "English, please?"

"*Médecin*," she said again.

"*Oui*," I said, thinking she was going for some Mercurochrome, only to figure out later the word meant doctor.

Daphne came to life for a split second. "The Klee," she whispered, all breathy. "Make sure it's safe." Then she passed out again.

I was starting to hate art.

CHAPTER TWENTY-SEVEN

"FOR THIS YOU CALLED a doctor?" said the doctor after he gave up trying to find a gunshot wound.

"It's true that I was biting my nails during the abduction. That is, before they'd tied me to the chair," said Daphne, her hand pressing down on a cuticle. "You know how I always faint at the sight of blood, Thomas." She held her hand out for the doctor to see.

"There is a slight infection, madame," he said, dabbing on alcohol and ointment, and then wrapping her finger in gauze.

"This is a bit extreme," she said, looking at her thumb. She had me fish money out of her wallet. We paid double the fee to keep his mouth shut.

Daphne was pale as a ghost, but her legs worked fine. We ran out the front way, straight for a boulevard with a crowd we could get lost in. We didn't stop moving until we were back at the hotel. Daphne asked for aspirin at the front desk. She made up a story about spraining her thumb playing tennis and falling into soot as a result. How it was that I ended up covered in soot, too, she left unexplained.

Back up in the room, I fluffed her pillows before

she rested her head on them.

"I've been shot at before, as you know," she said, closing her eyes. "Can't say that I like it." She sniffled back a sob and I sat on the edge of the bed holding onto her hand. She sucked back the tears and squeezed my hand. I figured that whatever the Gestapo did to her was pretty dastardly; and I knew, too, that she wasn't gonna tell me about it. The bruise on her face was enough to make my imagination go berserk.

She let loose a big sigh and was quiet. I knew better than to interrupt while she was getting herself together. Still with her eyes closed, she said, "Oddest thing, Thomas, but I believe the Gestapo mistook me for some sort of a communist. At least, that seemed to be the aim of their interrogation—to persuade me to give the names and whereabouts of a communist Resistance group." Her eyes popped open and she flung herself to an upright position. "It can only mean that Jean-Michel is one himself!" Daphne set her head back on the pillow, with her hands behind her head. "I've never been one for politics. It's true that my father votes Labour party, yet that hardly makes *me* a Bolshevik. What little I know about communists is that they murdered Anastasia, the daughter of the Czar of Russia, uncle of our King George." She shook her head sadly and I wondered if this Anastasia character had been a friend of hers. "Russia is on our side in the war, our greatest ally until you Americans joined in. I suppose that does make them the enemy of Hitler." She swung her feet to the floor. "A good lie-down helps calm the nerves so. I had a frightful scare until you showed up on the scene."

"Don't mention it," I said.

"I gave nothing away, mind you. Why, Jack would have been proud of me. I'll need a new identity though, now that they've seen both my passports, the real one and the fake. French would suit me." She began panicking, eyes darting around the room like she'd lost something important. I figured she just realized that the picture, "The Klee" as she called it, was left back at the alleyway garbage cans. But instead she said, "Where's Juliette? Did we leave her in the café?"

"That's right," I said.

"She was my responsibility. I promised Madame Doumer to look after her. She'll never forgive me."

I told her not to worry: that the Nazis didn't get Juliette; that she knew her way home; and in case the Gestapo did chase her, that she *was* the fastest runner I knew. Daphne said we'd better go to the Doumers' flat and make sure that Juliette was home safe. She got back into Sophie's coat and hat, pulling the netting down over her eyes. Then she changed her mind and put on the red coat with the rabbit fur lining.

"Goodness, this coat is frightful," she said. "But it's best to be incognito." She pulled the pins out of her hair and shaked her head so's her hair was wild. "I'll have to borrow something else from Sophie's closet. And I'll need a different hat, too. Let me borrow yours for the time being."

I handed over my tweed cap. She angled it so's it covered her left eye. Looked better on her than me, but my head was going to get cold. "Now come along," she said.

We found Juliette back at the apartment, safe with her mother.

"We thought we'd never see you again," said Madame Doumer. "How dare they snatch you from a café? In broad daylight, too." She brushed a finger against Daphne's cheek. "And what have they done to your face, my child? Unconscionable." She broke out a box of caramels she was so happy to see us again. "I was saving them for the end of the war, for when my husband returns home."

We saved one caramel for Mr. Doumer. For a minute we were quiet, staring at the caramel and thinking the same thing: that as much as we wanted to eat it, we wanted Mr. Doumer to come home from Germany even more.

"We're not out of the woods yet," said Daphne, explaining everything that Jean-Michel told us about Hermann Göring's visit to the gallery. "Sophie will be doomed if she's blamed for the missing painting. They'll hunt her down until they find her."

"Then we must return the painting to the gallery," said Juliette.

We sat mute again. No one wanted to hand over a real Vermeer, if that's what it was, to the Nazis.

Then I got to thinking. Daphne was pretty handy with a paintbrush. I'd seen one of her pictures back in London, hanging on her bedroom wall. Could've knocked me over with a feather duster, I was so blown over. "Say, Daphne. Why don't you make a copy of the painting?" I said. "Just in case the one we got is the original."

"A copy? You mean, *another* copy?" She tried to stick her thumb in her mouth but remembered the bandage. "Why, Thomas, this might be a solution. It's something I've done before. I copied *St. John the Baptist* by Leonardo da Vinci when I was at art school here. My painting won a prize, in fact." Daphne blushed. "The only problem is that I won't have time to do a proper job. Vermeer worked in multiple glazes, as did most Renaissance artists. Each layer was allowed to dry before the next was applied. It would have taken him months to complete a single painting. I'd be forced to work *alla-prima*, meaning a single layer instead of glazes… the way the Impressionists painted. And I'd have to use a medium that makes the paint dry faster, instead of a simple mix of linseed oil and turpentine." She looked at the oil heater, which wasn't turned on. "Force drying might crack the paint nicely and make the painting appear aged. Afterwards, I could put a coat of shellac over the whole thing. Shellac, Tommy, is made from beetle wings."

I cheered her on. Juliette was clapping the tips of her fingers again. Madame Doumer nodded her head. Daphne came up with some more ideas:

"I'll doctor the canvas to make it appear old, even when viewed from the backside. Or, better yet, find an old canvas, sand it, and paint over that. The whole thing will be amateurish to the upped degree, and an expert

will know immediately that it's not a genuine Vermeer."
She cracked a smile. "And won't Göring be livid?"

The idea of making Göring livid made me smile too. But, meanwhile, my stomach started going topsy-turvy. *Reichsmarschall* Hermann Göring: World War I fighter pilot ace, now head of the Luftwaffe; the man responsible for the Blitz; my brother Jack's greatest nemesis. This wasn't someone you messed with, not without reinforcements anyway. I crossed myself, something that seemed to be happening a lot lately, as if my hand had a mind all its own. *What the heck*, I thought, and threw in a prayer to Saint Joan.

Meanwhile, Daphne was working up a steam.

"That anyone in the gallery would think my painting were a genuine Vermeer... The very idea! The gallery's reputation will be left in tatters, but what do I care? From what Jean-Michel told us, they're nothing but a den of thieves, collaborators to the last one of them. Sophie was *obviously* the exception. They're helping the Germans to steal family heirlooms—cataloging the paintings, crating them up to be sent to Germany. But that's not the worst of it." She started crying. Madame Doumer took her hand. Daphne choked out, "What's to become of the families, the women and children shipped off to God knows where? My own dear Aunt Dalia escaped with her life. She's had to hide out at—"

I said, "Ho-hum," and drew a line across my lips.

"Thank you for reminding me, Thomas. 'Loose lips' and all."

Madame Doumer put the lid on the caramel box

and tied the ribbon back around. "I can think of at least one obstacle," she said.

I could think of ten, but I said, "Lay it on us, Mrs. D."

"Presuming you succeed in making a good copy, how will we get it into the gallery?"

"We'll find a way. Don't worry, Maman," said Juliette, at the same time turning to Daphne. "You can work in Sophie's studio. There you will find all the art supplies you need."

"Then let's get cracking," said Daphne, wiping her eyes.

CHAPTER TWENTY-EIGHT

THE FIRST THING we had to do was get the Vermeer, which meant breaking the curfew again. On top of that, Daphne worried that the Gestapo knew where we were staying, and that they'd nab us when we got to the Hôtel Saint Jeanne d'Arc.

"You didn't have the key on you, did you?" I asked, remembering that it had the name and address of the hotel and also our room number. A dead give-away.

"No, I left it with reception," said Daphne.

"No receipts, notes with the address?"

She patted her pockets, bit her lower lip and said, "I don't think so. The Gestapo agents asked me where I'd been staying but I lied. I was afraid that they'd discover the Vermeer."

The Hôtel Crillon, that's what she told them. We'd have to stay clear of the place, a crying shame. Daphne even made up a room number: 17B. I felt sorry for whoever was staying in that room.

"The thing is," she said, "I overheard them consulting with each other after I told them that I was a guest at The Hôtel Crillon. My German isn't very good, as you well know, but from what I gathered the hotel is being used as headquarters for something called the *Generalleutnant Fromm*. Your German is better than mine, Thomas. Do you have any idea what that means? When I told them I was a guest at the Hôtel Crillon, the whole course of the interrogation changed. They seemed troubled somehow." She stopped to ponder.

I knew that *general* meant general, and that *fromm* meant religious. But for the life of me I couldn't figure out what was happening at the Crillon. Nothing good from the sound of it. Madame Doumer piped up just then.

"The hotel is now the headquarters of the German military governor."

Daphne blushed from her Adam's apple to her hairline. "Oh, I think I understand now. Only I'm too, too, *too* embarrassed to tell you."

It didn't take much to get her talking though.

"Ever hear of Mata Hari?" she asked.

I knew that Mata Hari spied against the Germans in the Great War, but that was about it. Daphne filled in the details. Turned out that before the war, Mata Hari made a living by posing nude for artists, Daphne's favorite art teacher being one of them. "He used to bring her name up whenever one of our models was too fidgety. Mata Hari—Margaretha Zelle was her real name—was able to pose like a Grecian statue, he'd say. Well, one of the Gestapo agents called me Mata Hari, if you can imagine that. I knew that she'd spied against the Germans in the Great War, that she did striptease—a sort of dance, Thomas. She used her…well, *gifts* to get in close with the German military."

"So when you told the Germans that you were a guest of the military governor…" said Madame Doumer, bug-eyed.

"It's too awful," said Daphne, her face red as a beet. "I wish now that I hadn't named the Hôtel Crillon." She looked my way. "But Thomas, the way you drone on about the Hôtel Crillon, it was the first thing popped into my head."

"Sorry, Daphne," I said. "I wouldn't go near the place now that I know who's living there. Not for all the feather beds in the world, not for all the chocolate éclairs and crème brulee on planet earth, not even if they lured me in with marshmallows stuffed with maraschino cherries."

Juliette's stomach growled and Madame Doumer offered to cook us dinner. Boiled cabbage and leeks never tasted better. Madame Doumer decided that we should move back to the apartment. No one had been around asking for Sophie in at least a day, she told us. She worried about us staying alone at the hotel. If they nabbed us, nobody would know. Daphne agreed straightaway. Besides, she wanted to paint in Sophie's art studio. There was an easel and northern light streaming into the window. It turned out that northern light was what she needed. We piled into the art studio to get a look.

"We'll be your apprentices," said Juliette. "I already know how to clean brushes. Sophie taught me the correct way. Here is the *savon*"—she picked up a bar of yellow soap—"And here is where we set the brushes to dry."

She pointed to a towel. Looked like a plain ol' towel to me.

"I'll keep guard," I said.

"I'll prepare the food. You'll not have to pause but to eat," said Madame Doumer. She was happy, but then her face fell. "Only, how will this get us any closer to finding my daughter?"

Everyone stared at their shoes, waiting for someone else to come up with an idea.

If there was a curfew, people were ignoring it. But we didn't want to take chances, so we kept to the darkest parts of the streets, crossed whenever we saw Germans, and ran once or twice.

We passed by a whorehouse and Daphne told me to call it a *brothel* instead. I told her I'd seen places like it on a visit to Times Square in New York City, movie theaters with XXX on the marquees. It wasn't a day I was likely to forget. Jack told me about the birds and the bees that day. And all we were trying to do was find a certain comic book shop. We ate hotdogs and knishes from a street vendor, I remembered that.

Daphne was the first to notice that the building was originally a Jewish synagogue. We stood dumbfounded, watching as half-dressed ladies lured German soldiers in. Daphne was spitting mad. "I ought to give them a piece of my mind," she said.

I grabbed her coat and pulled her in the opposite direction. But there were other things got her mad too. We came across German posters, all of them lies. I knew by then that the word *Juifs* meant Jews. One poster said, "Jews kill in the shadows."

I told Daphne about Mr. Fisch, who lived down the street from me in East Hempstead, and who taught me German in preparation for my trip to occupied Europe. Him and his wife were the first Jewish people I ever met. We had other Irish on our block, a Polish family, a couple of Italians, and a lonely Swedish widow. But the Fischs were the nicest of all of them. They weren't killing anyone in the shadows, that's for sure. Whenever I came for a lesson, Mrs. Fisch rewarded me with a piece of cake. Sometimes it was sponge and sometimes pound, but it was always better than anything store-bought. When I told Daphne about the Fischs, she said, "I hope to meet them one day."

I pictured the five of us sitting on the Fisch's screened in porch—Jack, Daphne, me and them—eating sponge cake straight out of the tin. We'd be telling the Fischs about our time during the war, the way old soldiers do when they meet up at the VFW hall. I decided, then and there, not to tell the Fischs about the posters. It would only make them feel bad.

And while I'm on the subject…

I was feeling pretty bad myself for dragging Daphne back to Paris. The first time was one thing, but I should've known better than to bring her back again, her being half-Jewish. It'd been bugging me ever since we got to Paris. My ma called this my *conscience*, although sometimes she doubted I even had one. Now it was working overtime, telling me one minute what a *damn* fool I was, telling me the next minute that I shouldn't say *damn*. Daphne had covered her bruises with face powder, but knowing them black and blue marks were underneath made my conscience even worse.

We were standing under an awning, waiting out a downpour of sleet, when Daphne hugged me to her. She said, "After everything, I'm glad I came back."

"Really? You're not mad at me?"

"I wanted to come when you told me what was in the letter, the letter made from invisible ink, but I was afraid. And yet, I've wanted more than anything to play a part in the war effort. You know how I tried to become a nurse...But then the sight of blood." She shuttered. "I volunteered to be in the Women's Auxiliary Air Force, but because I was only seventeen at the time—"

Just then, a black sedan, trying to avoid a pot-hole, hit a puddle and splashed us with water. Daphne jumped back, letting go of my shoulder. I was suddenly colder. I leaned up against her, our backs to a plate glass window. She was still on the same train of thought:

"I convinced myself that loving Jack was something. You understand, by keeping his spirits up I was playing a part, because they do flag from time to time, especially when one of his buddies is killed in action. The boys always say that someone has 'bought it,' as if they've stepped out to buy a newspaper—never that they've been killed. When, really, it's murder, plain and simple. And having one's friends murdered is a bloody awful thing. Jack won't talk about it, but I know he gets bouts of melancholia whenever that happens. And then, there I am"—she threw her hands up in the air—"to cheer him up."

"You're the one keeps him going," I said, wiping water from my head. "It's *your* picture taped to his cockpit control panel."

Daphne pushed me forward. "We should keep cracking on. The rain is letting up." Then she pulled me backward, giving me a bear hug. "What I wanted to say," she said, "was thanks for convincing me to come. I feel as if I truly have a *raison d'être*, as the French say—a reason to live."

My conscience quieted down after that.

It was getting colder by the minute and it began pouring again. We'd lost our umbrella, but Daphne brought along something even better. If you ask me, it was a step up from an umbrella: a big, flat, black shield. It took the wind without bending, sleet bounced right off it. The trick was to hold it at the right angle.

Daphne said, "I'm glad for my gum boots. You know, I heard someone suggest putting mustard in one's shoes to keep the feet warm."

That made me think about hotdogs again. Daphne was right. Half the time I was daydreaming about food. We passed by a *boulangerie*, French for bakery. A sign in the window said they were out of bread. "Then let them eat cake," said Daphne, quoting the French queen who lost her head in the Revolution. I said, "Okey-dokey, your Royal Highness, give me the cake."

After walking about three miles, we got back to the Hôtel Jeanne d'Arc. We hid in a doorway across from the place, making sure that no one was watching for us. The block was empty and none of the parked cars seemed occupied. I looked for the flare of a cigarette, the telltale sign of a spy, but saw nothing. I was willing to chance it, but then Daphne got the idea to look for a back entrance. "There must be one," she said. "Notice that the trash bins aren't out front, which can only mean that they're kept at the back." We looked up and down the street, a solid wall of apartment buildings and shops, with not a single alleyway between them. We had a time finding the back of the hotel, taking wrong turns before we spotted garbage cans with Saint Joan's name stenciled on them, which seemed sacrilegious almost. A dozen cats came flying out of them cans as we got near, the scrawniest cats I'd even seen.

Daphne spotted a light on in a window next to the back door. She tapped a few times before the reception lady pulled back the curtain. Daphne smiled and chirped, "Here we are!" A minute later and we were in.

"*Bonsoir,*" said the lady, who was wearing a bathrobe over her pajamas. We followed her down a dark hallway and ended up back by the reception desk. Daphne asked if there'd been anyone to visit us, visit being a nice way to put it. The lady'd already handed over our key, but now she looked again into the cubbyhole. "*Rien du tout,*" she said, which I took to mean, "No messages."

As we hiked the stairs, I heard them creaking behind us. I whispered for Daphne to stand still. We listened together, but heard nothing. "Probably a rat," I said. After that, Daphne took two steps at a time.

The thread was just were we'd put it, between the door and the frame, about an inch above the floor. I checked to see if anything had been moved. Daphne went for the Vermeer. We whispered the whole time, seeing that the room next-door, the one with the connecting door, was occupied. Light came from under the door, and I could've sworn I seen a shadow pass, like somebody was spying on us, standing close enough to the door to hear us. Daphne said not to worry, that people were just naturally curious. I was glad to see the shadow move, to hear the bedsprings creak right after the light went off. I happened to be laying on the ground, my nose pressed under the connecting door when it did.

"He's wearing black boots," I whispered to Daphne. "And he sleeps in them."

"That *is* strange," she said. "But, come to think of it, during the Blitz we did the same. We were worried we'd have to flee from the house barefooted. People were getting their feet torn up with the glass from shattered windows. I helped take shards out of a little girl's foot. During my nurse's training, that was."

"You still got the pistol?" I asked.

Daphne reached into her pocketbook and showed it to me. I told her to keep it handy, still worried about the man next-door, the man with the black boots. I put my ear to the connecting door, listening for a snore or some other sign that he was sleeping. There was a glass on the bed stand and I put it against the wood. "Nothing," I said. "Not even heavy breathing."

"Some people sleep quietly," said Daphne. "Now come away from that door and help me." She pointed to the suitcase. You might've thought I was her personal valet. Next she'd be ordering me to shine her shoes.

But I knew Jack would've wanted me to help with the luggage. At the grocery store he'd always volunteer to carry old-timer's bags to their car. He was the kind of guy who helped people cross the street, who always gave up his seat to a lady. *Chivalrous*, they call it. And I wanted to be like Jack. So I hefted the suitcase, which seemed to be heavier than when we checked into the room.

"Why's the suitcase so heavy?" I asked.

"Been doing a little shopping for essentials while you sleep late."

"What kind of essentials? Anything essential to me?"

"Bits and bobs."

"Care to elaborate?"

"Used books, is all. French, every one of them. I did keep an eye out for something English, but couldn't find a thing. I have *Cyrano de Bergerac*, *Père Goriot* by Honoré de Balzac, *Nana* by Émile Zola—" She went on to list a few more, none I ever heard of. The suitcase got heavier with every book she named. I wondered when she thought she'd get the time to read. In less than a week she needed to make a painting that took Vermeer a year to paint.

"How much you figure the Vermeer is worth?" I asked. "A hundred dollars?"

Daphne was wrapping the Vermeer up in the bed-sheet. She thought about it a minute and said, "I'm not certain. But in 1930, a Rembrandt fetched £18,500."

I did the math in my head. "Holy cow," I said.

"Quiet down," said Daphne, putting a finger to her lips. "You'll wake our neighbor."

I heard rain beating against the window. The painting would be ruined if we tried to get it back to the Doumers' apartment wrapped in a sheet.

"Come and help me get this into the portfolio," said Daphne, pointing to the big, black, shield thing. *So that's what a portfolio looks like*, I thought. And all that time, I thought it was some kind of Frenchie umbrella.

CHAPTER TWENTY-NINE

Rue de Rivoli, Paris, France

HE'S BEEN FOLLOWING them for two days and only once were they able to shake him, by ducking into a *boulangerie.* A crowd of women waited on line and they had nearly torn him to pieces. He escaped with his life, to a position just across the boulevard where he had the perfect view. Half an hour later it began to dawn on him that the two had succeeded in evading him. They had tried it before, entering shops through the front entrance and leaving through the back, jumping on and off buses. But he'd always managed to follow. No one dared stop him…until the crowd of hungry women, that is.

He slips his boots off and follows them down the staircase. By now, he knows which floorboards creak. Earlier he had forgotten, the third step after the second landing, but he will remember this time. The boy has exceptional hearing. And he is smart. Plus, he is naturally suspicious. The girl, not so much—trusting, too trusting.

He plans to keep fifty steps back, using an umbrella for cover, a black umbrella. Theirs, in fact. They had left it at a café under the table. More than once it has hidden him from their sight. For instance, tonight when they hesitated before entering the hotel. It was easy enough to hide in an unlit vestibule, crouched behind the opened umbrella, open as if it had been left to dry.

But that one time... He wanted to kick himself. How could he have let them get out of his sight for two whole hours? It was unforgivable. He had circled back to the houseboat, returned to the Hôtel Jeanne d'Arc, checked their favorite café. His heart raced the entire time, he broke out in a cold sweat. He second-guessed himself, third-guessed himself, fourth and fifth.

He thinks about grabbing the both of them, right here and now, on the staircase, before they leave the hotel. But they'll wake the whole place.

He hears the boy say, "I think Jack'd be proud of us, Daphne. If he didn't join up to fly for the Royal Air Force, he would'a probably joined the Resistance."

Daphne, the man thinks. *If I show myself now, she'll scream. Besides, the operation to...remove them*, he thinks, laughing to himself.

The plan, regretfully, is not yet in place.

CHAPTER THIRTY

A COUPLE OF HOURS LATER, we made it back to the
Doumers' apartment, where everybody piled into the art
studio to watch Daphne begin working. The rest of us
kept our mouths shut, like we was in a library.

First Daphne examined the painting, measuring
and writing the dimensions on a scrap of paper. Then
she made a frame out of four pieces of wood, about the
same size as the Vermeer, each one half the length of a
baseball bat. The place was like a woodworking shop, me
holding down the boards as Daphne sawed the ends. I
never took her for a carpenter until then. I'm sure she
had hundreds of other talents I didn't know about yet.
She rubbed turpentine and brown paint into the wood.
A couple of times she told me to stand back while she
glued the pieces and clamped them together.

"I'm having second thoughts," she said, making a
sour face.

I yawned. It was getting on midnight.

"This won't do," she said, all frustrated. "It still looks
brand new. Old wood would have wormholes." We followed her back into the living room where she took
a painting off the wall. "Sophie won't mind. This was

painted in our early days at art school. It's not one of her best. I happened to remember that she painted this over an old, horribly amateurish landscape she found in a secondhand shop."

"It's one of my favorites," said Madame Doumer.

"It's Sophie's life or the painting's," I said.

Madame Doumer stifled a cry. We followed Daphne back into the studio and watched as she pulled the painting from the stretcher frames.

I was getting an art lesson whether I wanted one or not.

I took the couch, keeping my clothes on but taking my boots off to get my feet dry. They were wrinkled, like after you take a bath. My socks were smelly and I put them outside the back door, the door that led to a back staircase, figuring that would be our escape route if anyone tried to break in through the front door.

I wondered if Madame Doumer would volunteer do my laundry. Back home, my ma did it. At the Sopwith's joint, Mrs. Balson washed my clothes. They'd come back ironed and starched. Last time we were in Paris and staying with the Doumers, Mrs. D. done the duty. Maybe I'd get lucky again. But with her having two jobs, maybe I'd have to wash my own socks.

The couch was uncomfortable, stuffed with old feathers, some of them pointed like needles. I was half asleep when I remembered the pistol. Daphne's pocketbook was sitting on the end table. I turned the light back on and searched through the front section, finding nothing but lipsticks, rouge tins, and face powder. She had tweezers, which might come in handy, seeing that they could poke an eye out. I found a clean hankie and borrowed it, knowing that the feather couch was gonna make me sneeze before long. In the middle section of the pocketbook I seen a bottle of English Lavender perfume, a gift from my brother Jack. I'd once used a similar bottle for lighter fluid: blew the lid off a German munitions warehouse. I found the pistol in the back section and put it under my pillow. Then I went to sleep feeling safe and sound.

I woke up to the smell of burnt toast, and Juliette saying, "*Pardon moi!*" And, "It's the last of our bread." I could tell she was mad at herself for ruining our breakfast. Daphne said, "I'm watching my waistline and bread is so fattening." It was just like Daphne to let Juliette off the hook.

I decided to do calisthenics: a hundred jumping-jacks, ten push-ups, and a headstand. The day before, Juliette—a girl—beat me running. I wasn't gonna let that happen again. I was so winded by the time I finished that I needed a nap. Next thing I knew Juliette was shaking me awake.

"Come and see," she said. "Daphne is so clever."

I followed Juliette to the kitchen, where Daphne was mixing up something that looked like pancake batter.

"Did you find it on the black market?" I asked. The thought of pancakes made me woozy, like a drunk walking into a bar and smelling the booze.

"It's *gesso*, silly," said Daphne. She had the batter in a bowl and was mixing it with a hand-cranked beater. "It's used to protect the canvas, so that the oil paint doesn't soak into the fabric." She had another pot on the stove. I looked in and saw something that looked like boiling maple syrup.

"It smells horrible," I said when I got a whiff.

"It's rabbit skin," said Juliette. "Those cute, cute bunny rabbits."

"I'm not eating that, no way," I said, crossing my arms. As hungry as I was, even I had my limits. I'd use the pistol to hunt pigeons in the Luxembourg Gardens before I'd eat rabbit skin.

"This is for glue," said Daphne. "Before applying the gesso, I'll coat the canvas with it. When it dries, it will make the canvas tight as a drum."

I asked what was for breakfast and Juliette handed me a plate of black toast. I already knew it was her who burnt it, but I didn't want to make her feel bad. I shoved it into my mouth and smiled. "Not as bad as a burnt marshmallow," I said. A strange thing happened when I said that: a full-blown flashback. Juliette's face turned into my sister Mary's, the thorn in my flesh. Mary was infamous for burning toast. I swallowed the last bite and Juliette appeared again, offering me a glass of water.

"I hope that it wasn't too *terrible*," she said, pronouncing the last word the French way. "We won't have another loaf until next week."

"It was swell of you to save me the last piece," I said, feeling pretty good about myself for saying it.

Daphne stirred the rabbit skin and said, "Now move aside," taking a potholder and lifting the top pot. She had one on top of another, for some reason. Then she ran with the concoction to the art studio.

I pinched my nose and followed her back to the room, remembering the time I went wilderness camping with Jack. We took nothing but a bow and arrow, a magnifying glass for starting a fire, and the clothes on our backs. He was teaching me what to do if the end of the world came. Like if a meteor hit the earth, or a flood maybe. For supper we ate roasted rabbit, covered in mushroom sauce. Jack skinned that rabbit before he skewered it on a stick. Now I knew why.

"The gesso will have to dry overnight," said Daphne. She looked at the backside of the canvas: "It's too white. Have we any tea, by chance?"

"I can fetch some!" yelled Juliette, overjoyed to have a job finally. A few minutes later she was back with a cup of black tea. "What shall I do with, rub it on the canvas?" she asked.

"Heavens, no," said Daphne, taking the cup and sipping. "The tea is for drinking. A little brown umber paint, diluted with turpentine, will age the canvas nicely."

Daphne gathered together drawing supplies: paper, pencils, charcoal sticks, erasers, and a little piece of suede she called a *chamois,* used for erasing charcoal. The rest of us watched her every move without saying anything except "ooh" or "aah."

"It's not as if the time spent waiting for the rabbit-skin glue to dry will be wasted," said Daphne, ex-plaining that she'd spend the day doing charcoal studies. "It helps to be intimately acquainted with the original before starting in with paint. One gets to know the tone and edges."

"Tone and edges, sure," I said, not having a clue what she was rattling on about.

"This feels so like my art school days. Why, I have gooseflesh, I'm so excited."

CHAPTER THIRTY-ONE

Just when I was getting the idea to become an artist myself, making my fortune with a paintbrush, Daphne kicked us out of the art studio, locking the door behind us. She didn't like spectators, said that was the reason she didn't do *plien air* painting, whatever that was.

"It's when an artist takes an easel outdoors and paints the landscape," Juliette told me back in the living room. "Crowds of people stop to look on. Same as when acrobats perform in public places, or organ grinders with their *très* adorable monkeys. For some reason, the artists never get coins as the others do. Sophie doesn't like *plien air* painting either. She prefers to work in solitude."

Which meant me spending days sitting on the couch, twiddling my thumbs while Juliette pouted. We hardly saw Daphne, unless she was running from the studio to the bathroom. Madame Doumer was delivering meals to the studio, and reported that Daphne was hardly eating a thing. On the second night, Mrs. D. came out carrying a plate of uneaten dinner, saying, "She's having trouble matching the colors, apparently. It looks very nice, if you want my opinion. And meanwhile, the poor dear won't take a nibble she's so caught up in the process. Sophie is exactly this same way when she's painting. *Exactement*. It's as if they don't even remember to breathe."

Meanwhile, the clock was ticking. It was Wednesday morning when I asked Juliette to tell me everything she'd done to find her sister, up until Daphne and me showed up on the scene. About an hour later, I said, "Seems to me you've beat every bush and turned every stone."

"That's why I wrote to you," she said. "My mother and I were out of ideas."

I thought about Howard Carter, one of my heroes, the Egyptologist who discovered the tomb of King Tutankhamen. Not that it was Carter who found the tomb exactly. It was his faithful assistant, Ali, who noticed the step buried in sand. They'd walked past that step a million times before anybody seen it.

I said, "The thing to do in times like this is backtrack. You know, go over the same ground again. In case you missed something. My guess is you got close to finding Sophie but overlooked an important…step. The step that would'a led you to the buried treasure."

A look of doom crossed her face. "You don't think Sophie is buried, do you?"

"Just a figure of speech, a turn of the phrase, a little something called a metaphorical expression." I'd heard all those sayings from Lady Sopwith, my reluctant guardian's wife and my English tutor. I could see that Juliette was impressed.

"A metaphor," she said, jumping over to a bookcase.

She opened a dictionary. "Why, the word is derived from the 16th century French word *métaphore*, which comes from the Latin *metaphora*. Actually, I'm supposed to be doing my schoolwork right now."

I remembered her telling me that ever since the school she'd been going to kicked her friend Ruth out for being Jewish, Juliette's mother let her study at home. As a matter of fact, on my last stay with the Doumer family I joined in with the home studying, worried that I'd be left back a grade for playing hooky from Saint Brendan's parochial school—even when I did have a good excuse.

"You're gonna have to play hooky," I said. " 'Cause I didn't come all the way here to sit and watch you doing Latin homework. And what with the curfew, if we're gonna find Sophie we've got to do while there's daylight."

Juliette thought for a minute and said, "*Très vrai,*" which roughly translated meant, "Right-O."

"Then we start by backtracking, like I already said. We go over the same ground a second time looking for clues you missed, asking different questions, looking for new angles."

Juliette narrowed her eyes. "There's Jean-Michel, the man who worked with Sophie at the gallery. We never finished talking with him. Remember that he ran from the café?"

I slapped my head. "Just as he was about to tell us everything!"

We decided to go back to Jean-Michel's apartment,

that place with the whacky cat lady. We were in the 20th *arrondissement* and Jean-Michel lived in the 16th, but four of them *arrondissements*—neighborhoods, in other words—meant crossing the entire city. The soles on my boots were beginning to peel off and I asked Juliette if she had rubber cement. "I've something much better," she said, and bolted from the room. A minute later she came back carrying two pairs of roller skates. "I think Sophie's pair will fit over your boots. They're adjustable. You *do* know how to skate?"

"Like Sonja Henie, practically," I said. "And in case you didn't know, Sonja Henie won an Olympic gold medal at the 1936 Berlin Games. Then she got hired by a Hollywood picture studio to be the first ever skating, singing, film star." I told Juliette that *moi* won a race at Hempstead Lake, beating twenty other kids. I had a trophy cup to prove it.

"We don't like Sonja Henie around here," she said. "She's a friend of Hitler's. She's performed for him many times. Haven't you heard the Nazi sponsored radio stations going on about her? And don't you remember when she gave Hitler the *Sieg Heil* salute at the Olympic Games? Sieg Heil means 'Victory to the Nazis.' She wants them to win the war."

I took back what I said about Sonja Henie.

Juliette said, "Besides, these are rollers and didn't you win your race ice skating?"

I thought about the race. It was over ice, for sure. One kid fell into a crack and would've drowned if his mother weren't watching. Another kid crashed into a tree and broke his collarbone. Meanwhile, I skated over thin ice and around obsoletes like a pro, like… The problem was Sonja Henie was the only Olympian ice skater I knew of.

By then I had the rollers on and was tightening the buckles. I'd never roller skated, but figured it couldn't be much different than ice skating. I practiced by circling the living room. After three turns I had the knack of it. The whole time, Juliette was giving me advice:

"You've got to be careful of uneven pavement, places where the paving stones have been lifted by tree roots. And remember, the best thing to do if a policeman tries to stop you is to *totalement* ignore him. Kids do it all the time. Listen for a whistle and then look down and skate away in the opposite direction." She finished putting on her own skates and did a spin. When she recovered from a dizzy spell, she said, "One good thing to come of the petrol shortage is that there are very few cars on the roads. That, and the ban on private cars. We Parisians walk or bicycle these days. Why, we can skate down the middle of boulevards if we wish. Sophie and I skated down the Champs-Élysées and no one stopped us."

"Why'd you hold out on me?" I said. "And me with my blisters. Doesn't Daphne know you have these?"

"Oh, *she* can't skate. We tried to teach her once, but she kept clutching onto our coats and toppling us over."

The hard part was getting down five flights of stairs wearing the roller skates. But Juliette showed me how to put the break on, so's the wheels wouldn't move. After that it was no different than wearing high-heeled shoes, not that I ever did. When we got to the lobby, we took the breaks off. I followed behind Juliette, watching her technique. She had a way of moving her arms in the opposite direction of her legs. She used her arms for balance. A couple times she jumped right over potholes. I was improving just watching her. Then we heard a whistle.

Juliette yelled, "Look down!"

Which is why I didn't see the parked car.

After examining my shin, I said, "Just a scrape's all." It hurt something awful, but I kept quiet. "And what's the car doing parked in the middle of the road, anyway?" I pounded my fist against the trunk.

Juliette circled around and came at me going the speed of light. I swear, she was a blur. She grabbed my sleeve, pulling me behind her. I barely had time to get my balance, we was moving so fast. She shouted, "Jump!"

I saw the sidewalk coming at me and did what she said. Finally she let go of my sleeve. She was pumping her arms now, moving faster and faster, over a bridge, picking up speed on the downhill. The whole time, she kept turning her head backwards.

"You didn't see?" she said, when we came to a stop, about a mile away. We were both out of breath and it took a while before I could answer.

"See what?" I said, gasping for air.

"See the German officer whose car you bashed into."

"Golly," I said. "I was too busy looking at my leg."

"I hope you damaged the car, Tommy. Did you?"

I wanted it to be true, but I decided to be honest: "It's hard to damage a car with a human body. The car wins every time." I bent over so's I could see my aching leg. Already it was bruising.

Juliette touched my black and blue skin. "*Mon Dieu*, it's a war wound, Tommy! You should be awarded the Croix de Guerre."

"Or a Purple Heart." Even though my leg throbbed, I grinned like a son of a gun.

CHAPTER THIRTY-TWO

WE KNOCKED AND KNOCKED, but no one answered Jean-Michel's door. *Maybe he's sleeping,* was what I thought. After all, he worked nights as a drummer. A more obvious explanation was that he was working at the gallery.

I told Juliette to wait while I searched for a back entrance. After our stay at the Hôtel Jeanne d'Arc, I figured there had to be one. I looked up at the sky, trying to guess what time it was, but there were socked-in clouds with no sun in sight. We'd probably be cooling our heels until he got back from the gallery sometime just before supper. And what if he went straight to a nightclub or decided to hole up in a café, drinking coffee and smoking Gitanes?

The back stairs were rickety, missing boards, falling down; life-threatening in other words. I thought back to our first visit:

Baby carriage: first floor.
Underwear hanging to dry: second floor.
Jean-Michel's fleabag apartment: third floor.

My leg was hurting something bad by the time I got to the third floor. What I needed right then was ice, and my ma. She was the one who fixed me up with an ice pack, mercurochrome, and Band-Aids. The one time I needed a hospital, it was Jack who drove me there in his pickup truck. Now I was on my own.

On the third floor landing I had to pick one of two doors. I about-faced, getting my bearings. Then I picked the left-hand door. As luck would have it, the door was opened. I did a shout/whisper combo: "Anybody home?" I said. The cat came running at me, rubbing itself against my good leg. I stooped down and patted its head. It purred loud as an Indian Motorcycle: the Scout model.

"How's it going, pussy," I said.

"*Que fais-tu ici?*" I heard.

I looked up and seen the lady standing there. "*C'est toi*, English boy."

"Spanish," I said.

"*Garçon espagnol, oui.*"

She didn't seem to mind that I was in her kitchen without an invite, her messy kitchen. Dirty dishes filled the sink. The garbage was last taken out before the Occupation. A baking pan was filled with wood chips and cat poop, mostly cat poop. The place reeked of it.

The lady was half-dressed again, the straps of her nightgown hanging somewheres near her elbows. I seen she wasn't wearing a brassiere and averted my eyes after that. She ignored me and went over to the sink, fishing for a spoon. "*Voilà*," she said. I noticed there were scabs up and down her arms. Still speaking French, she asked me if that was me knocking on the door. I figured out that *frappez* meant knocking when she repeated the question, this time knocking her knuckles against a cabinet.

"*Oui*," I said.

She did a pantomime swoon. I wondered if she was an actress or something. Then she went off in French again, rapid-fire and without pantomime.

"Look, can you *parle anglais?*" I asked.

"*Un peu*," she said, bringing two fingers together, meaning "a little." The fact that she said "a little" in French didn't give me much hope. At this rate it would be years before we completed a sentence.

That's when I remembered Juliette.

The front door was blocked by a desk. I pushed it out of the way, opened the deadbolt, took the chain off, and said, "*Voilà!*" Juliette was standing on the other side of the door, just like I hoped. I turned around to see the lady sprawling herself out on the couch, with the cat jumping up on her stomach and circling into a ball.

"*Verrouille la porte*," she said, waving a lazy hand horizontally.

Juliette locked the door again and together we shoved the desk back in place. Silly, I thought, to barricade the front door and leave the back door wide-open. I knew my fair share of drunks, my da being one of them, and the lady laying on the couch was one, or something like it. She tied a rubber strap around her arm. Juliette and me watched in horror as she put white powder in the spoon, mixed in water, and then sucked the liquid into a needle. It was like she forgot all about the two kids watching. Juliette whispered to me, "We should go,

Tommy."

The lady injected herself and said, "Ahhhhh." I could tell she was about to pass out, so I told Juliette to give her the grill. "Find out where Jean-Michel is," I said. "And do it fast before she conks out."

Juliette sat on an ottoman with her knees touching the couch. She took the lady's hand in hers and kissed it. The lady smiled all drowsy-like. I stood back, listening to the conversation but not getting much of it. Sitting cross-legged on the ground, I called the cat over. I was happy after that, pretending I was back in East Hempstead, back in the room I once shared with Jack. I wasn't allowed a cat. My sister Mary, the thorn in my flesh, was allergic. But it was nice to dream. I closed my eyes, listening to the cat purr, picturing where our kitchen would be and imagining my ma was in there filling the ice pack, getting ready to fix my boo-boo.

A loud snore, more like a snort, brought me back to reality. I opened my eyes and seen that the lady was sound asleep. Juliette was crouched down in front of me. She lifted the cat from my lap and kissed its head. "We can go now, Tommy," she said. "It's not safe for us to be here, and besides…" she turned her head back to the lady. "We won't get anything more from her."

I started to move the desk away but Juliette stopped me. "If we go out the front, it will mean leaving the door unlocked. And then Mademoiselle Adalie, for that is her name—"

"Adalie," I said. "Now we know why Jean-Michel wears a pinkie ring with the letter A."

"From what I understand, they are *les amoureux*," said Juliette. I shrugged a shoulder. She translated: "Lovers, Tommy."

"Okay, spare me the details," I said, my face flushing.

"The police have been here—quite a few times actually—shouting at the door for Jean-Michel. Adalie pretends that no one is home. She is terrified that they will knock down the door with a *bélier*. Sorry, but I don't know the English word."

"Battering ram!" I said.

We ran through the kitchen and out to the landing. "Watch your step," I said. "This staircase is a teardown job. Some of the boards are rotten. Hold onto the railing." Juliette pointed her toes like a ballerina, testing each board before putting her weight on it.

After getting our roller skates from the entranceway, we crossed to a park. From the look of the streets, it'd rained while we were in the apartment. We sat on a bench, Juliette drying it first with the hem of her skirt.

"Here's what I learned, Tommy." She whispered and I leaned in. "The police have been paying visits, twice yesterday and once this morning. They shout Jean-Michel's name."

"French police or Gestapo?"

"French, from what I gathered. Only the *Préfecture de police*, they are working for the Germans, doing their bidding. It was they who took the Jewish families to the Vel'd'Hiv in June. No one can trust the police after such a horrendous deed."

"Daphne's aunt was almost picked up that day. My brother Jack saved her in the nick of time."

"*Dieu merci*," said Juliette. Without thinking, I crossed myself.

"Jean-Michel is indeed a communist," she went on. "Adalie admitted to being one too. Last year they took part in an assassination. They helped to kill a German officer named Anton Moser, murdered him in the Paris Metro. Adalie told me that she and Jean-Michel were the reconnaissance, that they hadn't done the actual killing. She feels terrible about it now. She said that it's the reason she takes the drugs. It is the only way to forget her guilt."

"But it was a Nazi they killed, right?"

"*Oui*, but in retaliation the Germans murdered three Parisians, people who had nothing whatsoever to do with the assassination. Adalie is cut up about this. *Cut up*, is this the correct saying?"

"Spot-on. I'd be cut up too."

"And after that, the German Military Governor—General Otto von Stülpnagel is his name—announced that for every German killed, ten Parisians would die. Hundreds of prisoners have been executed since then, and Adalie blames herself. She needs help... perhaps Sigmund Freud. Have you heard of him, the psychoanalyst?"

"Nope."

Juliette gave me the blow-by-blow of her interrogation. The long and the short of it was this: Jean-Michel was hiding out. Meanwhile, Adalie stayed back at the

apartment not caring if she lived or died. The desk barricade, the deadbolt, and the chain on the door meant she
wanted to live; the back door being left open meant she
wanted to die. That much I figured out myself, without
Sigmund Freud. Juliette'd pumped Adalie for Jean-Michel's hide-out and said, "He's staying in a wagon belonging to the Roma Gypsies who were taken by the
Germans a few months ago. Their wagons are all that
is left of them. Along the Seine, roughly ten kilometers
outside of Paris."

"Can we take the houseboat?"

Juliette shook her head no. "I'm not even certain
of the location, only that it is in the direction of—" she
craned her head and then pointed behind us.

I remembered the jazz guitar player, Django Some-
thing-Or-Other, who was playing at the party we'd been
at. "He's one of them Gypsies," I told Juliette, "Maybe
he'll know the whereabouts of the camp."

Juliette didn't think so. Even before the Germans
came, she said, the French police were giving the Gypsies a hard time, forcing them to hide their wagons, here
and there, willy-nilly. We'd have a tough time finding
Jean-Michel.

"All is not lost," said Juliette. "Adalie told me that
she has visited Jean-Michel and that she plans to visit
him tomorrow. They are mad about each other, *les amoureux*, they are compelled to meet."

"Would you stop with the les amoureux already?"

"Do you hear that?" she said, putting a hand to her
ear. "*Un, deux, trois, quatre...*" She was counting church

bells. "Maman will return from work in half an hour. We must hurry." She began strapping the roller skates to her shoes.

There was nothing else for me to do but copy her.

So we were studying Latin when Madame Doumer walked into the apartment.

"*Métaphore*. From which century?" I asked Juliette.

"The 16th, Tommy. The word comes from the Latin *metaphora*."

I lifted the Latin textbook. "Good stuff, Mrs. D."

She walked over and patted my head. "Nice of you to help Juliette. I'm not the most skilled of Latin teachers. I do my best."

"Years of Catholic school," I said. "The nuns drill it into you."

She asked where Daphne was and I thumbed at the art studio. Juliette and me had gotten home a split-minute before her, but I figured Daphne was working on the painting. "We didn't bother her once all day," I said.

"Hum," said Madame Doumer. "Has she eaten anything?"

"Not that I know of, Mrs. D. Not so much as a breadstick."

Madame Doumer tapped on the door and said something in French. She knocked a little harder and dittoed the question in English. Juliette looked at me with a raised eyebrow. We seen Madame Doumer turn the doorknob slowly, opening the door just a crack. "I don't mean to disturb, *ma chérie*," she said. And a beat later, "She's not in there." Madame Doumer went to the kitchen. A second later she said, "You didn't see her leave?"

I shook my head no. "We were totally absorbed in Latin verbiage, Mrs. D. She must've slipped out, quiet-like."

Juliette stammered, "Perhaps she needed turpentine or paint or canvas or rabbit-skin glue or gesso or—" on and on she went, slipping into French. "*Pinceaux, vernis, charbon. . .*" Her hands were shaking so much she had to sit on them. The whole time she didn't make eye contact with her mother, which is the first thing a pathological liar knows to do.

"I'll put the dinner on," said Madame Doumer, tying an apron around her waist. "Hopefully she'll return before it's ready. She must be famished, sweet child."

I figured this was a good time to get a look at Daphne's progress. But Madame Doumer threw herself against the art studio door. "Sophie gets upset when we look without permission," she said.

"But Sophie ain't here," I said, immediately sorry. Because Madame Doumer busted out in tears that reminded me of Niagara Falls. Juliette rushed over to give her mother a hug, shooting daggers at me. "*Pardon, Madame,*" I said. "It was a dirty rotten, lowdown thing to say. I'll wash my mouth out with *savon* if it'll make you feel any better."

That quieted her down. "It's not your fault, *mon chéri*. You were only stating the obvious. Americans have a habit of doing that, I know. It's just that my emotions are in such a fragile state at the moment. I find myself breaking down at the least reminder of Sophie."

"Maybe a bit of vino will help you," I said, being that I seen a bottle in her string bag. "Just go easy. Half a glass should fix you up." I shouldn't've encouraged her, but my ma always said that Da liked to cry in his beer, that it made him feel better about being out of work. At the Coldstream Pub in East Hempstead they even had something called "Happy Hour."

Madame Doumer agreed and we followed her back to the kitchen. I took the corkscrew from my pocket, the one I'd been carrying ever since we stayed at the houseboat. I said, "Want me to do the honors? O'Reilly, Lord and Lady Sopwith's nasty-piece-of-work butler, taught me. They're short a footman, you see. They got a wine cellar in the basement at Warfield Hall loaded with the good stuff—vino going back before the Magna Carta, older than King Henry himself. Some of it's so old it's turned to vinegar. Mrs. Balson, the cook, uses it for salad dressing. We're not allowed to waste anything, what with rationing. I sometimes use the spoiled wine for invisible ink. Used a bottle from 1849 once, a *riesling*. That's as good as wine gets, wouldn't you know." I picked up the bottle. "It's all in the wrist." I rotated my wrist back and forth showing her.

Madame Doumer asked us to set the table while she made supper. I was folding a napkin into a swan, another trick O'Reilly taught me, when Daphne walked in. Her hair was a mess. "The temperature has dropped and the wind's picked up," she said, taking off the red coat and preening herself in the foyer mirror.

I seen she'd been carrying the portfolio.

"Smells delicious," she said.

"Leeks again," I said. "This time with potatoes." I told her about the wine, how I'd been the one to open it, how the cork broke into pieces and was floating inside the bottle. "Don't swallow it," I warned.

"I'd like nothing better than a cup of hot tea," she said. "I'm frozen to the bone. I walked all the way to the Sorbonne and back. If only we had Epson salts. I'd love to soak my feet."

Madame Doumer came out of the kitchen carrying a casserole dish between two potholders. "*Où étais tu passé?*" she said.

Daphne kicked off her rubber boots, together with her shoes. "I've been to see my former art teacher. He taught art history at the *atelier*." She looked at me and explained that the word meant art school. "He also teaches at the Sorbonne. As luck would have it, he was in his office today." She took her place at the table. "Lovely swans, Juliette," she said, unraveling my handiwork and laying the napkin on her lap.

"You had a nice visit with your teacher?" asked Madame Doumer, dishing out the supper. She put the biggest piece on my plate.

"It wasn't a social call," said Daphne, "as much as I adore Dr. Baptiste. I wanted to consult with him regarding the painting. I brought along some of Sophie's sketches, too afraid of exposing the Vermeer to rain. But don't worry. I wrapped the sketches in oilcloth first, which seems to have kept them dry. What I was really hoping was to entice Dr. Baptiste to come and see the painting for himself."

"Should I lay another place?" said Juliette, looking at the door.

Daphne laughed. "That won't be necessary, darling. Dr. Baptiste, I came to discover, isn't a Renaissance expert. At the atelier he taught a survey of Western Art, covering the Renaissance period. But today I learned that his specialty is Assyrian antiquities. He'd only just begun a new excavation in Babylon when war broke out and the project had to be suspended."

"Babylon on Long Island?" I asked, a town on the South Shore.

"No, silly, Babylon in Mesopotamia." She took a bite of the casserole and said, "You really are a miracle worker, Maman," even though Madame Doumer wasn't her mother. She went on to tell us that this Dr. Baptiste recommended she show the painting to another professor, someone named Professor Berton. "The problem was that Professor Berton wasn't at the university today. He's a Northern Renaissance expert and knows everything there is to know about Vermeer. In fact, he was teaching at the University of Leiden in the Netherlands and returned to France only recently. I left a message with his secretary, requesting an appointment."

I was worried that she'd given away too much. There were people looking for the painting, people you didn't want to mess with. When I brought this up, she said, "Of course I was careful, Thomas. I told Professor Berton's secretary that my aunt had a painting we suspected of being a Jan van Eyck, *Christ Contemplating the World*."

It made sense: the robe, the long hair. "Maybe that's who it is in the painting. Jesus," I said.

Daphne laid her folk down. "I don't think so. From what I've seen in other Renaissance paintings, the Christ is almost always depicted wearing a red robe. And our painting has the man in a blue robe."

I closed my eyes and was back in Saint Brendan's Catholic Church in East Hempstead, kneeling down at the altar with my hands clasped, waiting for the priest to put the wafer in my mouth and praying that the Brooklyn Dodgers would win against the Cincinnati Reds that day. "Lord, help Whit Wyatt's arm," I prayed, trying to think if it was his right or left arm that was giving him trouble. "You know which," I'd mumbled under my breath, opening my eyes and looking straight at the stained glass window: Jesus wearing a red robe.

Daphne was saying, "Come to think of it, the Christ is more often painted wearing a white loincloth. In any case, it wasn't the iconology that had me visiting Dr. Baptiste."

I swallowed a mouthful of casserole. "Why'd you go then?"

"Well, I knew how much Sophie adored old Dr. Baptiste. She called him her mentor, in fact. He'd been such an enthusiast of her work, he bought one of her drawings once. I suppose I hoped she'd been in touch with him. I even imagined she was hiding in his office. I don't know—hiding behind his big oak cabinet. I was disappointed there." She sighed.

Madame Doumer said, "Eat something, *mon chéri*. You must be famished."

Daphne lifted her folk an inch from the plate and let it hang there. "And another thing...the painting. Now that I've had a chance to examine it, something doesn't seem right for it being an original. The varnish, for one thing. It's not aged as it would be. There are no cracks, no blemishes. I thought that perhaps the painting had been recently restored and the varnish replaced. But then I remembered that an oil painting is left to dry six months before a varnish is applied. So I knew that if the painting were a recent copy—Sophie's copy, for instance—then the oil paint under the varnish wouldn't be completely cured. Scraping the paint would tell all."

Madame Doumer poured wine into Daphne's glass. "Then is the painting my daughter's work? Was the paint wet underneath?"

Daphne nodded yes, then no—like she couldn't decide. "I stopped myself from testing my theory. What if I'm wrong and our painting *is* the original? I dare not damage a masterwork."

"I'll do it," I said. I picked up my butter knife.

"No, you won't," said Daphne. "I decided to consult with an expert in the field. And knowing I could trust Dr. Baptiste, I went to him. I remembered how much he despised Hitler, how worried he was by the course of events back in 1939 when I studied with him. He canceled class the day Holland surrendered, he was *that* disturbed." She wiped her mouth with the back of her hand. "I'm glad I went to him today. He's heard rumors about the Jeu de Paume gallery being a clearinghouse for stolen artworks. He told me this came as quite a shock to him."

But this Professor Berton fella, I thought. I didn't like the idea of trusting our lives to a complete stranger and I made that plain and clear.

"Dr. Baptiste would never put me or Sophie at risk. He swore to the professor's integrity and discretion."

"Swore in blood?" I asked.

Daphne's face got white as a ghost. "Do you mean that silly practice of pricking one's finger with a pin and then—" She started swaying back and forth.

Madame Doumer put the wine glass to Daphne's lips. "Have a sip, *mon chéri*. We have no brandy."

"Oh, dear," said Daphne, with her hand pressed against her forehead. "I hope I'm not catching cold."

"It's not a cold, it's the thought of—"

Juliette kicked me under the table. "Don't say it," she whispered, pulling me bodily from the chair and dragging me to the kitchen. I thought she wanted me to help with the cleaning up, but then I seen her rummaging through a junk drawer. She found a pin and said, "Swear that you won't tell Daphne where we went today. She'll only tell Maman and I'll be in trouble."

I held out my index finger and closed my eyes. I opened them to see a drop of blood forming on the tip of my finger. Juliette pricked herself and we rubbed our fingers together. "This covers tomorrow, too," she said.

"You mean when we tail Adalie to the Gypsy camp?"

She licked blood from her finger. "*Exactement*," she said.

It was later that same night, after Madame Doumer excused herself and went to bed, that Daphne said, "Now why don't you tell me where the two of you were all day." Juliette stared at the ceiling, but I looked Daphne straight in the eye.

"Roller skating," I said. "In the park."

"Which park, may I ask?"

"The one down the street."

Juliette started humming a tune, letting her eyes drift around the room.

"I see," said Daphne. "You mean the park two blocks down, on the right hand side?"

"That'd be the one," I said.

"The park with the locked gate?"

"Easy-peasy to jump," I said.

"Over the fence topped with spearheads?"

Juliette sucked in her lips.

"I thought maybe that would be the park you'd choose," said Daphne. "Only certain people have the key to the gate. Fortunately there was a woman inside feeding the birds, and she was kind enough to admit me."

Juliette squirmed in her seat, sucking the tip of her finger. Daphne stopped talking so's she could watch. Juliette was in her own world. She checked out the prick mark, holding her fingertip about five inches from her face, looking at it from every angle. After sucking it again, she wiped saliva on her skirt.

"You didn't?" said Daphne, slapping my knee. "Please tell me you didn't."

"It was her idea, I swear," I said. I kicked Juliette's foot and she came too.

"*Oui?*" she said.

"The game's up," I said. "Time to spill the beans."

"Spill the beans? We have no beans, Tommy."

CHAPTER THIRTY-THREE

ALL NIGHT MY LEG throbbed something awful. At the crack of dawn I gave up on sleep. I checked the icebox, wanting to make an ice pack, and seen that the ice trays were empty. I knew there was a fishmonger around the block and I remembered that he kept the fish on ice.

The fishmonger was opening his shop just as I got there. I watched as he pulled a rolling cart to the sidewalk. In there would go the ice and fish. I'd seen it passing by.

I said *"Bonjour."*

He pulled two stools to the sidewalk and invited me to sit. He took rolling papers from his shirt pocket and a pouch with tobacco, or something that looked like it. The whole time he rolled his cigarette, he was telling me a story, one I got a fraction of. It had something to do with his son, that much I got. The boy's name was Jules, same as Jules Verne who wrote *Around the World in Eighty Days.*

The fishmonger pressed his fingers to his wet eyes. He crushed the cigarette butt under his foot and stood. Then, after rolling down the awning, he showed me the writing that ran across the front of it.

Brassens et Fils. Brassens and Son.

The fishmonger shook his head sadly. I figured out his son was gone, killed in the war probably. He opened his wallet and showed me a photo of a baby-faced man wearing a French army uniform.

I seen then that the fishmonger was wearing a black armband, like people wear at funerals.

I said, "*Je désolé,*" meaning, "I'm sorry."

The fishmonger pointed to a handwritten sign, taped to the store window. Then he poked his finger toward me. I knew what he was getting at. The sign said, *Demander de l'aide.* Help Wanted.

I could use the cash, I thought. The Sopwiths weren't giving me an allowance and I was stone-broke. The only money I ever got was a farthing, 1/960 of a pound sterling, after running an errand for Lord Sopwith. I wasn't complaining, mind you. He'd bought me a bicycle for the purpose. O'Reilly made me mow the lawn, but I never got paid. It was a big lawn, too, one that took a month to finish. And Daphne pinched pennies, worried that we'd run short and become a burden to Madame Doumer, her with rations for only three.

Meanwhile the fishmonger was egging me on, pressing a coin into my hand.

Maybe I reminded him of his son, gunned down by the Wehrmacht. Could be he was offering to make me the *fils* in Brassens et Fils. My own da was an out-of-work odd-jobs man. The idea of an inheritance was sweet, I'll admit.

The fishmonger motioned for me to stay sitting. I

crossed my bum leg over my knee and seen it was swollen and black and blue, plus gray. I wished then I knew the French word for ice.

Suddenly I wanted to get out of there, away from the fishmonger with his black armband. I couldn't be his son, because I was already somebody else's. I remembered when Jack went missing, how my da stared at the ketchup bottle all through supper, how he started going to the Coldstream Pub in daylight hours. Ma said he was dying a slow death. So what if I never got a letter from him? He always signed his name at the bottom of my ma's: *T.R.M*, that's how he signed it.

Which was funny when you thought about it, that he didn't sign Da or Pa or Dad or Daddy. T.R.M, that's how he signed. Like he was reminding me that we had the same name, that I was Thomas Robert Mooney, too. Joined forever by them initials.

I seen the fishmonger go to his horse-drawn wagon, lifting a bucket full of ice chips and dumping them into the rolling cart. I figured he had oysters in the wagon, too. I'd seen them on the ice, passing his store. He'd probably let any son of his keep the pearls.

He rolled his sleeves up and smoothed the pile of ice with the back of his arms. He was wanting me to watch, to learn the trade. He was happy, like we'd struck a deal already.

I said, "*Je désolé*," again, this time pressing the coin into his hand. Didn't even have the heart to ask for ice after that. I just turned around and limped away. I glanced back once to see him watching me. The look on the fishmonger's face stung me like a jellyfish.

CHAPTER THIRTY-FOUR

WE WAITED UNTIL Madame Doumer left for work and then the three of us got our coats on. First we went to a tobacconist's shop to buy a phone token. I begged Daphne to let us get a sucking candy. They had them in big glass jars. "Who am I to refuse?" she said, giving me one of her dimple grins. Juliette and me sat on the curb, moving the suckers from cheek to cheek, while Daphne "rung up the professor." A few minutes later she told us she'd struck out. The professor was out of the office.

It meant she'd help us tail Adalie. "Six eyes were better than four," she said.

The first Metro station we walked to was closed, and we wasted time finding the next one along the line.

"I think it's best we level with Adalie, tell her that we need to speak with Jean-Michel and ask to be taken along," said Daphne after we got settled on the train. I heard a whoosh sound and we were off. "I'll go up and have a word with her alone, girl to girl. I'll tell her about the time Jack had to hide"—she lowered her voice—"from the Nazis. We have that in common, boyfriends on the run."

A bell dinged. People got on and off. Some of them

wore German uniforms and carried *Baedeker* guide-
books, like they were on vacation instead of fighting a
war. The train jerked forward.

I said, "I say we tail her, let her lead us to him. She's
the type gets spooked easy, all jumpy-like. If we ask, she's
gonna say no."

"I couldn't disagree more," said Daphne.

"Let's put it to a vote," I said. "All in favor of tailing Adalie, raise your hand." Daphne and Juliette folded
their hands into their laps.

Two transfers later, we were back in Jean-Michel's
neighborhood. We knew that Adalie wasn't answering
the door, so we went straight to the back and up the
rickety stairs again. I knocked this time. When Adalie
didn't answer, I tried the doorknob.

"Locked," I said.

"Let me try," said Daphne, pushing me out of the
way. She rapped three times and shouted, "Mademoiselle Adalie? *C'est moi*, Daphne," then to us, "Perhaps
she's still sleeping."

"Or maybe she's out cold from them drugs she
takes," I said. "You're a nurse, Daphne, you could save
her life."

Daphne thought for a second. "I don't have training
in resuscitation." She rapped on the door again, saying,
"Is anyone home?" using the French word *maison*, which
didn't exactly describe the dump.

I reached up and pulled a pin from Daphne's hair.
A strand fell in front of her face and she blew it away.
She said, "Okay, you might have a point. I'll pick the

lock." A minute or two later we were standing in the kitchen. I wouldn't've thought, but it was an even bigger train wreck than before. Every drawer was hanging open, kitchen utensils everywhere, a flour jar spilled on the counter, an ironing board blocking our path. Meanwhile, nobody had lifted a sponge; the same dirty dishes were in the sink. I stepped over the ironing board and into the living room. The desk was pushed away from the door and the drawers were laying on the ground upside down. The couch cushions were ripped open and feathers floated in the air. I sneezed. An overturned fan was running at full speed. I bent down and pulled the cord from the wall.

Daphne went to the bedroom. I told Juliette to search in the bathroom. She opened a closet door and said, "A shared toilet and bath must be down the hall." Daphne was back in the room and said, "She's not anywhere."

I took in the scene. "Somebody's ransacked the place," I said. "Check out the pictures. They're all off the hooks. And somebody pulled the curtains off the rods." I lifted a piece of red material and it turned out to be part of a Soviet Union flag: a sickle with no hammer.

Juliette looked under the couch for some reason. "She's missing," she said.

"We can see that," I said.

"No, I mean the *chatte*, the cat. She's missing."

Daphne was turning over books with the tip of her shoe. Somebody'd overturned a bookcase. She picked up a paperback, flipped though it and found a bookmark.

"How do you like that? Shakespeare and Company," she said.

Before she could say another word, a word like *henceforth*, I pulled Juliette in the opposite direction.

We found the cat hiding under the bed, sitting in its own piss. Juliette dragged it out by the scruff of the neck. "She's scared half to death, the dear," she said. Even when I pet the cat's chin, it wouldn't purr. It puffed its fur and hissed instead. Its paw struck out, aiming for Juliette's cheek. Juliette let the cat fall from her arms and it scurried back under the bed.

"Did it break the skin?" I asked, checking Juliette's cheek. "Good thing it didn't take out your eye."

"Someone has given the dear thing an awful fright." Juliette crouched down and lifted the bed ruffle. She clicked her tongue. I heard the cat hiss back. All of a sudden, Juliette was sliding herself backwards, clutching at her hand. She opened her palm and I seen a scratch, right along her lifeline. A shiver went down my spine seeing that.

Daphne came into the bedroom and said, "It's strange that Adalie's purse is still here." She opened a leather pocketbook. "With her lipstick and money-purse. What woman leaves the house without her lipstick?"

"We should beat it," I said.

"Give me a moment," said Daphne, emptying the pocketbook onto the bed. "Her identity papers aren't here. I'd have thought they would be." She held up a matchbook. It was exactly the same as the one Jean-Michel left on the bench the day we met him, the one for the nightclub. Daphne opened the cover and we seen there was one match left. Scribbled inside the matchbook was an diagram of some kind. By then, the three of us had our noses pressed to the matchbook, so close I smelled sulphur. Most of the pencil lines were thin, but a thick one, filled in with zigzags, went down the middle of the diagram.

"That's the river, I betcha," I said.

"And the V-dash-S, here…" Juliette touched the letters. "Could that mean Vigneux-sur-Seine or Vitry-sur-Siene? Both places are in the right direction. Adalie told me that the Gypsy wagon was downriver from Paris."

I sat on the bed, trying to fit the pieces together. Didn't make sense that Adalie would leave without her pocketbook, and without the map telling her where to find Jean-Michel.

Unless, I realized, she was forced to leave.

Daphne slipped the matchbook into her pocket. "You're right. We need to go."

We headed out the front door. I noticed that the chain was off the latch. The door wasn't locked either. We stepped out into the hallway and I leaned over the banister, making sure the coast was clear.

Juliette was the one who noticed the notice, nailed to Jean-Michel's door. "*Par ordre de Préfecture de police…*" she read. "No one may enter without—" She looked to Daphne for help with the translation.

"—incurring arrest!" Daphne stood there with her

mouth opened. "Cor blimey!" she said finally. British for "H-E-double toothpicks."

We changed our minds and exited by the back stairs instead. But before we left, Juliette filled a bowl with water and another with what looked like cat food.

CHAPTER THIRTY-FIVE

WE BOUGHT APPLES and a wedge of cheese from the market, using more of Madame Doumer's ration coupons. Down the street was a park and we made our way to it. It was empty except for a hobo sleeping on one of the benches. I wondered if maybe he was a refugee.

"We passed a phone booth coming," said Daphne. "I'll try the professor again. Feel free to join the queue at the bakery in the meantime. There's one across the street."

My blisters were starting up again and I said I'd cool my heels in the park. Juliette wanted a baguette something bad and I watched as she skirted between bicycles to get at one.

"You don't have a pin, do you?" I asked Daphne. By then my boot was off and my sock pulled down around my toes.

She looked both ways before turning her coat collar back, revealing a brass pin in the shape of a Spitfire. Half the English wore pins just like it, showing they'd contributed to the Spitfire Fund. "You should hold a match to the point before using it," she said, reaching into her pocket and handing me the matchbook with its one match.

"You think it's safe wearing that pin?" I whispered, afraid even to hold it. "What if the Gestapo'd seen that?"

"Well, they didn't. And I'm not a fool, I wear it on the inside of my collar. But I won't part with it for the world. Call me superstitious if you want. Now pop your blister and give it back."

She was serious. She wasn't gonna part with it even while she made a phone call. I lit the match like she told me to, watched the pin tip turn blue and then blew the match out. Just as I was sticking the pin into my heel, Daphne turned her back to me. The sight of water flowing from my blister made me happy somehow, or maybe it was the teeny-weeny Spitfire in my hand.

I handed back the pin and the empty matchbook. "Pin it inside the lining of your coat at least. What if a storm blows and you put your collar up without thinking? You might as well sew one of them yellow stars to your coat."

She bent over and pinned the Spitfire to the inside hem of her coat. "Does that satisfy you?" she said. Then, before straightening up, she kissed the top of my head. "Now, don't move an inch. And let the blister dry a little before putting your dirty sock on again." She handed me a clean hankie. "Wrap this around the blister first. And remind me to take bicarbonate of soda to your socks tonight."

"Thanks, Nurse Clarke," I said.

"Do they even let kids in?" I asked an hour later when we

stood in front of an arched doorway. Engraved in stone, I read *SORBONNE*, and under that *UNIVERSITÉ DE PARIS*.

"I explained on the phone to Professor Berton that I had charge of two children today and had no choice but to bring them along. I think he assumed I was a nanny. This was the only time he had free and he's leaving town at the week's end."

The lobby was like Grand Central Station in New York City, only grander. I'd never been to a university and neither had anybody in my family. High school was the highest we ever got, and at the rate I was going, I wouldn't even get there. President Roosevelt might give me a medal when I got home but my guess was Saint Brendan's had already expelled me. At last count, I'd missed seventy days of school. I wondered if they were even bothering to call my name when they checked attendance.

Daphne walked us over to a guard, asking where we could find Professor Berton. Up a marble staircase, it turned out. The ceiling above us was topped with a dome that reminded me of a church. I looked up and seen a bird flying around in circles, trying to find a way out. We finally located the secretary's desk. It was cluttered with manila folders and test exams. I seen typed reports with red markings on the first pages. The place was getting more like Saint Brendan's by the minute.

The secretary tapped a pile of paper against her desk until it lined up. Then she walked us to Professor Berton's office. "*Vous étiez étudiant du Dr. Baptiste, quel merveilleux!"* she said. Daphne answered back in French. I hoped the whole day wouldn't go like this. How was I going to pick up clues if I couldn't understand half of what anyone said?

The secretary waved us toward a closed door and then backstepped to her desk.

Daphne tapped on the door after saying, "He's expecting us."

We heard a man's voice say, *"Entrer,"* which even I got. Daphne turned the doorknob and whispered to us, "Let me do the talking, if you don't mind. Act as if you are my good obedient charges, please."

My mouth flung open the same time as the door.

"Mademoiselle Clarke, come in," he said, taking Daphne's hand. "Antoine Berton, at your pleasure." The pockmarked face, the crooked nose, still wearing the white suit, only somebody'd taken bicarbonate of soda to the wine stains.

"We met at the jazz gathering," said Daphne. "What a remarkable coincidence."

"I prefer to call it destiny," said Professor Berton, planting a kiss on Daphne's hand.

Professor Berton offered Daphne a sherry, me and Juliette a soda water. He sprayed it into glasses using something along the lines of a fire extinguisher. Daphne accepted the sherry, but I noticed she didn't drink it.

"You heard of the Galerie du Jeu de Paume, of course," said Daphne.

"But of course," said Professor Berton.

"My best friend, Sophie, was working there until

recently. She too was a student of Dr. Baptiste's."

"Then I am sorry for your friend," he said.

"Why's that?" I asked.

"Because it means she is a collaborator. And the worst kind—one who pillages and plunders from her own people, France. Assuming that she is French."

Juliette shot from her chair and said, "*Excusez moi s'il vous plait*," and headed out the door. For all he knew, we were Nazi sympathizers too. Only he didn't seem to care.

"The *Einsatzstab Reichsleiter Rosenberg für die Besetzten Gebiete*—or, in English, the Reichsleiter Rosenberg Institute for the Occupied Territories—is headed by one Alfred Rosenberg. It sounds like a Jewish name, *non*, Rosenberg? Don't be fooled, this man is behind the racial policies of the Third Reich. He is an enemy of the Jewish people."

I waited for Daphne to tell the professor she was half-Jewish herself, but she was holding back. "Go on," she said.

"The ERR, as it is called, was formed immediately after the occupation of France. Hermann Göring has charged the organization with the systematic plundering of 'Jewish art,' which means both artworks *created* by Jews and artwork *owned* by Jews. The ERR has the authority to steal indiscriminately, although Göring and Hitler have a penchant for 16th and 17th century Dutch and Flemish works. I shudder to think what is happening in Holland as we speak."

All of a sudden the room got dark. A black cloud

must've hovered over the building. Sure enough, rain started pelting the window.

Daphne crossed her ankles and said, "I understand that a certain painting attributed to Vermeer was stolen from the de Rothschild family. *The Astronomer*, it's called."

"From Baron Édouard de Rothschild. He inherited it from his father. I was privileged to view the painting during happier days, when I was commissioned to authenticate another painting of his, this one a Rembrandt he had bought at auction. Unwisely, I might add."

"Painted by a student of Rembrandt's?" asked Daphne.

"Exactly. Abraham van Dijck, I suspect."

Daphne put her hand under her chin, her elbow leaning on her knee. I knew she was weighing up the professor, trying to decide how much to tell him. Finally she said, "At the atelier where I studied, we transcribed masterpieces. The Louvre allowed us to bring oils into the galleries. My friend Sophie is particularly skilled in this way. Whilst we were students together, she painted from Ingres."

"Which of his works?"

"*La Grande Odalisque.*"

"A naked lady?" I asked.

"Arguably the greatest painting of a naked lady ever to exist in this world," said Professor Berton, giving me a wink afterwards.

Daphne pretended to take a sip of sherry. I could tell she was still on the fence. "I wonder if I might entice you to look at a painting, one I suspect to be a transcription of Vermeer's *Astronomer*."

"The original, I am told, is now in Germany," said Professor Berton. He stood and walked behind his desk, opening an appointment book and running his finger across the page. "I won't ask why it is you have sought my opinion for what you believe to be a student exercise. Could it be you have doubts about the attribution... Mademoiselle Sophie, you said?" He put on a pair of half-moon glasses, pushing them to the end of his nose. "Tomorrow morning at seven. I can stop by on my way out of town." He picked up a fountain pen. "*Adresse, s'il vous plaît.*"

Daphne gave him the address. I hoped he wouldn't show up in a black Renault.

As he was showing us out, he said, "It's interesting that you should mention the Galerie du Jeu de Paume. Recently a colleague of mine was asked to give a reference. Apparently, they were considering me for employment." He laughed.

"You turned down the job?" I asked.

"I was never offered the position. And, besides, I would not deign to cross the threshold of the Galerie Nationale du Jeu de Paume. Or shall I say, not until France is liberated."

CHAPTER THIRTY-SIX

I JUMPED OUT OF A DEEP SLEEP, thinking that some-body'd knocked on the door. Then I thought, *I must've been dreaming*, and I laid my head back on the pillow. I felt the pistol underneath, just under my neck.

"*Qui est là?*" I heard, just as a lamp was switched on. Madame Doumer was standing outside the bed-room door, tying her bathrobe belt. "Did you hear that, Tommy?" she asked me. She looked worried. I pulled the pistol out and made sure the safety was off. Then I tip-toed to the door, listening for another knock. Madame Doumer ran in front of me and I seen what she was aiming for: a note somebody'd slipped under the door. Typed on the envelope was one word: *Daphne*.

By then Daphne was hovering over Madame Doumer's shoulder. "Open it," she said. "Hopefully, it's from Sophie."

At that, Madame Doumer rushed the door, flinging it open and throwing herself at the banister. Next thing I knew, she was back in the apartment, pulling back the curtains.

"Who do you see?" asked Daphne.

"Someone riding a bicycle, that's all."

I bolted to the window. From that angle, I couldn't see much. "For sure, it's not Sophie," I said. "It's definitely a man."

Madame Doumer said, "The letter is addressed to you, my dear," and handed it over. I seen Daphne's hand shaking as she took it.

I was right beside her, my eyes scanning the letter left to right. The letter was typed. There were places where the writer messed up and typed uppercase crosshatches over a word and then started over. The letter said:

You need to leave XⱵⱵⱵⱵⱵX the building by the back exit. You are being XⱵXXⱵrefollowed. It isn't safe. DonXⱵXXⱵ't return untXⱵXⱵl tomorrow.

There was no signature.

"It's in English," I said.

"I noticed the same thing," said Daphne. "It's from someone who knows me. Enough to know that I'm British, at least." She scanned the letter again.

In the background, Madame Doumer was making frantic hand signals to Juliette, firing off words like *rapidement*. Juliette was in a tizzy, flying around the room and grabbing things: a photo album, a stack of letters from her father, and a silver frame with a black and white of Sophie. "Tommy, hurry," she said. "Pack your valise."

"I don't have a valise or nothing," I said.

A few minutes later, Daphne was coming out of the art studio carrying the black portfolio. She leaned it against the wall and disappeared into the bedroom. I figured it was time to put on my boots. My socks were laid out on the radiator to dry. *This is why soldiers sleep with their boots on*, I thought. The socks were still wet. I put them on anyway. At the bedroom door, I shouted, "Everyone decent?" before looking in.

Daphne said, "All clear," and I seen they were in a frenzy, stuffing things into suitcases and hatboxes and square suitcases specially made for makeup. Madame Doumer said, "I suppose we can't take the steamer trunk?"

Man, oh man, I thought. If it was up to me, we'd be leaving with the clothes on our backs and a pistol in my pocket.

Daphne was riffling through Sophie's dresses, laying a few on the bed with the hangers still in them. "I think the letter was from Jean-Michel," she said, holding up a blue chiffon number and trying to decide if she was taking it or not. "Adalie had to have told him you visited. Did you give her our address?"

Juliette tapped her lips and said, "No, I don't think we did tell her. But Jean-Michel knows our family name. He could have easily found us."

"We need to get a move on," I said. "To Portugal would be my vote."

"Then should I pack my swimsuit?" said Juliette, brightening up.

I covered my ears and pretended to scream.

In the end they narrowed it down to one suitcase and a pocketbook each. I carried the portfolio/umbrella. It was heavy enough to tell me that inside was the Vermeer. After filling the cat bowl to brimming, we left by the back entrance without knowing where we was headed. We only figured that out near the garbage cans.

My idea about Portugal was shot down when we remembered that the Doumers didn't have the proper papers to cross the border. Next I suggested Les Misérables, the dress store we knew was a front for the Belgian Resistance—they being the ones who got us out of France the first time. The leader, Dédée, showed us the path over the mountains and into Spain. They had bolt-holes all over Paris, meant for downed RAF pilots, but good enough for the likes of us.

"Brilliant," said Daphne. "To Saint-Germain-des-Prés it is then."

Madame Doumer checked her wristwatch. "The buses and trains won't be running for another two hours. And there is a curfew, you know."

"We could wait it out at the houseboat," I said. The others shook their heads no. Our cover was blown there, I remembered. I patted my left pocket where the corkscrew was, my right pocket where I'd put the pistol. But did I really want to fight the Nazis head on?

No, was my answer.

"We'll hoof it to Saint-Germain-des-Prés," I said. "We ain't got a choice." I looked down at my boots. All we'd done was walk down a few flights of stairs and already my blisters were screaming. "How far is it?"

"Far," said Daphne.

Madame Doumer suggested we wait it out at a café, but then she couldn't think of a single one open at that hour. I threw out another suggestion and they went for it.

The sign out front said that first Mass wasn't until 8AM. We tried the front doors and they were locked. "They'll have a side entrance," I said. "Churches are never locked. In case a dying man needs to make a last confession."

"*Mon Dieu*, I forgot to take my rosary beads and my missal book," said Juliette.

Sure enough, the side door was open. I took off my cap and dipped my fingers in holy water. There wasn't a priest in sight and I decided to hog a whole pew for myself and sleep. I genuflected before sliding into a pew at the back of the church. I seen the others march up to the altar, kneel on the pillows, and begin praying. Even Daphne did it, and her half-Anglican, half-Jewish. I wondered if she'd converted without telling me. Maybe she had to, to marry my brother. I watched her bow her head. Then she crossed herself the wrong way and I knew she was still half-Anglican. I wondered if she'd say her Hebrew prayer, "*Am Yisrael Chai*," the one she taught me when we first landed in German-occupied Belgium, all those months ago.

The bench was hard as a rock, as usual. *For once I can get a good snooze in church without somebody poking me awake*, I thought. I kicked off my boots, took off the wet socks and draped them across the back of the pew. Then

I laid flat on my back with my arms folded across my chest. It was only then I noticed the tears running into the cups of my ears. I said to myself—or maybe it was to God—"I take that back. I wish my ma was here to poke me like she does." I was scared, that was the truth.

Then—like a miracle—the next thing I knew, somebody was poking me and saying, "Wake up!"

I rubbed my eyes and yawned. Daphne was sitting at the end of the pew. "The Mass is about to begin. If you'd like to stay, we can."

I seen a couple of old-timers hobbling in. The priest was up at the altar getting the wine and wafers organized. An altar boy my age kneeled down to tie his shoe lace. I was torn in two. I crossed my fingers and said, "Can't. You gotta go to confession first and we missed it." Daphne, being half-Anglican, half-Jewish, believed me.

A newsstand was just opening and Daphne fished around in her change purse for the money to buy a paper. After scanning every page, she said, "Nothing about *Reichsmarschall* Göring's impending visit to Paris. But perhaps they don't announce such visits, afraid that the Resistance will plot an assassination. There are plenty of people in Paris who would like nothing better than to take a shot a Göring."

After that we went straight to Saint-Germain-des-Prés, or as straight as you can in Paris. Unlike New York City, Paris wasn't built on a grid.

A couple of months earlier, the Belgian Resistance was working out of a dress store called Les Misérables.

We knew something was wrong from a distance. There was junk in the display window, knick-knacks and whatnot. And somebody'd whitewashed over the store name.

"Let's check the apartment," I said, remembering that the real resistance happened there. We went to the side of the building and rang the bell for the apartment where we'd last seen Dédée's father. No one answered and we had to ring a bunch of apartments before somebody let us in. Daphne and me entered, while the Doumers kept watch outside. If they saw anything suspicious they were instructed to run.

I knew my way to the apartment: up the elevator and down a hallway where the floorboards creaked. As we got closer, we seen the door to the apartment was open. Daphne stuck her head in and was invited to enter. A man dressed all dapper spoke to her in French. She whispered to me, "He thinks we've come about the flat. Wanting to rent it."

"Ask him what happened to the last tenants," I said. I watched his face while she asked. He lifted the corner of his lip and said, "*Je n'ai aucune idée*," meaning he didn't have a clue. He wanted to show us around the empty room. We backed out, turned and hightailed it for the elevator. For all we knew, he worked for the Germans, waiting for the wife of a Waffen-SS officer to decide whether or not the apartment suited her taste. Back in the elevator, Daphne said, "We can only pray that our friends relocated voluntarily." She wiped a tear from her cheek. I was so worried, I almost suggesting we go back to the church and pray. The idea of Dédée and her father being arrested by the Gestapo made my stomach hurt. We were silent after that, hearing nothing but the sound of the elevator motor. It came to me that the only place for us was with Jean-Michel, and going to him would solve two problems:

1. A place to hide out.
2. The chance to grill him.

I was still carrying the portfolio and it was getting heavier by the minute. Blisters were starting where my hand gripped the handle. Maybe Jean-Michel could tell us if the painting was the real deal or a fake. If it was a fake, I was leaving it in a dumpster.

"Jean-Michel," I said.

"I was thinking the same exact thing," said Daphne.

CHAPTER THIRTY-SEVEN

Meanwhile...

A black Citroën Traction Avant is pulled up to the curb opposite to the building where the Doumer family lives. The man seated in the driver's seat is alone. He pretends to read a newspaper, but the paper is French and he doesn't know the language. On the seat beside him is his dinner: a ham sandwich in wax paper, a slice of pickle, and a chocolate bar. The sandwich is partially unwrapped and he sees the thick slices of ham on a crusty baguette, stuffed with chunks of brie. He is hungry, yet hesitates before taking a bite.

He's alone tonight because his partner, *Kriminalassistentanwärter* Klaus Grönemeyer, has been taken ill. He was discovered in the hallway toilet, bent over the basin and retching his guts out, claiming that he'd been poisoned, blaming the French Resistance.

Earlier, a man on a bicycle stopped in front of the apartment building, swinging his leg over the top bar even before the bicycle had come to a stop. The same man exited the building a minute later and went on his way. Now he has returned. *Keiner von bedeutung*, thinks the Gestapo agent seated in the Citroën. No one of importance.

He turns his attention back to the sandwich.

His eyes are focused on the pickle. He turns it over, looking for telltale signs of tampering. He hears the passenger door open, someone saying, "*Guten Morgen, mein Freund.*" Klaus Grönemeyer's replacement, he assumes. He smiles as the fellow Gestapo agent climbs into the passenger seat.

"*Darf ich?*" says the replacement when he notices the sandwich—may I?

The man in the driver's seat says something to the effect of, "Have the whole thing. I've been here all night and I'd like a quick nap."

It is only when his eyes are closed and his hat tilted over his eyes, that he feels something pressing against his ribcage.

CHAPTER THIRTY-EIGHT

ASKING THE FISHMONGER to drive us in his horse-drawn wagon was my idea. Turned out Madame Doumer and him went way back, back to when the Doumers first moved into the neighborhood and needed a trout.

For one thing, the Metro didn't go to Vigneux-sur-Seine. And it turned out there was a good fishing spot near Vigneux-sur-Seine and the fishmonger didn't mind taking us. If we struck out there, we'd find a way to Vitry-sur-Siene, and onward, until we ran out of V-dash-S towns. Lucky for us, there was a run on fish that day and the fishmonger was free by lunchtime.

Before we got going, he asked me to fuel the vehicle. This involved mowing the lawn at a nearby park, using a hedge clipper. Juliette came with me, explaining about the shortage of oats, on top of everything else. When we returned with a basket full of grass, Daphne was chatting it up with the fishmonger and Madame Doumer, sitting in the back storage room so's they wouldn't be spotted.

"Good job, darlings," said Daphne. "Only, what is this?" She dug her hand into the basket and came out holding something the size of a baseball. "Tell me you didn't rip out the tulip bulbs?"

"A horse has gotta eat," I said.

In my pidgin French, I asked the fishmonger what the horse's name was. He told me it was Cheval and everybody laughed. Turned out the word meant horse.

"Here, Cheval," I said, taking a clump of grass and holding it about a foot from his teeth. I was half afraid he would take my hand off, but I came to learn that Cheval was the gentlest horse in Paris. He ate a mouthful and then bumped his nose against my shoulder in thanks. He was a strong horse, too, and even with five of us on-board the cart he pulled like a stallion. His only fault was speed. Cheval was no Spitfire, that's for sure.

The sun was setting by the time we got to Vigneux-sur-Seine. The fishmonger invited me to go fishing with him. He showed me the extra fishing pole he'd brought along and his can of worms. Once again I said, "*Je désolé.*" I could see he was heartbroken, probably thinking about all the times he went fishing with his son.

The dames air-kissed with the fishmonger until their lips hurt, then Daphne asked if he knew about a Roma Gypsy camp anywhere nearby. He motioned for us to follow him down a narrow trail growing over with weeds. *At least Cheval will get supper,* I was thinking. We came to a clearing with a huge tree in the middle. Three wagons circled the tree, of the sort that pioneers drove across the frontier to California during the Wild West days, only more colorful.

The fishmonger bid us goodbye. Madame Doumer said, "He says there is no one here, that the wagons have been abandoned."

My fingers started twitching. Maybe it was from schlepping the Vermeer around all day, or maybe it was a sign. Then my nose started twitching.

"*Délicieux!* I can smell stew cooking," said Juliette.

I narrowed my eyes and seen smoke coming from between the wagons. "Just in time for supper," I said.

If Adalie was surprised to see us, she didn't let on. She was squatting in front of a campfire, a cast-iron pot balanced on three rocks. I seen a bloody rabbit skin laying over to the side, ears and all. Adalie stirred the stew and motioned for us to sit down. Logs were set around the campfire, turned vertically like stools. Daphne craned her head around before sitting, looking for Jean-Michel, no doubt.

Being the only man in sight, I took charge of the fire. It was down to nothing but burning coals. The temperature was dropping and we'd need a raging fire once the sun set. Adalie still hadn't said a peep. All she did was to take a pinch of salt from a paper bag and throw it into the stew. She didn't look right. Even in firelight she seemed bleached out. Finally she spoke, pointing to one of the wagons.

Daphne volunteered to translate. "Adalie has invited us to take the largest wagon." She jerked her head toward it. "The only problem is that there's a mice infestation. They've gotten to the food left over when the Gypsies were taken. They've made nests in the cabinets. But there are warm blankets if we'd like." I noticed then that Adalie was wrapped in one.

"I'd love a blanket," said Madame Doumer, without budging. The only thing that moved were her chattering teeth.

"Maman is afraid of mice. I'll fetch us blankets," said Juliette as she leaped from the log and took two steps forward before stopping short. "*Petites...ou rats?*" she asked.

"I'll get the blankets," I said, wishing we'd brought along the cat. I grabbed a stick from the woodpile, meaning to use it as a weapon if it turned out the mice were anything like the rodents that hung out around the wharfs in Paris. On my way to the wagon, I noticed a candle burning in one of the other wagons, the one nearest to the fire. The shutters were closed partway and I'd need a step-ladder to get to them. I returned to the fire, where they were talking in low voices. Nobody noticed me taking away one of the logs.

Jean-Michel was laying on his back with heavy blankets covering everything but his head. Didn't matter, he was shivering. I wondered why he didn't just come out to the fire. I was getting a chill myself standing so far away from it. I stepped down off the log and braved the rats, which turned out to be miniature mice, most of them babies. Sure enough, they were breeding like rabbits. I found one nest in an overhead cabinet and another in a box full of balled-up yarn and knitting needles. The wagon, I was realizing, smelled of mildew, like it'd been sitting empty a long time. I remembered something about the Nazis rounding up the Roma Gypsies and taking them to prison camps. I seen clothes hanging near the double bed, clothes that looked like costumes you'd wear on Halloween to go trick-or-treating. One of them had tarnished coins for trim. Some of the dresses belonged to a kid, a girl about my own age from the look of it. Who ever heard of sending a kid to prison?

I got a bad feeling, like I was walking on somebody's grave. I grabbed a stack of blankets and got out of there fast.

Back at the fire Madame Doumer was at the reins, dishing out stew into clay bowls. Daphne and Juliette were on each side of Adalie, with their arms around her shoulders. Adalie held one of Daphne's hankies; I seen the initial D embroidered in the corner. Daphne gave me a shush symbol, with a finger touching her lips. Adalie started whimpering. I ate my stew in peace, thinking about the time I went camping with Jack, how we slept around a campfire even though it was summer, ate beans right out of the cans after setting them on a fire and watching the Heinz labels curl with blue flames.

I wished Jack was there with us. He'd know how to liven the place up. A cloud of doom was over the camp. Like a story I heard in history class: the Donner Party—a wagon train of pioneers stranded in a snow storm somewheres in the Sierra Mountains, turning to cannibalism in the end.

Daphne got my attention by poking me with a stick. "Jean-Michel was shot," she said, and my head jerked up.

"When?" I asked.

"The same day I was interrogated. They chased him

from the café. I had no idea. I thought he escaped unscathed. And now the wound has become infected and he's taken a fever."

I thought fast and said, "Maybe Mr. Brassens is still fishing. We could ask him to take Jean-Michel to a hospital."

"Jean-Michel refuses to go. The hospital staff would be obligated to report a gunshot wound to the police, and he knows where that will lead. No, I'm thinking that we might be able to find the doctor who attended *my* wound." She lifted her thumb. The bandage was long gone, but her cuticles were still bleeding. "He hadn't asked questions, if you recall."

"Didn't they teach you anything at nursing school? Can't you fix him?"

"I was taught to take blood pressure and temperature, to give a sponge bath, and to empty bedpans. And I can't even do that without a thermometer. Maman knows some of the old folk remedies, though. We might try soaking a sheet in cold water and wrapping it around him, but with the temperature plummeting..." She drew the blanket around her shoulders and over her head. "Yarrow or elderflower tea, Maman says, will reduce the fever. Or perhaps a mustard footbath." She glanced at Madame Doumer, sitting across the campfire. "Not that I'm qualified to have an opinion, but I think what Jean-Michel needs is a doctor."

"Somebody with tweezers to take the bullet out."

Daphne's face brightened up. "Well, those I've got."

I remembered the tweezers, probably for plucking

her eyebrows. But I kept quiet so's she wouldn't know I'd been in her pocketbook.

"Still," she went on, "I haven't the stomach to remove a bullet. And besides, he'll need penicillin. I still think it's best we find that doctor."

I pictured the weeds we'd passed coming along the trail, and said, "If you want I can scout out some yarrow or elderflower leaves. Only, you'll have to tell me what they look like."

"Maman might be able to identify the herbs," said Daphne. "In the meantime, I'm going to see if Monsieur Brassens is still here. And if he is, I'm going back to Paris and returning with the doctor. I'll take a peek at Jean-Michel first. Assess the wound, why don't I?" She swung an elbow in a go-get-'um way.

"You want me to run ahead and stop the fishmonger from leaving?" I asked.

"Yes, you do that."

I ran at the speed of sound, stopping only once because of a side stitch. I heard the fishmonger before I seen him, singing what sounded like a lullaby. As I got closer, I got a look at him from behind, him sitting alongside the river, gutting a fish. He'd made himself a campfire with a grill set on it. Seeing him all alone, I felt bad about not inviting him to our campfire, but the truth was I'd never thought of it. His eyes lit up when he seen me.

I said, "*Excusez-moi,*" waving my arms in the direction of Paris. "Problem grande, bang-bang, doctor, Paree?" The fishmonger cocked his head. He wiped fish guts from his knife. I tried a few more French words, stringing them together as best I could. Finally, I grabbed his hand and escorted him back to the Gypsy camp.

Juliette and her mother were huddled around the wagon door, the one I knew Jean-Michel was laying in. A bright light came from the wagon, brighter than any candle. I stood on my toes, peering over Juliette's shoulder. They'd lit a kerosene lamp, set high on a shelf. Daphne was sitting cross-legged on the bed, next to Jean-Michel, pulling a bloody strip of fabric from his gunshot wound. I was proud of her. She wasn't swooning and she had color in her face. But she was biting her lower lip so hard it bled.

The fishmonger was right behind me, smelling like a cod. He said, "*Oh, la, la. Oh, la, la,*" over and over.

Daphne's eyes were bugging out as she looked at the wound. "This is beyond my experience," she said. "At the very least, I can tell that the dressing needs changing. Have we got clean rags, a bedsheet perhaps?"

Jean-Michel started shaking, what with having no blanket on him and the temperature outside nearing freezing. Juliette rummaged through a chest, coming up with a pillowcase. She put it to her nose and said, "It's old, but it smells clean."

Madame Doumer took the pillowcase and shredded it into even strips.

The fishmonger said, "*Oh, la, la, oh, la. la.*"

"Have we alcohol?" asked Daphne.

Jean-Michel opened his eye, resting them on a bottle. I knew what it was after Daphne examined the label and said, "Absinthe. 74% proof. I wish I knew what the other 26% consisted of."

"A little green anise, sweet fennel, and other medicinal herbs," said Madame Doumer. "All beneficial."

"I'll need to sanitize the wound with it." Daphne soaked one of the fabric strips in absinthe. "Well, here goes. This might sting," she told Jean-Michel. He gasped, closing his eyes. Daphne took a swig of absinthe and wiped her mouth with the back of her hand. She rested the other one on Jean-Michel's forehead. "He's burning up. We really ought to fetch a doctor."

She redressed the wound and covered Jean-Michel again with a blanket. Only his arms were sticking out, laying flat against the lump of his body. Daphne inched off the bed, taking the kerosene lamp from the shelf. Just before she turned down the wick, a ray of light bounced off Jean-Michel's pinkie ring.

Thomas," she said, "I want you to find rocks, about the size of a tulip bulb. Put them in the fire and when they're hot, place them in your socks. Then set them under the blanket, one near his feet and one at his side. We don't want him getting a chill after having been exposed to this cold. I almost think it might be best to take him closer to the fire, rather than leave him in here."

The second she said that we heard pounding on the roof.

"Oh my, rain again," said Madame Doumer. We jammed into the tiny space, wiping our faces. Through the open door I seen the fire go out.

Daphne shouted, "Oh bloody hell-O. The Vermeer!" and shot out of the wagon, straight for the portfolio. I'd only ever heard her cussing once before, if *bloody* even was a cuss word. Madame Doumer ran out after her, pulling the suitcases into the wagon. *We all can't sleep in here*, is what I thought. There went my idea of sleeping cowboy-style, alongside a crackling campfire. I crawled onto the bed, next to Jean-Michel. Adalie took the other side. Madame Doumer sat on a chest with Juliette on her lap. The fishmonger and Daphne were together on the pile of suitcases. I seen he was a gentleman, keeping both hands to himself.

Jean-Michel stirred in the bed. He still had his eyes closed. He said, "We only wanted to fund the Resistance, buy guns and munitions, have money to print our underground newspaper. I explained all this to your sister." He swallowed hard. "May I please have a drink of water?"

I found a glass next to the bottle of absinthe, reached behind me, and swung open the shutter. It took less than a minute to fill the glass. "Here," I said, putting the glass to his lips after his girlfriend lifted his head. He swallowed and took a deep breath, like he was getting ready for a speech. Only later did we realize it would be a deathbed confession.

"Your sister," he said again, confusing me for Sophie's brother. "Mademoiselle Villand, she who runs the Nationale du Jeu de Paume gallery, had already entered the painting in the ledger, the painting discovered by the Möbel-Aktion, the one hidden in an armoire. No sooner had Georges at the gallery put it onto a new stretcher frame and the Germans were stamping it with their nasty little mark."

"A swastika?" asked Daphne, but Jean-Michel talked over her:

"It was only a matter of time before the painting would be sent to Germany. I, the supposed art expert, insisted that it was a copy of the original. *Mais non*, Mademoiselle Villand disagreed. She was certain that our Vermeer was genuine, that the painting already in Germany was the copy. A contemporary of Vermeer, but a copy. More water, please."

Adalie helped him to sit upright in the bed. I put the cup to his lips.

"Your sister Sophie, she overhead me speaking with a comrade. Our plan was to smuggle the painting to Switzerland. We already had a dealer lined up and a potential client, as well. Why did she have to interfere? So that a *bourgeoisie* baron could have a painting that should never have been his to begin with? Art belongs to the people."

Adalie put her finger to his lips and said something to soothe him. He was quiet after that. For a second there I worried that he'd never speak again. But then his eyes opened. "We needed to pay for weapons and explosives, to get our printing pressed repaired—smashed in a raid by the Gestapo, you understand? It was a day or two later that Sophie requested permission to draw from the painting in charcoal. Mademoiselle Villand, who, I suspect, has her own subterfuge going, was only too happy to oblige."

His voice was getting softer. I helped him along,

"And then the painting disappeared," I said.

"*Oui*, and Sophie with it. And then the trouble began."

I lifted his pinkie finger. "Art expert, are you?"

Daphne let out a yelp. "You're Professor Berton's brother!"

"Comrade Jean-Michel Berton, at your service," he said and then got still.

I dripped my fingers into the water glass and said, "In the name of the Father, the Son, and the Holy Ghost. Amen." Then I made the sign of the cross on his forehead. I wasn't a priest, but it was the best Jean-Michel was ever gonna get. Not only that, but I was assigned the job of gravedigger, too.

We buried Jean-Michel under the big tree, with a view of the Seine River. Monsieur Brassens, the fishmonger, and me took turns with the digging. We were head-to-toe in mud by the time we got done. Afterwards we all stood in the drizzle, around the mound over Jean-Michel's grave, saying any prayer we could think up. Even Adalie, a bonafide communist, recited a prayer. Daphne sang one in Hebrew.

Professor Berton. It would be us telling him.

Monsieur Brassens offered us a ride to Paris, but we decided to keep Adalie company. She was broke up about Jean-Michel. She put a hand on her stomach and said, "*Que dois-je faire?*" Turned out she was in the family way, but now there'd be no father.

When she waved the fishmonger goodbye, I seen that she was wearing Professor Berton's pinkie ring, the one with the A initial. Wearing it on the finger where a wedding ring would've gone.

CHAPTER THIRTY-NINE

THE SUN ROSE OVER THE TREES behind the camp, drying my blanket and the ground around me. It would turn out to be an Indian-summer day—that's what we called it in New York, anyway—a summer day plopped into winter. I didn't get a wink of sleep that night, thinking about Jean-Michel six-feet under, about the kid he would never meet, about the printing press that would never get fixed, wondering if we should just hand the painting over to Adalie and be done with it. Let the communists have their guns and grenades and whatever else they needed.

The fishmonger stirred in his sleep. He'd decided to stay after all, promising us a fish fry-up for breakfast. I heard Cheval chewing grass nearby. The dames were sleeping in the wagon, four of them in the one bed. We still didn't know what happened to Sophie, but something Jean-Michel said stuck with me and I kept chewing it over. *Bourgeoisie* baron. What did it mean?

Was he talking about the Baron de Rothschild fella who owned the Vermeer painting? The only other baron I could come up with was the Red Baron, the World War I German flying ace. His nickname was once used as a code by the Belgian Resistance, a clever way to get a message to us. And what did *bourgeoisie* mean? I sat up and pressed my eyes tight, hoping that might help me think better.

Cheval nuzzled my face with his moist nose. He smiled so's I could see his teeth. "What happened to Sophie?" I asked him.

I pictured her hanging the painting in the boathouse bathroom and thinking, "I'll go out for a stroll, maybe get myself a croissant with strawberry jam," and then—BABOOM!—somebody grabs her while she's waiting on line at the *boulangerie*. Which, come to think of it, sounded an awful lot like *bourgeoisie*.

Or another scenario: Sophie stealing the Vermeer then finding her way to the baron hoping for a reward. Maybe she read about one being offered, printed in the classified section of a Paris newspaper.

And another possibility: Sophie overhearing the conversation between Jean-Michel and his communist friend, and then getting the idea to fund her own Resistance group by selling the painting. Maybe right now she was skiing down the Matterhorn, waiting for instructions from General Charles de Gaulle, leader of Free France.

One thing was for sure, people wanted that painting and they were willing to kill for it. I let my eyes drift over to Jean-Michel's grave. They'd taken a shot at Daphne, who was practically my sister-in-law. And they'd come after Madame Doumer, and Juliette, my blood-sworn friend. Once *Reichsmarschall* Hermann Göring got wind of the painting being missing, there'd be Hell to pay—

bloody Hell. This was the man behind the Blitz, the man who'd shot down my brother Jack. Or someone under his command, anyway.

According to Jean-Michel, Göring was due to arrive that very day, not that we knew exactly when he'd visit the gallery. Maybe he had other business in Paris. Or maybe not.

I remembered Jean-Michel telling us that Mademoiselle Villand, the lady who ran the gallery, believed that the painting found in the armoire was the original Vermeer. If she said as much to Hermann Göring, after he'd flown all the way from Berlin to see it, there would be no telling what he'd do for revenge when he learned it was missing. Line a thousand Frenchmen against a wall, most likely.

I was sure of one thing. Somebody had to get that painting back to the gallery before Hermann Göring showed up. And Daphne, being that she was as much an art fanatic as Sophie, wasn't gonna let that happen; not if there was the slightest chance of our Vermeer being the original.

But what did I care about art?

I called Cheval over. He bent his head close to mine. I whispered, "You know your way home, boy?" He smiled again and shook his wet mane so's that water sprayed my face.

And that's when I made the decision to strike out on my own.

CHAPTER FORTY

THE CLOSEST I'D COME to horseback riding was on a merry-go-round at Playland in Rockaway, Queens. Turned out the real thing was slightly more challenging, there not being a pole to hang onto. Luckily, I have good balance—I can walk a tightrope strung between two trees, climb the oak tree in the O'Leary's yard and straddle the top branch. I'm fantastic at hopscotch, not to mention ice skating. The couple times Cheval tried to turn back, I used a stick to tap his head in the direction of Paris.

Like I said already, Cheval was the gentlest horse I'd ever met. He seemed to know I was new at horseback riding and kept a steady pace, never trotting or galloping, not once. The trick was to move my body opposite his, not much different than roller skating, the way I had to use my arms for balance. But I had to grip the horse's flank with my thighs and before long they were burning. And then my crotch began chaffing, sort of like when you ride a bike for the first time after a long, snowy winter. At least the blisters on my heels were getting a break. And I'd tied the portfolio to my back using a rope I found, so the blisters on my hands were beginning to mend too.

Cheval was faster without the wagon to pull, and before long we were back at the fishmonger's store. It was only then, when I seen the sign that read *Brassens et Fils*, that I began to feel bad about borrowing the horse without asking first.

I made sure to feed Cheval and tie him to a lamppost in front of the store. In a way, I was glad that the fishmonger was left behind with my friends, a strong man to protect them. It was Saturday then, and I checked the sign in the store window which told customers the hours of operation. Sure enough, the store was due to open that day. That made me feel rotten again. The fishmonger would miss a day of sales.

My conscience was working overtime and I wondered if it had something to do with my ma praying up a storm for me back at Saint Brendan's Church. Or maybe it had to do with being so close to evil—*Reichsmarschall* Hermann Göring, I mean—like a compass needle pointed toward the North Pole and my conscience saying, "Go south, young man." Anyway, I didn't like the way guilt felt, not one bit. It made my insides hurt and my head pound, and it made me think that I'd better visit Notre-Dame Cathedral sometime soon and confess.

But first I had to get the painting back to the Galerie du Jeu de Paume, the gallery where Sophie was working before she disappeared. I figured I'd just leave the portfolio on the front stoop, sort of like people leave abandoned babies in front of churches. If I hurried, I might get there before they opened, if they were even open on the weekend. With any luck, the German tank would be gone. If I had to, I'd make up a story about finding the portfolio and wanting to return it to the rightful owners. I wasn't sure how I'd explain knowing where it belonged. There wasn't a tag on the handle. I thought about stopping off at a stationery store and buying one. The problem was I only had enough money for a Metro ticket.

By then I knew my way around the Paris Metro. I got out at the *Concorde* stop. I hiked up to street level, just next to a park surrounded by a stone fence with a lion statue at the corner. The gallery was just behind that fence. I walked to the park entrance, to a gate with Pegasus statues on either side of it. The gate was opened when we visited the first time, but now it was closed.

Standing outside the gate were German soldiers, a battalion from the look of it. I crossed the road and sat under an obelisk, an Egyptian monument. I was baffled why there were so many soldiers on duty this early in the morning. The time I'd visited the Metropolitan Museum of Art with my sister Nancy, they'd had an Irish security guard with nothing more than a billy club, not even a pop-gun.

I must've been beat, because next thing I knew I was being woke by an old lady selling pansies. She had them wrapped in bundles, stuck in a bucket. Why she thought I'd want them, I have no idea.

The sun was higher in the sky and I knew I'd slept for a while. The streets were busier than before, with bicycles and pedicabs and horse-drawn wagons. I returned to the park entrance, or just across the street from it, and seen there were even more soldiers and a few Waffen-SS officers, to boot. Even stranger, I seen a group of Luftwaffe pilots standing over to the side and smoking cigarettes. Each one of them had medals pinned to their uniforms, the formal uniforms they kept for parades and not the ones they wore flying. I watched as one of them removed a hankie from his pocket, using it to buff his boots. They'd pulled armored cars in front of the entrance and now there was a Nazi flag draped over the gate. The soldiers were getting into formation, lining up three deep, shoulder to shoulder. I counted forty of them.

They were expecting somebody important. I figured I knew who he was.

I watched as a woman approached the gate from the inside, calling to one of the highest ranking officers. She wasn't in uniform but was dressed for the occasion, with a carnation in her coat buttonhole. I wondered if she was Mademoiselle Villand, who ran the operation. Her and the German officer stood on either side of the gate having themselves a pow-wow. Then she turned and hurried back in the direction of the gallery, stopping only once when she twisted her heel on the cobblestones. There was no way I was getting in that way, so I decided to skirt around the park and look for another way in.

The darnedest thing: the whole park was surrounded by German soldiers, spaced at intervals of ten feet or so, all of them facing out to the street with their eyes scanning left and right. When I tried to cross to their side, one of them waved me away.

"*Halt*," he said, raising his gloved hand like a stop sign.

I crossed back to the other side, circling the perimeter of the park. There'd be no way in without guns blazing.

I felt the weight of the pistol, still in my right pocket, and the corkscrew in the other one. I slipped my hand into my pocket, gripping the pistol handle and fingering the trigger. I wished my brother Jack was there to help. He'd know what to do. RAF pilots were issued pistols, .45 caliber Enfields, to be exact, and trained to use them. Meanwhile, the only pistol I'd ever fired shot water.

By then I'd swung back around to the front gate. I could see the gallery over the stone fence. It looked like something dropped in from Athens, Greece. If only I could get over the fence, but how?

I sat on a grassy spot, letting the wheels in my head spin. My stomach was rumbling and I needed to eat something. My last meal was beans and rabbit stew back at the Gypsy camp. I came close to calling it a day, just going to find something to eat. I'd volunteer to wash dishes in exchange for breakfast if I had to.

So I was picturing scrambled eggs and buttered toast, Kellogg's Rice Krispies with maraschino cherries, when I seen a line of black sedans with them little Nazi flags mounted to the hoods. They were coming down the road in my direction.

The whole thing made me think of a funeral procession, except instead of a hearse in front, there was a canvas-topped army truck, packed with soldiers. More soldiers stood on the running boards, holding machine guns against their chests. To the rear of the sedans was an identical army truck. It was almost like they were preparing for an attack, the French Resistance coming out from behind scrubs, armed and ready. In a flash it came to me:

Reichsmarschall Hermann Göring had arrived.

Suddenly the painting didn't seem all that important. For one thing, there was no way to get it back to the gallery in time. And now an opportunity presented itself:

For glory.

For immortality.

For medals and monuments.

A place in history books.

I imagined kids at Saint Brendan's parochial school, cracking open their textbooks and reading about me: Thomas Robert Mooney, one of their own.

I leaned the portfolio against a tree trunk and reached into my pocket for the pistol, deciding to keep it concealed until the last minute. I'd have to get close, seeing that I hadn't practiced. I'd go for a head shot.

The procession came to a stop in front of the gates. By then the soldiers were standing at attention, with their rifles held neatly to their shoulders. There was little chance that I'd survive the day.

I seen the gate swing open. Behind it stood a group in plainclothes—the gallery staff, probably—nervous to the last one of them. One lady was holding a bouquet of roses. None of them were smiling, I noticed.

I scanned the procession and spotted Hermann Göring in the second car. He was wearing a white uniform and I seen the Iron Cross hanging where a bow tie might've gone. I'd seen that mug in the newspaper. And in *Addy and Hermy. The Nasty Nazis*, my favorite British cartoon featuring him and Adolf Hitler.

His hat was off and I had a straight shot at his head.

That's when I heard someone call my name, from all the way beyond the obelisk, on the other side of the huge square.

"Thomas Robert Mooney," she shouted again, and I knew it was Daphne. Here to thwart my plans, for sure.

I turned my attention back to the scene unfolding at the gates. The Luftwaffe pilots were now standing next to the car, *Heil Hitler*-ing, bowing at the waist, clicking their heels. The window rolled down, and now I had an even better shot at Hermann Göring.

I heard my name called again, this time from half the distance.

A Luftwaffe pilot was opening the car door and I seen Hermann Göring's huge leg, dressed in white trousers, stretch out from the sedan.

It's true what they say: your life does flash before your eyes. I seen myself in the cradle with my ma hovering over me, singing me an Irish ballad. I seen myself being confirmed, kneeling at the rail next to girls in white lace dresses. I was climbing a tree, camping with Jack, sitting on his lap while he taught me to drive his Ford pickup truck. Twelve and a half years flashed by in as many seconds, and then I crossed the street that separated me from the black sedan.

I heard Hermann Göring laugh. I seen him slap a pilot's back. They were speaking German, of course. One of them said, "*Willkommen in Paris.*"

Halfway across the street, they noticed me.

"*Wer ist das?*" I heard Hermann Göring ask: Who is this?

"*Nur ein Kind,*" said the Luftwaffe pilot: Only a kid.

Not one solider pointed his rifle at me. The Luftwaffe pilot had the nerve to laugh.

I didn't know what to say, what my last words would be. But as I fingered the pistol's safety catch, sliding it to the firing position, I found myself shouting:

"Take this, you swine!"

Before I knew what was happening, my arms were pinned to my sides and I was being hoisted from the ground. I tried to fight, kicking backwards and aiming for the groin. Brawny arms gripped my torso like a vise. All I could see was the black wool sleeves of the man's jacket. He wasn't one of the pilots, wasn't in uniform, and my best guess was that he was Gestapo. His hat fell off, a black fedora. It rolled on its brim until it came to a stop at Hermann Göring's feet. I tried to bend my neck and bite the man's hand, but I couldn't reach. He tightened his grip until I stopped breathing. Any tighter and he'd break a rib.

I heard "*Wer ist das?*" again from Hermann Göring.

And then a girl's voice, sweet and gentle and speaking French, said, "*Un cadeau d'une nation reconnaissante.*"

She curtsied.

As I was thrown into the trunk of a black Citroën parked directly across the street, I seen Juliette hand the Vermeer to Hermann Göring. He belly-laughed, taking the painting in his chubby hands. The trunk slammed shut just then. In the pitch-darkness of my new prison cell, I translated Juliette's words:

"A gift from a grateful nation," she'd said.

CHAPTER FORTY-ONE

THE CITROËN STOPPED only once, about ten minutes later. I figured the trunk would pop open and I'd be dragged to my death. But a few minutes passed and I heard the car doors open and slam, the springs rock as more passengers got in. My heart sank; any hope of fighting off the one Gestapo agent was gone.

We kept driving.

When the trunk did pop open, I was curled into a tight ball with my eyes pressed shut and my hands shielding my head. I figured we were at the dreaded Fresnes Prison, first stop on my journey to purgatory. I realized then that I'd been counting on instantaneous death, not on torture and imprisonment, slow starvation, cold, and misery. With no one watching, I'd cried myself dry in that dark trunk, ruing the day I decided to return to German-occupied Paris.

But now I was honestly more embarrassed than anything, by my tear-stained face and the fact that I'd wet my pants on the drive to Fresnes Prison. It took a minute before I got up the courage to open my eyes.

Nobody was standing over me, and that was my first shock. And the second was that we weren't at the

Fresnes Prison but parked across the street from the Hôtel Jeanne d'Arc. I heard my name called, "Thomas, get a move on!"

It was a voice I recognized. I thought, *Oh no. They've got her too.*

And it was my fault. There'd be a wedding without a man of honor, without a best man, and without a bride. My brother Jack would never forgive me for dragging his fiancée back to Paris. My stay in purgatory had just been extended by about a zillion years. *But why'd they bring us back here*, I wondered? And then I remembered the man with the black boots, the man staying in the room adjoining ours. My suspicions were confirmed then and there: we'd been followed all along. There was never the slightest chance of me getting a shot at Hermann Göring.

Right then, I could've made a run for it. Only they had Daphne hostage. I had no choice but to follow. I dashed across the street and into the hotel, past the coat of armor. Turning on my heels, I tried to pry the sword from Saint Joan's hands. But she wouldn't give it up, and I seen that it was bolted to her wrist.

I looked up the stairwell to see Daphne's rubber boots. I followed. The door to the room next to the one that'd been ours was open. Daphne swung around and waved me forward. "Hurry up, slow poke," she said.

The room had twin beds like ours. On one bed sat Madame Doumer, Juliette, Adalie, and now Daphne. Across from them sat the man with the black boots, the man with the black wool coat minus the fedora. The man who'd manhandled me away from my appointment with Hermann Göring. The man who'd thrown me into the trunk.

My brother Jack, in other words.

I was speechless, a rare thing in my life up to that point.

"Take a load off, Tommy," he said, patting the place beside him.

I throw myself at him, pressed my head into his chest and gripped him even harder than he'd gripped me back at the Galerie du Jeu de Paume. I started bawling, letting all my fears spill out onto his scratchy wool coat.

He whispered in my ear, "I've got a spare pair of britches hanging inside the bathroom door." Then he said to the gals, "Let me show you something," reaching into his inside coat pocket and distracting their attention just long enough to give me time to make it to the bathroom.

A couple minutes later I came out wearing the bottom part of a suit, with a belt tied around my waist because even the last notch wasn't tight enough to hold the pants up. I'd folded the cuffs. I'd washed my face, and even used a bit of Jack's aftershave. I exited to find Daphne next to him, with her head on his shoulder and one leg swung over his knee. He was saying, "Sweetheart, you wouldn't believe how many times you looked straight at me, stared right into my eyes without recognizing me. A couple times I passed by you, winking. You just raised your chin and ignored me. Like I was any 'ol Joe Shmoe, hitting on you uninvited." He laughed.

"It's 'cause we weren't looking for you," I said, taking a seat on the other side of him. "Not like the last time we was here in Paris, searching every face and hoping it was yours." I suddenly remembered something: "Hey, was you at the jazz party? I think I seen you in the fog of cigarette smoke."

Jack started laughing, telling us how he'd spilled wine on Antoine's white suit because he flirted with Daphne, and how he'd slapped the lady when she called Daphne a *damn fool*. "I almost gave myself away that time. My temper got ahead of me," he said.

"How'd you get to Paris, anyway?" I asked.

He shook his head remembering. "When the airliner took off and neither of you were at the airport, I knew straight off what happened. I bought a seat on the next flight and had to borrow civvies from one of the ground crew. Trouble was, they detained me at the Lisbon airport, thinking for some reason that I was a German agent. I had a time convincing them otherwise. Luckily they didn't search me or they would'a found my Gestapo warrant disc." He drew a chain out from under his collar. "I keep it hanging in my Spitfire, a sort of talisman for good luck. Got it after my Spit went down in Belgium that time." He hid it under his shirt again. "I knew you'd be heading to Paris on some lame-brain mission to rescue Sophie, so here I came."

"Oh, Jack," said Daphne.

"Listen up," he said. "Before leaving England, I made sure to get a contact here in Paris. Through a buddy with the SOE, who stuck his neck out for me."

"SOE?" asked Juliette.

"Special Operations Executive," said Jack. "But forget you heard that. They don't exist." He ran his fingers across his lips.

Then he told us that the following night, a Royal Air Force spy-plane would be leaving from Northern France and returning us to England. "And me, most likely, to a court-martial," he added. He was AWOL, meaning absent without leave, and it could mean the end of his flying career. I hung my head in shame because it was my fault. When I tried to apologize, he said, "What was I supposed to do, just send you off with a 'Cheerio, ta-ta'?"

Daphne pretended to slap Jack's face. "Why didn't you let us know you were here? Why the cloak-and-dagger?"

"Because I couldn't be seen, me an officer of the Royal Air Force, walking around the streets of Paris and asking after a runaway girl, is why. There's procedures for these things, directives for pilots who find themselves in occupied territory, ways to evade capture. And I couldn't trust this…this Tom Fool here, to not give me away."

I hung my head again.

"And then, I thought somebody'd better follow behind you, making sure you were safe. Watching your back, literally. Which, as it turned out, was a good plan."

Daphne went and mentioned her interrogation with the Gestapo and Jack began rubbing the top of his head franticly, as if he had lice. "That was the day you slipped away. You're telling me the Gestapo got you?"

He took Daphne's hand in his and examining each finger, like he was checking to see that they hadn't pulled the nails out. Then he took her face in his hands and kissed each part, beginning with her nose and ending with her forehead. "I blew it," he moaned. I seen a tear forming at the end of one of his eyelashes. I reached out and caught it.

"Where'd you get the getup," I asked, pulling at his sleeve. "And the Citroën?"

"It was a honest-to-God mistake, is what it was. Saw them staking out the apartment building where you were staying. I waited until there was only one of them. Turned out he was tailing somebody else, but by the time I got that out of him..." Jack went silent. "What does it matter? You're safe and sound and that's all that counts. The rest we can chalk up to the casualties of war."

He was looking at me with tremendous love in his eyes and my heart melted seeing that. But a second later, he said, "Tommy, you could'a gotten us all killed." He was shouting now, calling me names I can't write down without cringing. His face twisted into something monstrous, like our father's face on a drunken rampage. I was so terrified I jumped from the bed and cowered in a corner. Jack rose from the bed too, taller, it seemed, than I remembered him being. I feared he was about to strike me, something he'd never done before. I held my hands over my head, same as I did whenever my father came at me.

But then Jack started weeping, pulling me to him, saying, "I'm sorry, shortstop. It's just that you—you seem to think this war is a sport or something. I mean, going for Göring! What in Hell's bells were you thinking?" He cuffed my shoulder and then went into the bathroom. He stayed in there for a long time.

"Sometimes you bring out the worst in him," said Daphne. "And sometimes the best. I just hope they allow him to fly after this. Because if he's dismissed, I think it will kill him. And what happens if they put him in the brig? Our wedding will have to be postponed yet again."

She seen how upset I was and bobbed her head, saying, "Get over here and let me give you a little loving." I knelt on the ground in front of her and put my head in her lap. She stroked my hair.

"I've decided," said Madame Doumer, suddenly, "that Juliette and I will be moving from Paris until the end of the war. I'd thought of moving in with my eldest daughter and her husband in Dunkerque, but the German presence is more formidable than ever there." She looked at me. "I believe you've met them?"

"The Faures are some of my favorite people," I said. "Gave me shelter when I needed it. And peppermints."

Madame Doumer smiled at that, saying, "My sister lives along the coast, quite a bit west of Dunkerque, in the small, quiet, fishing village of Vierville-sur-Mer—thus far, free of Nazis. She's invited me to work in the grocery she and her husband own." She hugged Juliette to her. "I can't risk losing another child."

I knew she was thinking about her grandson, Jacques-Yves Faure, killed by aircraft fire while he picnicked with his parents on a beach in Dunkirk back in

1940. Madame Doumer turned toward Adalie, who'd been silent this whole time. She laid a hand on Adalie's knee before saying, "And you, child, I'm sure will be welcomed, too. Stay with us, at least until your baby is delivered." Madame Doumer remembered that Adalie didn't know English and repeated the invitation in French. We watched as Adalie's face became a Joan of Arc look-a-like: beatific, the nuns call it.

Jack came back into the room then. "The north coast, you say? That'll work out fine and dandy. We meet the RAF plane in Brittany. We'll drop you first." He looked at his watch, a German issued chronometer, I noticed. "We meet the plane at O-four-hundred. We'd better step on it. We'll take the Citroën. And don't worry, I've already changed the license plate."

Daphne turned to Madame Doumer, asking, "Where did you say your sister lives, Maman?"

"Vierville-sur-Mer, in Normandy," she said. "But, please, I can't have you go out of your way for us, not when you are on such a tight schedule. We can easily get a train from Paris St. Lazare to Bayeux and find our way from there. Juliette and I have done it many times. Usually with Sophie, it's true." She sucked in her lips before adding, "Only I hate the idea of leaving Paris when Sophie is still missing. What if she were to come home and find the door locked?"

"Ain't she got her own key?" I asked.

Jack looked at Madame Doumer. "For Pete's sake, she didn't leave a note or nothing?"

Madame Doumer straightened her back. "Well, actually, *oui*, she did."

We all let out mouths hang open and she went on, "The envelope was addressed to me, but inside I found nothing but a blank sheet of paper. Blank, both front and back."

"And you didn't think to hold it to a lamp?" I asked.

"*Mais pourquoi?*" she said, "but why? I realized that in her haste to leave, Sophie had made the mistake of putting the wrong sheet of paper into the envelope. I searched everywhere for a note but failed to find one."

Juliette fired a question at her, something along the lines of, "Why didn't you tell me about the note?"

"And where's the blank sheet of paper now?" I asked.

Madame Doumer opened her purse, where the letter had been all this time. "I wanted it near," she said. "The envelope is in my daughter's handwriting."

Juliette snatched the envelope, slipping the blank sheet out. She put her nose to the paper, "Vinegar," she said.

"Hold it up to the lightbulb," I said.

We watched as letters appeared, one by one:

First an M.

Then an O.

Juliette read, " '*Ma chérie, Mère.*'" switching to English. " 'Forgive me for leaving in this way. I have no choice. As Henri Matisse said, 'Creativity takes courage.' "

Daphne sighed.

Juliette kept her eyes on the letter, "Sophie wrote: 'I must leave France and make my way to New York. I know that you will try to stop me if I were to tell you.'"

"It's quite true," said Madame Doumer.

Juliette continued reading: " 'I must return a valuable article to its proper owner, something of great value. And by doing so, I will save a national treasure from falling into the hands of our artless enemy...' "

"New York," said Daphne. "Hadn't we heard that this is where the Baron de Rothschild escaped to?"

"*Oui, oui,*" said Juliette.

That's when Daphne reached into her pocket, "Jack, darling, can you make sense of this?" she said, showing him the slip of paper with BU 8-0555 written on it.

"Butterfield 8-0555," he said straightaway. "A Manhattan phone number."

I moaned. "You mean to tell me that all this time she's been heading to New York with the painting? Son of a gun."

I squeezed my eyes shut, trying to get it all straight. "So the Vermeer painting found in the armoire was the original. And the one in Germany is a copy, and the one Juliette gave to Hermann Göring—the rat-fink—was Sophie's copy?"

"So you've figured that out, have you?" said Daphne. "I realized the painting in our possession was a copy as soon as Jean-Michel mentioned the fact that paintings cleared though the Jeu de Paume were each stamped with a swastika. That's something I would have noticed, given that I meticulously examined the painting front and back. Do you honestly think I would have stood back and allowed Göring to take the original? Why, I would have fought tooth and nail to save the painting from the Nazis."

Suddenly, I smelled burning, as a brown spot appeared where the paper touched the lightbulb. Juliette moved the letter away from the bulb, blowing on it furiously. We watched as the letters disappeared again. Madame Doumer began crying. Luckily we'd already read the part that was now incinerated.

"Try again," I said, and Juliette brought the letter close to the lightbulb, this time a half-inch away. She scanned the page and said, "She closes the letter with little hearts. And a postscript saying that we are not to worry. There's no signature, but it is certainly her handwriting." She smiled. "Sophie has ended the letter with another quote. I will try to translate," she said finally. "The quote is from Pablo Picasso."

"That artist fella who lives in the Montparnasse?" I asked.

Juliette nodded. She began to translate slowly, stopping and starting until we had the whole quote. It must've been important to Sophie. I paid close attention. We all did...

What do you think an artist is?
He is a political being, constantly aware of
the heart breaking, passionate, or delightful things
that happen in the world...

Painting is not done to decorate apartments.
It is an instrument of war.

EPILOGUE

I WAS ALLOWED TO SIT by the window, seated in a West-land Lysander Mk III, flying five-thousand feet above sea level, over the darkened French countryside and then over the English Channel. The pilot, when he first laid eyes on me, said, "Son, be on the lookout for German kites," meaning fighter planes and bombers equipped with anti-aircraft guns.

But I didn't see one. Only a squadron of American B-17s making their way to Berlin, just about the most thrilling thing of this whole adventure.

My brother Jack took the co-pilot's seat, maybe his last time in a cockpit. Beside me sat Daphne, and next to her a lady who spoke only to ask that I raise the window. I figured her to be a secret agent, this being the nightly flight that dropped them into German-occupied France and took them out when it was time for a debriefing. I figured this out all on my own, since no one would say boo about why it was an RAF plane was landing on an airstrip in a field in Northern France and then taking off half an hour later.

Lieutenant Verity was the pilot at the controls. I leaned over his shoulder and watched his every move.

He knew I was doing it and pointed out landmarks along the way. "There's the coast of England," he said, turning his head my way. "She's welcoming you home." He had to shout over the roar of the engine and the whirl of the propeller.

"Well, sir, it's not my home," I said, not that he heard me. I wondered if the airplane had enough fuel to get us to Mitchell Airfield, just a few blocks from our house in East Hempstead. But before long we were landing at RAF Tempsford in Bedfordshire.

Jack kissed Daphne goodbye, long and hard on her lips. I turned away to give them privacy. We were going to London and he'd been asked to ferry a Hawker Hurricane back to RAF Rochford, where his squadron was stationed. He seemed relieved when they gave him the assignment. They hadn't stripped his wings yet, not that he was wearing them.

My conscience was acting like a hundred air raid sirens during the Blitz. I must've said "sorry" a million times before we parted. Jack threw me a bone when he said, "It was pretty brave of you to try and rescue Sophie." He added, "Wish me luck!" and ran toward the Hawker Hurricane.

It was later that night, when we arrived at Daphne's house in London, that her mother said, "You received a letter from New York City." This was after she'd applied ice to Daphne's black eye and swollen cheek, and fattened us up with apple pie and a Wartime Casserole.

Daphne grabbed a butter knife the second the envelope hit her hands, using it for a letter opener.

" '*Ma chérie*, Daphne,'" she read. " 'You will be surprised to hear that I am living in New York City, a student at the famous Art Students League! The wonderful thing is that my room and board, plus my tuition at the League, is being paid for by my patron—my very own de' Medici, so to speak—this in return for a little favor I did him. I'm loving New York. All this inspiration crammed into a space no larger then thirteen-by-three miles. My greatest wish is that once you marry Jack, and this horrible war is over, the two of you will set up housekeeping here. Jack is a New Yorker, *non*?'" Daphne stopped reading aloud, scanning the page for something we'd be interested in.

I broke in with, "Who's de' Medici and what does he have to do with anything?"

"The de' Medici family were patrons of the arts in Florence, Italy, during the Renaissance. They funded artists like Michelangelo and Raphael. Cosmos de' Medici was the most famous of the lot."

"*de*," I said. "Remind you of anyone?"

"Yes, *de* Rothschild."

"Sophie's patron."

"I thought the same thing, Thomas." She looked at her chewed up fingernails, then turned to her mother. "Mum, where is that powder you use to keep me from biting my nails?"

"You mean cayenne pepper? Let me see if we have any," said Mrs. Clarke.

There was only one question left, for me anyway:

How the devil did Sophie get to New York?

It came to me then. She must've hightailed it to Portugal, got a visa from the US Embassy, then bought herself a berth on an ocean liner. But how'd she pay for the ticket? She was a starving artist, for Pete's sake. I picked up the envelope and seen there was a return address. While Daphne was busy peppering her fingernails and screaming in agony, I slipped the envelope into my pocket. First thing back at Warfield Hall, I'd borrow stationery and a stamp from Lady Sop.

With any luck, I'd be home for Christmas.

GOOD REVIEWS ARE BETTER THAN MARASCHINO CHERRIES!

If you enjoyed *Letter Via Paris*, kindly write a review. It will make the author do an Irish jig. Just go to www.amazon.com and type in the title of the book. And, while you're at it, write one at: www.goodreads.com.

TOMMY MOONEY'S ADVENTURE
BEGAN WITH:

Telegram For Mrs. Mooney
By Cate M. Ruane

WITH ONLY A TELEGRAM to guide him, Tommy Mooney leaves his Long Island home in search of his big brother Jack—a RAF Spitfire pilot missing in action somewhere in Nazi-occupied Europe. He cycles to the Brooklyn Harbor where he spots a yacht flying a British flag and stows away in a Louis Vuitton trunk, discovered only when the ship is mid-Atlantic. Once ashore, he heads for London where he enlists the help of Daphne Clarke, Jack's British fiancée. Making off with a speedboat, the two cross the English Channel, dodging German U-boats.

Hope turns to foreboding as it begins to look as though the two are being deceived by the Gestapo, used in a plot to expose a Resistance network created to help downed airmen evade capture. "What a conundrum," says Daphne, as it becomes clear that by continuing the search for Jack, they risk the lives of many like him—as well as their own.

Message For Hitler
By Cate M. Ruane

WHEN VISITING RAF Rochford, Tommy begins to suspect that a Nazi spy is working mischief at the base. Airmen are mysteriously wounded, Spitfires are sabotaged, someone has been poisoning the food. No one escapes Tommy's radar, especially after Daphne falls ill and is hospitalized. That night the base is attacked, setting off a chain of events that will either prove Tommy to be a fool or a hero.

BONUS CHAPTER:
DAPHNE GETS A LETTER

By joining our mailing list, you'll receive bonus chapters, rare photographs of the true-life characters, historical backstories, advance notice of new books in the series, and more. We'll begin with a peek into Daphne's mind, as she dreams about her fiancé Jack, and reads a letter she's just opened from his little brother, Tommy Mooney. We hope you enjoy!

Sign up at: www.catemruane.com

LETTER VIA PARIS is a work of fiction, but some of the characters are loosely based on real people who lived and died during World War II. Many of my characters are drawn entirely from my imagination, and even the ones based on (then) living and breathing people are largely a fictional construct. Here and there, there are some facts:

As it turns out, Rose Valland, who ran the *Galerie Nationale du Jeu de Paume*, was working for the French Resistance, secretly making an inventory of art plundered by the Nazis. As the war came to an end, these records were instrumental in saving thousands of works of art.

In February 1941, Johannes Vermeer's masterpiece, *The Astronomer*, was packed into crate H13 (H for Hitler), loaded onto a train and shipped to Germany. It was rescued in May 1945 from a salt mine, and returned to Édouard Alphonse James de Rothschild, who was living in New York City until the war's end. The Butterfield phone number may have been his—I found the listing in the 1942 New York City phone directory.

The Astronomer was later acquired by the French state, in lieu of inheritance taxes owed, and has been on exhibit at the Louvre ever since. Hitler never did get his Führermuseum—thank God for that.

Thomas Octave Murdoch Sopwith (who was appointed Commander of the Most Excellent Order of the British Empire in 1953, and was not actually a "Lord") was an English aviation pioneer and yachtsman. His *Endeavour* challenged the America's Cup in 1934 and 1937. Warfield Hall is in Berkshire. I have taken the liberty of relocating it to Hampshire.

Andrée Eugénie Adrienne De Jongh, nicknamed Dédée, was the young Belgian woman who founded the Comet Line to help downed Allied airmen evade capture. In *Telegram For Mrs. Mooney*, I gave her Resistance group a shop called Les Misérables. In *Letter Via Paris*, she and her father are no longer occupying the space or the apartment above.

But don't worry. . .yet.

In truth, she wasn't betrayed until two months later, when she was sent to the notorious Fresnes prison in Paris and then to Ravensbrück and Mauthausen concentration camps. Released by the advancing Allied troops in April 1945, she was later awarded the United States Medal of Freedom. Her father, Frédéric De Jongh, was also betrayed to the Gestapo and was executed in 1943.

Tommy is based on my own da, Thomas Robert Mooney, who was a child when his oldest brother, Flight Lieutenant John "Jack" Mooney, flew with the RAF Eagle Squadron.

Jack was a twenty-one-year-old Spitfire engaged to marry a seventeen-year-old London girl named Daphne Clarke. About all I know of the real woman comes from a *New York Times* article quoting a letter that she'd written to my grandmother when Jack was missing: "I've put away the trousseau for a while but I'll be taking everything out again soon as I know he'll be back." The character of Daphne is built entirely from that one line. In truth, Jack was killed in action on June 16, 1942 and is buried in Dunkirk. But, don't cry yet. . .

. . .I am keeping him alive with this series.

ACKNOWLEDGEMENTS

MANY THANKS to the people who read early drafts of this novel.

Especially, to my brother Kevin, a World War II expert who knows things like whether or not the Wehrmacht had jeeps. (No, they didn't.) And thanks to him and my sister-in-law Glenda, for helping to pay the bills while I indulge my fantasy of becoming an author.

Thanks to all of my art teachers, who taught me, among other things, how to grind paint, prime a canvas, work in glazes, and make stretcher frames. Who would have thought, all these years later, that these lessons would come in handy in this way. (On my website—www.catemruane.com—are two of my paintings, a self-portrait I painted whilst in Italy—from life—and a painting of Tommy Mooney, painted from my imagination after writing the first two books in the series.)

A million thanks to Julie Eargle and Chrys Goodman for their excellent copy editing. And to Trisha Walsh Devenish for a final polish. Konstantin Orizaris for advice about German expressions, Chrys for the same. I need more people like them in my life!

And thanks go to the late Charlie Ellis, the first one to read this book. His enthusiasm still inspires me.

In 1937, Pablo Picasso painted *Guernica*, a mural in protest of the aerial bombing of the Basque town during the Spanish Civil War, done at the request of Francisco Franco's nationalist government by its allies, the Nazi

German Luftwaffe. The quote at the end of chapter forty-one comes from an interview with the artist, given to Simone Téry for her piece "Picasso n'est pas officier dans l'armée française," March 24, 1945, in *Les Lettres Françaises*, a magazine published by the National Front, vol. V, p. 48. But perhaps he quoted it at an earlier date to a student artist hanging around the Montparnasse? I'd like to think so, anyway.

ABOUT THE AUTHOR

CATE M. RUANE graduated from the School of Visual Arts in New York City, worked as an art director at advertising agencies in NYC and San Francisco, and later studied painting in the Master Class at The Jerusalem Studio School. Vermeer is her favorite painter. Born and raised on Long Island, she now lives in Asheville, N.C. She is the author of *Telegram For Mrs. Mooney* and *Message For Hitler*.

www.catemruane.com

Fonts used in this book

The headline and subtitle font is LD Telegram,
by Inspire Graphics, licensed from LetteringDelights.com.

The text font is Adobe Caslon Pro.
Englishman William Caslon (1672-1766) first cut his
typeface Caslon in 1725.
His major influences were the Dutch designers
Christoffel van Dijcks and Dirck Voskens.